"Something bad's come to Seattle."

"What kind of trouble?" Wizard asked.

"You tell me," she challenged.

Wizard shook his head, trying to breathe. "I can't. I don't know anything about it. Anyone with any magic at all can tell there's something hanging over the city. But I don't know what it is, and—"

"It's coming for you." Cassie's voice brooked no denial. "Whatever it is, it's yours. The sooner you stop it, the better for us all. Do you know what I'm saying?"

"I know you're scaring the hell out of me."

Ace Fantasy books by Megan Lindholm

MEGAN LINDHOLM
WIZARD OF THE PIGEONS

ACE FANTASY BOOKS
NEW YORK

This book is an Ace Fantasy original edition,
and has never been previously published.

WIZARD OF THE PIGEONS

An Ace Fantasy Book/published by arrangement with
the author

PRINTING HISTORY
Ace Fantasy edition/January 1986

ISBN: 0-441-89467-4

Ace Fantasy Books are published by The Berkley Publishing Group,
200 Madison Avenue, New York, New York 10016.

PRINTED IN THE UNITED STATES OF AMERICA

WIZARD OF THE PIGEONS

ON THE FAR WESTERN SHORE of a northern continent there was once a harbor city called Seattle. It did not have much of a reputation for sunshine and beaches, but it did have plenty of rain, and the folk who lived there were wont to call it "The Emerald City" for the greenness of its foliage. And the other thing it boasted was a great friendliness that fell upon strangers like its rain, but with more warmth. In that city, there dwelt a wizard.

Not that folk recognized him as a wizard, for even in those days, wizards were becoming rarer with each passing year. He lived a simple life upon the streets of the city, passing among the folk like the wind passes among the flowers, unseen but not unfelt. He was known, to the few who knew him, simply as Wizard.

Little was known of his past, but atoning for this lack was a plenitude of rumors about it. Some said he had been an engineer and a warrior who had returned from some far battle with memories too fearsome to tolerate. And some said no, that he had been a scholar and among those who had refused to go to that far strife, and that was why he dwelt nameless and homeless in the streets. And some said he was older than the city itself, and others that he was newly arrived, only a day or so ago. But what folk said of him mattered little, for it was what he did that was important. Or didn't do, as Cassie would have quickly pointed out.

To Seattle there come blue days in October, when the sun shines along the waterfront and one forgives the city its sins, both mortal and venial. On such a day the cries of the gulls seem to drown out the traffic noises, and the fresh salt breath of the ocean is stronger than the exhaust of the passing cars. It was such a day, and sunlight shattered brilliantly against the moving waters of Elliott Bay and the brisk wind blew the shining shards inland over the city. It was a day when no one was immune to magic, and a wizard might revel in its glories. The possibilities of the day tugged at Wizard's mind like a kite tugs on a string. So, although he had been standing for some time at a bus stop, when the bus finally came snorting into sight, he wandered away from the other passengers, letting his feet follow their own inclination.

When he reached the corner of Yesler Way, he turned and followed it downhill, toward the bay. The sidewalk was as busy as the narrow crowded street, but Wizard still halted in the middle of it, forcing the flow of pedestrians to part and go around him. He gazed up fondly at the peak of the Smith Tower. A merry little flag fluttered from the tip of its tall white tower. Mr. L. C. Smith, grown rich from manufacturing typewriters, had constructed the tower to be the tallest building west of the Mississippi. The flagpole had been added in an attempt to retain that title for a little longer. The tower was no longer the tallest, of course, but its proud lines gave Wizard the moral courage to pass the notorious structure known as the Sinking Ship parking garage. This was a triangular monstrosity of gray concrete wedged between Yesler and James Street. When one considered it as a memorial to the Occidental and the Seattle, the two old hotels torn down to allow for its construction, it became even more depressing. The hill's steepness always made it appear that the garage was foundering and would vanish into the earth tomorrow, but, alas, it never did. Wizard hurried past it.

Safely beyond it, he slipped back into a stroll again, gazing around himself and taking more than a minor satisfaction in knowing his city so well. He knew it not as a common street survivor might, but as a connoisseur of landmarks and their history. How many skid row denizens, he wondered, of all the skid rows across the nation, knew that Seattle had boasted the original Skid Road, after which all others were named? From the hills above the city, logs had once skidded down that nearly vertical street to Yesler's Sawmill. Living conditions in the area had been so poor that an eastern reporter had taken his impressions and the name Skid Road home, to coin a brand new cliché.

Wizard passed under the gray thunder of the Alaskan Way Viaduct with a small claustrophobic shudder, and emerged into the sun, wind, and sea smell of Alaskan Way South. He turned north and plodded up the waterfront, watching the tugs, ferries, and gulls with equal interest. Ye Olde Curiosity Shop. That was what was luring him. He hadn't chatted with Sylvester for days; the old coot would be wondering where he was.

By the time he reached the glass doors of the shop, he was just chilled enough that the warmth of the interior made his ears tingle. He stood, rubbing the chill from his fingers, and let his eyes rove over the shop. It was a marvelous place. It was so crammed that not one more item could be packed into it, yet each time Wizard dropped by, something new had been added. The place was a cross between a museum and a shop, with rarities on display, and bargains for browsers. The aisles were cluttered with machines that, for a single shiny coin, would let you test your strength, find your weight, take a peek at the lady in her bath, or hear the nickelodeon tunes of the olden days. For fifty cents, another machine would squish a penny into a souvenir of the shop. One could buy postcards and shells and knick-knacks and jewelry, carvings and pottery, toys and trinkets. Suspended from the rafters were trophies of the seas, including a mermaid's body. But Wizard walked past all of these fascinating things, straight to the back of the shop.

The very best things were in the back of the shop. The shrunken heads were here, and the ancient skulls in glass cases. A baby pig with two heads was pickled in a large jar atop a player piano. To the left of this piano was a Gypsy fortune-teller holding her Tarot cards and waiting for the drop of a dime to deal out your fortune card to you. To the right of the player piano was Sylvester.

"So how's it going, old man?" Wizard greeted him softly.

Sylvester gave a dry cough and began, "It was a hot and dusty day . . ."

Wizard listened, politely nodding. It was the only story Sylvester had to tell, and Wizard was one of the few who could hear it. Wizard looked through the glass into the dark holes behind the dry eyelids and caught the gleam of his dying emotions. The bullet hole was still plainly visible upon Sylvester's ribby chest; his dessicated arms were still crossed, holding in the antique pain. His small brown teeth showed beneath his dry moustache. Sylvester was one of the best naturally preserved mummies existent in the western United States. It said so right on the placard beside his display case. Sylvester had met with success in death, if not in life. One could buy postcards and pamphlets that told all about him. They told everything there was to know, except who he had been, and why he had died in the sandy wastes from a bullet wound. And those secrets were the ones he whispered to Wizard, speaking in a voice as dry and dusty as his unmarked grave had been, in words so soft they barely passed the glass that separated them. Wizard stood patiently listening to the old tale, nodding his head slightly.

Sylvester was not alone. There was another mummy in a glass case next to his, her shriveled loins modestly swathed in an apron. She listened to Sylvester speak to Wizard with her mouth agape in aristocratic disdain for his uncouthness. She had died of consumption and been entombed in a cave. She still wore her burial stockings and shoes. Privately Wizard did not think her as well preserved as Sylvester, but she was definitely more conscious of social niceties.

Sylvester finished his account, and Wizard stood nodding in grave commiseration. Suddenly, raucous laughter burst out behind him. Wizard gave a startled jump, and turned to find that two teenage girls had slipped a coin into Laughing Jack. The runty little sailor with the fly on his nose and the cigarette dangling from his lips guffawed on and on, swaying in the force of his hilarity and wringing answering giggles from the girls. The girls had eyes as bright as young fillies'. They were incredibly young, even for a bright October day in Seattle. Wizard could only marvel at it. When the coin ran out and Jack was mercifully still, they stepped up to Estrella the Gypsy.

"Oh, I did her before. Come on, Nance. That's a dumb one. She just gives you this little printed card."

"It's my dime," Nance declared loudly, and slipped the coin in the slot. Estrella lifted her proud head. She gave the girls a piercing look and then began to scan the tarot cards before her. She made a few mystic passes and a small white card dropped from a slot in the machine. Estrella bowed her head and was still. Nance picked up the card. Haltingly, she began to read

Estrella's prophecies aloud. "'Your greatest fault is that you talk too much. Learn to—'"

"Geez, Nance! You coulda learned that from me and saved your dime!" Her friend rolled her eyes, and with much giggling the two girls departed, Nance waving the little black and white printed card before her like a fan. Wizard shook his head slightly after them. Sylvester breathed a small and dusty sigh. Estrella lifted her head and gave Wizard a slow wink. A second card emerged from the slot.

Wizard stooped cautiously to take it up. He glanced at the brightly painted tarot card in his hand, and then peered sharply at Estrella. But she was as still as a painted dummy, her eyes cast modestly downward. Wizard stared at his card. It was more than twice the size of the one the girls had received. Depicted on one side in gaudy colors was a man, caught by one heel in a rope snare and dangling upside down. Wizard was fascinated. Slowly he turned the card over. In ornate letters of dark red was printed A WARNING! That was all. Estrella wouldn't meet his eyes, and Sylvester gave a hollow groan. Even the pickled piglet in its glass jar squirmed uncomfortably.

Wizard tucked the card into his shirt pocket and gave a farewell nod to Sylvester. The wind hit him as he emerged from the shop, pushing him boisterously as it rushed past him. He strode down the street, letting the exercise warm him. A tiny pang reminded him that he had not yet eaten today. Time to take care of that. He heard the approaching rumble of a bus. Tucking his shopping bag firmly under one arm, he sprinted to the stop just ahead of it.

The bus gusted up to the stop and flung its door open before him. Wizard ascended the steps and smiled at the bus driver who stared straight ahead. He found a seat halfway down the aisle and sat looking out the window. "'. . . Cannot rival for one hour October's bright blue weather,'" he quoted softly to himself with satisfaction. He stared out the window.

The bus nudged into its next stop and five passengers boarded. The four women took seats together at the back, but the old man worked his slow way down the aisle to stop beside Wizard's seat. Wizard felt his presence and turned to look at him. The old man nodded gravely and arranged himself carefully in the seat as the bus jerked away from the curb. The old man nodded to the sway of the bus, but didn't speak until Wizard had turned to stare out the window again.

"My boy isn't coming home from college for Thanksgiving this year. Says he can't afford it, and when we said we'd pay, he said he needed the time to study. Can you beat that? So I asked him, 'What are Mother and I supposed to do, eat a whole turkey by ourselves?' So he said, 'Why don't you have chicken instead?' No understanding. He's our youngest, you see. The others are all long moved away."

Wizard nodded as he turned to look at the old man, but he was staring at the back of the next seat. As soon as Wizard turned back to the window, he started it again.

"Our second girl had a baby last spring. But she won't come either. Says she wants to have their first Thanksgiving together, just her family alone. So when I said, 'Well, aren't we family, too?' she just said, 'Oh, Daddy, you know how small our place is. By the time you drove clear down here for Thanksgiving, you'd have to spend the night, and I just don't have any place to put you.' Can you beat that?" The old man gave a weary cough. "Eldest boy's in Germany, you know. Stationed there fourteen months now, and only three letters. Phoned us three weeks ago, though. And when his mother asked him why he didn't write to us, he says, 'Oh, Mom, you know how it is. You know I do love you, even if I don't find time to write.' After he hangs up, she says to me, 'Yes, I know he loves us, but I wish I could feel him love us.' It's for her I mind. Not so much for me. Kids were always a damn nuisance anyway, but it hurts her when they don't call or write."

The bus pulled into Wizard's stop. He kept his seat with his jaw set against the grumbling of his stomach. As soon as the bus lurched forward again, the old man resumed.

"I guess I wasn't around that much when they were growing up. I guess I didn't put as much into them as she did; maybe I didn't give them as much as I should have. So perhaps it's only fitting that they aren't around when I'm feeling my years. But what about Mother? She gave them her years, and now they leave her alone. Can you beat that?"

Just as the old man's voice trailed out, the Knowing came to Wizard. He always wondered how the talkers knew to come to him, how they sensed that he had something to tell them. Even Cassie had no answer to that question. "Every stick has two ends," she had mumbled when he had asked her. "Mumbo-jumbo!" he had replied derisively. But now he had something for the old man, and it must be delivered. He took his eyes from the window, to stare at the seat back with the old man.

He whispered as huskily as a priest giving absolution in a confessional.

"Buy the turkey and the trimmings. Tell her that with or without kids at the table, you wouldn't miss her holiday cooking. Your eldest son got some leave time, and he'll be flying in from Germany. But he wants to surprise her. So keep it to yourself, but be ready to go to the airport on Thanksgiving morning. Don't spill the beans, now."

He never looked at Wizard. At the next stop the old man rose and made his slow way to the door in the side of the bus. Wizard watched him go and wished him well. At the next stop he hopped off himself and went looking for the right sort of restaurant.

It took him a moment to get his bearings, and then he recalled a little place he had used before. He mussed his hair slightly, took his newspaper from his shopping bag and tucked it under his arm, and clutched the plastic bag by its handles. His stomach made him hurry the block and a half to the remembered location.

With a flash of light and a roar of wind, he appeared in the door of the restaurant. A secretary hurrying through her half-hour lunch break paused with her burger halfway to her lips. Framed by a rectangle of bright blue October, the man in the door blazed blue and white and gold. A strange little squirt of extra blood shot through her heart at the sight of him. Wasn't he the illustration of the wandering prince from some half-forgotten book in her childhood? Sunlight rested on his hair like a mother's fond benediction. He was too vital and sparkling for her to break her stare away.

Then the tinted glass door on its pneumatic closer eased shut behind him, revealing to her the cheat. Bereft of wind and sun at his back, the man who had seemed to fill the doorway was only slightly taller than average. The gold highlights on his hair faded to a brown tousle; even this boyishness was denied by a sprinkling of gray throughout it. His lined and weathered face contradicted his youthful stance and easy walk. Just some smalltime logger from Aberdeen who had wandered into Seattle for a day of shopping. His longsleeved wool shirt was a subdued blue plaid; thermal underwear peeked out the open collar. Dark brown corduroy slacks sheathed his long legs. The blue spark of fascination in his eyes was only something she had imagined. When the secretary realized her gaze was being returned with interest, she stared past him, scowling slightly, and returned to her hamburger. Wizard shrugged and strolled to the end of the line at the counter.

Once in line, he took the folded *Seattle Times* from under his arm and stuffed it into the top of his plastic shopping bag. He scanned the restaurant expectantly. The place was an elegantly disguised cafeteria. The tables had donned red-checked cloths and boasted small guttering candles in little red hobnail holders. Their dimmed gleam was augmented by the shining fluorescent light over the stainless steel salad bar. The girl clearing tables wore a lacy little apron and a dainty starched cap. But the fine masquerade was betrayed by the metal dispenser for paper napkins on the condiment bar, and the swing-front plastic trash containers that crouched discreetly beneath potted plants. Wizard was not deceived. He caught the glance of a small girl seated at a corner table with her brother and parents. His face lit when he spotted her. With a broad grin and a wink, he reduced her to giggles.

"Ready to order, sir," the cashier informed him. Her square plastic name tag introduced her as Nina Cashier Trainee.

"Coffee." He tried a melting smile on her, but she was too nervous to thaw. He jingled the change in his pocket as her finger wiped his order onto her machine.

"You want that to go," she told him.

"No, I'll drink it here." He refocused the smile on her. "It's pretty nippy outside."

She mustered an uncertain authority. "You can't sit in a booth with just coffee and be alone." She gabbled the words as her pen jabbed up at a sign posted high above anyone's eye level. In stout black letters it proclaimed LONE PATRONS OR PERSONS ORDERING LESS THAN $1.50 EACH ARE NOT PERMITTED TO SIT IN BOOTHS BETWEEN 11:00 AND 2:00 PM, DUE TO LIMITED TABLE SPACE. THE MANAGEMENT REGRETS THIS NECESSARY MEASURE IN OUR EFFORTS TO KEEP OUR PRICES LOW. So did Wizard. The sign had not been there last month.

"But I'm not alone, Miss Nina." His use of her name unbalanced her. "I'm joining some friends. Looks like I'm a bit late." He winked at the little girl in the corner booth, and she squirmed delightedly. "Isn't the kid a doll? Her mom looked just like that when we were kids."

Nina hastily surrendered, barely glancing at the child. "A real cutie. Fifty-seven cents, please. Help yourself to refills from our bottomless pot."

"I always do." He pushed mixed coins onto the counter to

equal exactly fifty-seven cents. "I used to be a regular here, but the service got so bad I quit coming in. With people like you working here, maybe I'll become a regular again."

For an instant a real person peered out of her eyes at him. He received a flash of gratitude. He smiled at her and let the tension out of her bunched shoulders. She served him steaming coffee in a heavy white mug. He let her forget him completely as she turned to her next customer.

Wizard took his mug to the condiment counter. He helped himself to three packets of cream substitute and six packets of sugar, a plastic spoon, and four napkins. He sauntered casually over to the corner booth where the small girl and her brother pushed their food about on their plates as their parents lingered over coffee. He halted just short of intruding on them and allowed himself a few silent moments to make character adjustments. "Turning the facets of your personality until an appropriate one is face up" was how Cassie described it when she had taught him how. Prepared, he took the one more pace that put him within their space, and waited for the husband to look up. He did so quickly, his brown eyes narrowing. The muscles in his thick neck bunched as the man hiked his shoulder warningly, and set down his coffee mug to have his fists free. Very territorial, Wizard decided. He smiled ingratiatingly, cocking his head like a friendly pup.

"Hi!" he ventured in an uncertain voice. He cleared his throat and shifted his feet awkwardly. A country twang invaded his voice. "I, uh, I hate to intrude, but I wonder if I could share your table. I'm waiting for my lady friend."

"Then wait at an empty table," the man growled. His wife looked both apprehensive and intrigued.

"Uh, I would, but, well, look, it's like this. The first time I ever took her out, we wound up here, sitting at this table until three in the morning. Since then, we've always sat here whenever we come in. And well, today is kind of special. I think I'm going to, you know, ask her. I got the ring and the whole bit." He patted his breast pocket with a mixture of pride and embarrassment. His soft voice was awed at his own boldness.

The seated man was not moved. "Buzz off," he growled, but his wife reached quickly to cover his hand with hers.

"Come on, Ted, show a little sense of romance. What harm can it do? We're nearly finished anyway."

"Well..." She squeezed his hand warmly as she smiled at

him. Ted's hackles went down. "I guess it's okay." Ted gave a snort of harsh laughter. "But maybe I'd be doing you a bigger favor if I refused. Look how they get, once you marry 'em. Changing my mind before I can even decide. Yeah, sit!" Ted pointed commandingly at the end of the booth bench, and Wizard dropped into it obediently. He leaned his shopping bag carefully against the seat, and smiled with a shy tolerance at Ted's rough joking.

"Well, you know how it is, sir. I've been thinking it's about time I took the step. I'm not a spring chicken anymore. I want to do this thing while I still got the time to get me some pretty babies like yours and be a daddy to them." He spoke with a farm boy's eloquence.

"Hell, ain't never too old for that, long as you find a woman young enough!" Ted laughed knowingly.

"Yessir," Wizard agreed, but he blushed and looked aside as he did so. Ted took pity on him. Poor sucker couldn't keep his eyes off the door, let alone make conversation. "Eat up, kids. I want to be on the road before the traffic hits, and your mom still has three more places she wants to spend my money."

"Oh, Ted!" the woman protested, giving their visitor a sideways glance to assure him that women were not as bad as Ted painted them. The stranger smiled back at her with his eyes, his mouth scarcely moving. Then his eyes darted back to the door.

Ted pushed his plate away. Leaning back into the booth seat, he lit a cigarette. "Finish your lunch, kids," he repeated insistently, a trace of annoyance coming into his voice. "Clean up those plates."

The boy looked down at his hamburger in despair. It had been neatly cut into two halves for him. He had managed to eat most of one piece. "I'm full, Dad," he said softly, as if fearful of being heard. His sister pushed her salad plate aside boldly. "Can't we have dessert before we go?" she pleaded loudly.

"No!" snapped Ted. "And you, Timmy, just dig into that food. It cost good money and I want it eaten. Now, not next week!"

"I can't!" Timmy despaired. "I'm full! If I eat anymore, I'm gonna throw up."

Ted's move was so casual it had to be habit. His right hand, with the cigarette in it, stayed relaxed, but his left became a claw that seized Timmy's narrow shoulder. It squeezed. "If I get that 'throw-up' bit one more time, you are going to regret it. I said eat, boy, and I meant it. Clean up that plate, or I'll clean you up."

Cold tension rushed up from the children. The little girl made herself smaller. She took a carrot stick in both hands, like a chipmunk, and quickly nibbled it down. She refused to look at her father or brother. The boy Timmy had ceased trying to squirm away from Ted's white-knuckled grip. He picked up his hamburger half and tried to finish it. His breath caught as he tried to chew, sounding like weeping, but no tears showed on his tight face.

The woman's face flushed with embarrassment, but Ted was too focused on his dominance to care if he caused a scene. The stranger was oblivious, anyway. His long narrow hand had fallen to the table, where he toyed with the candle in its scarlet holder. He lifted it and swirled it gently, watching the flame gutter and leap as the wax washed around the wick.

"It's a very big hamburger for such a small boy." The stranger did not speak in his self-effacing country twang. His tone made him an interloper at the table, drew Ted's eyes to him and refocused his anger. Wizard's eyes met his. Their stares locked. Wizard's eyes blazed an unnatural electric blue. Abruptly he switched his gaze to Timmy. Ted's startled gaze followed his.

Wizard had continued to toy with the candle. The light from his candle faded, then leaped up with a white intensity. It became the only important light in the dimmed restaurant. It licked over the boy's face, playing games with his features. His round child's chin jutted into the firm jaw of a young man; his small nose lengthened; the brows on the ridges above his eyes thickened, and deepened the eyes themselves into a man's angry stare. The anger and hurt in his face were not the emotions of a willful brat. Ted was looking into the eyes of a young man being forced to act against his own judgment and resenting it keenly. One day he would have to justify himself to that man. His hand dropped limply from his son's shoulder.

The candle flickered down, but Ted's vision did not pass. How long since he had last looked at this boy? There had been a baby, like an annoying possession, and then a toddler, like an unruly domestic pet. They were gone. This was a small person. Someday he would have to confront him as an adult. Ted's jaw gave a single quiver, then stiffened again. Wizard set the candle down on the table.

"If you're full, Tim, don't eat the damn thing. But next

time, tell me before I order it for you. It'll save us both a hell of a lot of trouble." Ted leaned forward angrily to grind out his cigarette on the untouched hamburger half. Wizard flinched slightly, but made no remark. The woman was looking from face to face in consternation. A message had passed, a change had been wrought; she knew it, but she also knew she had missed it. She began helping her daughter into her coat. She gave the stranger a long look from the corners of her eyes. He met it full face and nodded to acknowledge her uneasiness. Ted was moving to leave, almost fleeing. She rose and gathered her purse and bags. Nodding to the stranger, she managed, "Best of luck to both of you."

"And to you, also," Wizard replied gravely. He watched them walk to the door, the girl holding her mother's hand, the boy walking out of his father's reach. They would need more than his luck wish. He gave a small sigh for them, and turned his attention to more immediate matters. Nina was busy taking orders; the aproned girl had just carried a tub of dirty dishes back to the dishroom. Wizard assembled his lunch.

Only the top of Tim's hamburger had been fouled. He discarded it and placed the rest on the woman's plate beside the handful of crisply dark french fires she had rejected. Both the children had been served from the salad bar. Their two plates were a trove of broccoli spears, cauliflower florets, sweet pickles, and garbanzo beans. They had devoured the more prosaic radishes and carrot sticks, but left these adult-bestowed vegetables for him. Ted's plate donated a wedge of garlic toast, one corner slightly sogged with spaghetti sauce, and two sprigs of parsley. Not a feast, he reflected, but certainly far from famine. And he needed it. The candle business had drained his reserve energies. It hadn't been wise. If Cassie heard of it, she'd call him a meddler, even as her eyes sparkled with the fun of it.

He ate without haste, but he did not dawdle. He had to remember that he was the man who had arrived late for a lunch date. No reason to rush. In the course of his meal, he refilled his mug four times, feeling with pleasure the hot rush of caffeine that restored him. During his fifth and final cup, he neatly stacked the dishes out of the way. He drew his newspaper from his shopping bag, folded it to the want ads and studied it with no interest. He had possessed the paper for several days now. It was beginning to look a little worn; best replace it today. So essential a prop was not to be neglected.

As he gazed unseeing at the dense black type, he reviewed his morning. The Celestial Seasonings Sampler was the high point today. He had found the box of tea bags in the dumpster in the alley behind the health food store. The corner of the box was crushed, but the tea bags were intact in their brightly colored envelopes. The same dumpster had yielded four Sweet and Innocent honey candy suckers, smashed, but still in their wrappers. In a dumpster four blocks away, he had found two packets of tall candles, each broken in several places, but still quite useful. An excellent morning. The magic was flowing today, and the light was still before him.

Wizard drained his mug and set it on the table. With a sigh he folded his paper and slipped it once more into his shopping bag. The bag itself was on exceptionally good one, of stout plastic and solid green, except for the slogan, SEATTLE, THE EMERALD CITY. It, too, had come to him just this morning. Rising, he glanced around the place and left his best wishes upon it.

He paused at the pay phone on the way out, to put the receiver to his ear, then hit the coin return and check the chute. Nothing. Well, he could not complain. Magic was not what it once had been. It was spread thinner these days; one had to use it as it came, and never quite trust all one's weight to it. Nor lose faith in it.

He stepped back into October and the blueness of the day fell on him and wrapped him. The brightness of it pushed his eyes down and to one side, to show him a glint between the tire of a parked car and the curb. He stooped for a shining silver quarter. Now, two more of these, and a dime, and he could have his evening coffee in Elliott Bay Café, under the bookstore. He slipped it into his shirt pocket. He took two steps, then suddenly halted. He slapped his pocket, and then stuck his fingers inside it and felt around. The tarot card was gone. Worry squirmed inside him. He banished it. The magic was running right today, and he was Wizard, and all of the Metro Ride Free Zone was his domain. He believed he would find two more quarters and a dime today.

A sidewalk evangelist with a fistful of pamphlets caught at his arm. "Sir, do you know the price of salvation in Seattle today?" He flapped his flyers in Wizard's face.

"No," Wizard replied honestly. "But the price of survival is the price of a cup of coffee." He pulled free effortlessly of the staring man, and strolled toward the bus stop.

2

RASPUTIN SUNNED HIMSELF on the bench, making October look like June. He was wearing sandals, and between the leather straps his big feet were as scuffed and gray as an elephant's hide. His blue denims were raggedy at the cuffs, and the sleeves of his sweatshirt had been cut off unevenly. His eyes were closed, his head nodding gently to the rhythm of his music, one long-fingered hand keeping graceful time. Black and Satisfied, Wizard titled him. Blending in with the bench squatters like a pit bull in a pack of fox hounds. The benches near him were conspicuously empty of loiterers. Wizard shook his head over him as he sat down at the other end of the bench.

Rasputin didn't stir. Reaching into a pocket, Wizard drew out a crumpled sack of popcorn fragments. He leaned forward to scatter a handful. Rasputin shifted slightly at the fluttering sound of pigeon wings as a dozen or so birds came immediately to the feed.

"Don't let them damn pests be shitting on me," he warned Wizard laconically.

"Wouldn't dream of it. Don't you think you should carry a radio or something?"

"What for? So folks would quit looking for my headphones?

Ain't my fault they can't hear the real music. They too busy covering it up with their own noises."

Wizard nodded and threw another handful of popcorn. Rasputin's hand danced lazily on the back of the bench. Muscles played smoothly under his sleek skin, sunlight played smoothly over it. The day arched above them, and Wizard could have dreamed with his eyes open. Instead, he asked, "So what brings you to Pioneer Square?"

"My feet, mostly." Rasputin grinned feebly. "I'm looking for Cassie. Got a present for her. New jump rope song. Heard it just the other day."

Wizard nodded sagely. He knew Cassie collected jump rope songs and clapping rhymes. "Let's hear it."

Rasputin shook his head slowly in a graceful counterpoint to the dance of his hand. A passerby slowed down to watch him, then scurried on. "No way, man. Not going to repeat it here. Sounded new, and real potent in a way I don't like. Gonna tell it to Cassie, but I'm not going to spread it around. Won't catch me fooling with magic not mine to do." Rasputin's words took on the cadence of his concealed dance, becoming near a chant. Wizard had known him to speak in endless rhymes, or fall into the steady stamp of iambic pentameter when the muse took him. But today he broke out of it abruptly, the rhythm of his hand suddenly changing. A grin spread over his face slowly as he gestured across the square to where a woman in a yellow raincoat had just emerged from a shop.

"See her? Walking like rain trickling down a window glass? She makes loves in a waltz rhythm." A black hand waltzed on its fingertips on the bench between them. Wizard glanced from it to the tall, graceful woman crossing the square.

"That doesn't seem possible," he observed after a perusal of her swinging stride.

"The best things in this life are the ones that aren't possible, my friend. 'Sides, would I lie to you? You don't believe me, you just go ask her. Just walk right on up and say, 'My friend Rasputin says you can make a man's eyes roll back in his head while your thighs play the Rippling River Waltz.' You go ask her."

"No thanks," Wizard chuckled softly. "I'll take your word for it."

"Don't have to, man. She's one generous lady. Picked me up off the bus one rainy night, took me home and taught me to waltz horizontal. Kept me all night, fed me breakfast, and put me out with her cat when she left for work. Best night of my life."

"You never went back?"

"Some things don't play well the second time around; only a fool takes a chance at ruining a perfect memory. 'Sides, I wasn't invited. Kinda lady she is, she does all the asking. All a man can say to her is 'yes, please' and 'thank you kindly.' That's all."

Wizard shifted uncomfortably on the bench. This kind of talk made him uneasy, stirring places in him better left dormant. "So you're looking for Cassie," he commented inanely, looking for a safer topic.

Rasputin gave a brief snort of laughter. "Did I say that? Stupid way to put it. No sense looking for her. No, I'm just waiting to be found. She'll know I got something for her, and she'll come to find me. Don't you know that about her by now? Think on it. You ever been looking for Cassie and found her? No. Just about the time you give up looking and sit down someplace, who finds you? Cassie. Ain't that right?"

"Yeah." He chuckled slightly at the truth of it. "So what you been doing lately?"

"I just told you. Getting laid, and listening to jump rope songs in the park. How 'bout you?"

Wizard shrugged. "Not much of anything. Little magics, mostly. Told a crying kid where he'd lost his lunch money. Went to visit Sylvester. Saw an old man hurting on a street corner. Asked him the time, the way to Pike Place Market, and talked about the weather until he had changed his mind about stepping in front of the next bus. Was standing in front of the Salvation Army Store and a man drove up and handed me a trenchcoat and a pair of boots. Boots didn't fit, so I donated them. Trenchcoat did, so I kept it. Listened to a battered woman on the public dock until she talked herself into going to a shelter instead of going home. Listened to an old man whose daughter wanted him to put his sixteen-year-old dog to sleep. Told him 'Bullshit!' Old dog sat and wagged his tail at me all through it. That's about all."

Rasputin was grinning and shaking his head slowly. "What a life! How do you do it, Wizard?"

"I don't know," the other man replied in a soft, naive voice, and they both laughed together as at an old joke.

"I mean," Rasputin's voice was thick and mellow as warm honey, "how you keep going? Look how skinny you getting lately! Bet Cassie don't appreciate that in the sack; be like sleeping with a pile of kindling."

Wizard shot Rasputin a suddenly chill look. "I don't sleep with Cassie."

The big man wasn't taking any hints. "No, I wouldn't either. No time for sleeping with something that warm and soft up against you. You don't know how many times Euripides and I sat howling at the moon for her. Then you come along, and she falls into your lap. Her eyes get all warm when they touch you. First time she brought you to me, I saw it. Oh, oh, I say to myself, here come Cassie, mixing business with pleasure. Now you telling me, oh, no, ain't really nothing between us. You sure you wouldn't be telling me a lie?" An easy, teasing question.

"I don't do that." Wizard's voice was hard.

"Don't do what?" Rasputin teased innocently. "Screw or tell lies?"

"I tell lies only to stay alive. I tell the Truth when it's on me." Ice and fire in his voice, warning the black wizard.

"Say what?" Rasputin sat up straight on the bench, and his fingers suddenly beat a dangerous staccato rhythm on the bench back. Wizard felt his strength gather in his shoulders and watched the play of muscles in the black hand and wrist on the bench back. He felt the edge and dragged himself back from it. This man was his friend. He forced his voice into a casual scale.

"Remember who you're talking to, Rasputin. I'm the man who knows the Truth about people, and when they ask me, I've got to tell them. I have my own balancing points for my magic. One of them is that I don't touch women. I don't touch anyone."

"That so?" the black wizard asked skeptically. Wizard looked at him stony-eyed. "You poor, stupid bastard," Rasputin said softly, more to himself than to his friend. "Drawing the circle that shuts it out." He flopped back into his earlier, careless pose, but his dancing fingers jigged on the bench back, and Wizard felt his awareness digging at him.

The pigeons roared up suddenly around them, their frantically beating wings swishing harshly against Wizard's very face. Cassie stood before them, slender and smiling. She was very plain today, dressed all in dove gray from her shoes to the softly draped cloth of her dress. Her hair was an unremarkable brown, her features small and regular. But when she flashed Wizard her smile, the blue voltage of her eyes stunned him. She proffered him a couple of gray tail feathers. "Nearly had myself a pigeon pie for tonight," she teased, tossing the feathers in his face. Wizard winced, fearing there was more truth in her jest than he approved. "Come on," she cajoled, sitting down between the men. "If lions are majestic and wolves are noble and tigers are princely, what's so cruddy about a person who snags a few pigeons for a meal now and then?"

She bent suddenly to wipe a smudge from her shoe, and Rasputin grabbed Wizard's eyes over her bent back. "Stupid shit!" he mouthed silently at Wizard, but composed his face quickly as Cassie sat up between them. She gave her brown bobbed hair a shake, and the scent of wisteria engulfed Wizard and threatened to sweep him away. But she had fixed those eyes on Rasputin and pinned him to the bench. "Give it to me!" she demanded instantly.

"Right here?" His reluctance wasn't feigned. "It's a heavy one, Cassie. Bad. I didn't like hearing it, and I don't like repeating it."

"All the more reason I should have it. Out with it."

"It was these two cute little girls, one in pigtails, down in Gas Works Park, and they were jumping rope, and I was hardly listening, cause they was doing all old ones, you know, like 'I like coffee, I like tea, I like boys, why don't they like me?' and 'Queen Bee, come chase me, all around my apple tree . . .'"

"Oldies!" Cassie snorted. "Get to the good stuff."

"It didn't sound so good to me. All of a sudden, one starts a new one. Scared the shit out of me. 'Billy was a sniper, Billy got a gun, Billy thought killing was fun, fun, fun. How many slopes did Billy get? One, two, three, four . . .'" Rasputin's voice trailed off in a horrified whisper. Wizard's nails dug into his palms. The day turned a shade grayer, and Cassie rubbed her hands as if they pained her.

"It has to come out somewhere," Cassie sighed, ripping the stiff silence. "All the horrors come out somewhere, even the ones no one can talk about. Look at child abuse. You know this one, so it doesn't bother you anymore. But think about it. 'Down by the ocean, down by the sea, Johnny broke a bottle and blamed it on me. I told Ma, Ma told Pa, and Johnny got a licking with a ha, ha, ha! How many lickings did Johnny get? One, two, three,' and on and on, for as long as little sister or brother can keep up with the rope. Or 'Ring around a Rosie' that talks about burning bodies after a plague. Believe in race memory. It comes out somewhere."

"'When the bough breaks, the cradle will fall,'" whispered Wizard.

"'Take the keys and lock her up,'" Rasputin added.

The day grew chillier around them, until a pigeon came to settle on Wizard's knee. He stroked its feathers absently and then sighed for all of them. "Kids' games," he mused. "Kids' songs."

"Jump rope songs they'll still be singing a hundred years from now," Cassie said. "But it's better it comes out there than to have it sealed up and forgotten. Because when folks try to do that, the thing they seal up just finds a new shape, and bulges out uglier than ever."

"What do you do with those jump rope songs, anyway?" Rasputin demanded, his voice signaling that he'd like the talk to take a new direction.

Cassie just smiled enigmatically for a moment, but then relented. "There's power in them. I can tap that magic, I can guide it. Think of this. All across the country, little girls play jump rope. Sometimes little boys, too. Everywhere the chanting of children, and sometimes the rhymes are nationally known. A whole country of children, jumping and chanting the same words. There's a power to be tapped there, a magic not to be ignored. The best ones, of course, are the simple, safe-making ones."

"Like?"

"Didn't you ever play jump rope? Like 'Teddy Bear, Teddy Bear, turn around. Teddy Bear, Teddy Bear, touch the ground. Teddy Bear, Teddy Bear, go upstairs. Teddy Bear, Teddy Bear, say your prayers. Teddy Bear, Teddy Bear, say good-night. *Good night!*'"

The last words she shouted as gleefully as any child ever did. Both men jumped, then smiled abashedly at one another. The simple words were full, not of awe-inspiring power, but of glowing energy. When Cassie chanted them, her voice made them a song to childhood and innocence, suggesting the woman's magic she wielded so well. Wizard and Rasputin exchanged glances, nodding at the sudden freeness in the sky and the fresh calm that settled over them. They settled back onto the bench.

"Something bad's come to Seattle," Cassie announced suddenly.

Rasputin and Wizard stiffened again. Rasputin's feet began to keep time with his hand, to dance away the threat that hovered. Wizard sat very still, looking apprehensive and feeling strangely guilty.

"What you want to be saying things like that for?" the black wizard abruptly complained. "Nice enough day, we all come together for some talk, like we hardly ever do, I bring you a new jump rope song, and then you go *'Boogie-boo!'* at us. Why get us all spooked up when we just got comfortable?"

"Oh, bullshit!" Cassie disarmed him effortlessly. "You knew it when you came. That jump rope song scared the shit out of you. You knew it didn't mean anything good when kids in the city start singing stuff like that. So you brought it to me to hear me say how bad it was. Well, it's bad."

"Just one little jump rope song!"

"Omens and portents, my dear Rasputin. I have seen the warnings written in the graffiti on the overpasses and carved on the bodies of the young punkers. There are signs in the entrails of the gutted fish on the docks, and ill favors waft over the city."

"Just a strong wind from Tacoma," Rasputin tried to joke, but it fell flat. The small crowd of pigeons that had come to cluster at Wizard's feet rose suddenly, to wheel away in alarm. Startled at nothing.

"What kind of trouble, Cassie?" Wizard asked.

"You tell me," she challenged quietly.

"Ho, boy!" Rasputin breathed out. "Think I'm gonna dance me off to somewheres else. Give a holler when the shit settles, Cassie. I'll tell the Space Needle you said hi!"

She nodded her good-byes as Wizard sat silent and stricken. Rasputin stroked off across the cobbled square, his gently swaying hips and shoulders turning his walk into a motion as graceful as the flight of a sea bird. He vanished slowly among the parked cars and moving pedestrians. Wizard was left sitting beside Cassie. Her body made him uneasy. It had taken him a long time to accept that every time he saw Cassie she would be a different person. Today she seemed too young and vibrantly feminine, radiating a femaleness that had nothing to do with weakness or docility. He wished she had come as the bag lady, or the retired nurse, or the straggly-haired escapee from the rest home. Those persons were easier for him to deal with. Looking at her today was like staring into the sun. Yet anyone else passing by their bench might have tagged them as a very nondescript couple. He suddenly wished desperately to be somewhere else, to be someone else. But he was Wizard, and he was sitting beside Cassie, and he felt like a small and scruffy kid in spite of his magic. Or maybe because of it.

"Your den is the storm's eye," she said without preamble. "Whatever it is, it's coming for you. You want to tell me about it, so I can at least warn the rest of us?"

Wizard shook his head, trying to breathe. "I can't. Not because I won't, but because I don't know what you're talking about. I mean, I don't know anything about it. Not exactly. Anyone with any magic at all can tell that there's something hanging over the city. But I don't know what it is, and—"

"It's coming for you." Cassie's voice brooked no denial. There was a chill in it that was not the absence of feelings, but the hard edge of emotions kept in check. "Whatever it is, it's yours. If it has a balancing point, only you will be able to reach it. The sooner you stop it, the better for us all. But you can't stop it until you give it a name. Do you know what I'm saying?"

"I know you're scaring the hell out of me."

"Good. Then you do understand. Be on your toes. Keep your rules."

"I do. You know I do." He added the last reproachfully.

"Yes. As I keep mine. I suppose I know that best of all." There was regret in her words. It stung him.

"Cassie. I'm not holding out on you. If I knew anything, wouldn't I tell you?"

She leaned back on the bench, not speaking. Silence fell between them. Thin Seattle sunshine, a mixture of yellow and gray, cautiously touched the uneven paving stones. A sea bird flew overhead, too high to be seen against the sun's glare, but its mournful cries penetrated the city sounds to echo in Wizard's soul. A terrible foreboding built within him, forcing words out.

"There was something, once. Like a hunger, an appetite. Something like that. I don't remember."

"It didn't have a name?"

"It was gray," he admitted uneasily.

"So it was." Cassie sighed heavily. "So you've told me. Listen, Wizard. If you needed help, you'd come to me, wouldn't you?"

"Who else would I go to? But you've got something backward, Cassie. I heard about the gray thing from you."

"You did? Well, if you say so, it must have been so. Just remember, Wizard. If you need help, I'm your friend. Just let it out that you need me, and I'll come to you. And . . . it doesn't have to be danger. If you just want some company, that's fine, too. If you just want to see me . . ."

"If I need a friend. I know that, Cassie."

She lifted a slender hand that hovered uncertainly for a moment before falling to gently pat the bench between them. "Listen," she said suddenly. "You want a story? I've got a story for you if you want it."

"Sure," he lied, covering his reluctance. He never liked what Cassie's stories did for him.

Cassie settled in. She took a breath, and after a moment began, "Once there was a war, where a guerrilla force was fighting an army from across the seas that was struggling to keep a government in power."

"If you mean Viet Nam, say Viet Nam," he said with a bravado he didn't feel.

"I didn't say Viet Nam, so shut your mouth and listen!" When Cassie was interrupted, she was as fierce as a banty on eggs. "There was an old man in a village. He had an old rifle, and whenever the foreign soldiers came near, he would fire a few shots in the air. This was because the guerrilla forces expected him to snipe at the foreign soldiers. He could not bring himself to do that. So he would fire a few wild rounds at nothing in particular, and the guerrillas would hear the shots and be satisfied he was doing his part. The foreign soldiers understood. Sometimes they'd even let off a burst or two, to make things sound lively. And the old man's family slept safely at night.

"But into this there came a very young foreign soldier who didn't understand the rules of the game. So when he saw the old man fire the old rifle, he took him seriously. He killed him."

Wizard's mouth was dry. Cassie had stopped talking as suddenly as the jolt of a rear-ended vehicle. He sat silently, waiting for more, but she said nothing. After a moment she bent her head to dig through her purse, and offered him a Lifesaver.

"The moral?" he asked, taking one. His voice cracked slightly.

"There isn't one." She spoke to the roll of candy she was peeling. "Except that the next week, the guy sniping at them from that hamlet wasn't shooting into the air."

Another electric jolt from those incredible eyes. He withstood their voltage, gripping the edge of the bench to keep his hands from shaking. She rose and walked away, leaving as silently as she had come. He tried to watch her go, but the sunlight was making his eyes water, and it seemed that she just melted into the passing foot-traffic.

"Cassie," he sighed softly, feeling empty. And wondered why.

3

WIZARD CAME AWAKE. His blanket, tucked so carefully under
the edge of thin gray-and-white striped mattress, had pulled
free. A large damp tomcat had insinuated itself between the
flap of the blanket and the small of his back, to curl in contented
sleep. November's chill damp of night infiltrated his unheated
room; the cold air condensed on his unprotected back. But
neither the cat nor the cold had awakened him. Behind his
closed eyelids, his mind had clicked into instant awareness.
Something was out there.

His fingers tightened on the fraying edge of the blanket, his
knuckles white. Without opening his eyes, he turned his concentration in, to hold his breath to the steady cadence of sleep
and keep his strung muscles from a betraying twitch. No one,
nothing, could have known that he was now awake. Even Black
Thomas, curled serenely against him, was unaware of his
watchfulness. Reassured that his personal perimeter was still
intact, Wizard cautiously deployed his senses.

A subtle wrongness pervaded his room. To his nostrils came
the familiar mustiness of the dank walls, the city cat stink like
damp wool, and beyond that the cheesy odor of pigeon droppings. A light rain had fallen on Seattle since he had drowsed

off. It had cleaned the metropolitan air and cooled it, the falling
drops pressing down the fumes of the cars and buses and rinsing
the oily gutters. Beneath the streetlamps, the drops would sparkle on the green glass sides of discarded wine bottles. He could
find the sparkle breaking into a thousand night sequins beneath
a bench in Pioneer Square. But all of this was absolutely and
totally as it should be. The very rightness of it stiffened his
spine with dread. Whatever it was, it was very clever.

But sound would betray it. He smiled without a twitch of
muscle. Hearing was his gift, Cassie had told him. His ears
could pick up the tortured hum of a fluorescent light, could
sense the shop-lifting detectors that framed the doors of so
many stores these days. He could feel the rumble of a diesel
truck in his skull when it was yet blocks away. He passed his
power to his ears and let them quest outward. But his ears were
filled with his own deep breathing and the rising thunder of
his heart. Be still! he bade it angrily, but it would not heed.
Danger pressed all around him, waiting for such an internal
betrayal. Fear soured his stomach, sending his heart thudding
high in his chest, hammering against his throat, making his
pulse leap. He had to waste precious strength and time by
turning his power on himself, to quiet his fearful body. He
gave his heart a slow count and repeated it until it could hold
the rhythm of a natural sleep. His lungs sighed in harmony.
Secured, he peered from his position, listening.

There was the whoosh and hiss of traffic on Jackson and
Occidental Avenue South. Less traffic than usual, far less than
on a King Dome night, and it was moving cautiously over the
dampened streets made treacherous by a slightly suspended
film of oil. He could hear the rainbow arching of spattering
water as fat tires spun past. Subjugated to the traffic sound was
the gentle creaking and grumbling of the old building itself.
But these normal groanings he knew as well as he knew the
thump and rush of his own blood. He blotted these sounds from
his consciousness and listened anew.

He listened for the halted footstep, for the creak of sagging
floor boards under unaccustomed weight. He listened for the
whisper of shirt fabric against jacket lining as the intruder
breathed silently in the dark. He hoped for an unwary sniff,
for the catch of breath in a nervous throat. But he heard only
the breathing of himself and Black Thomas, only the flick of
the old tom's ear as a nocturnal mite nibbled.

So slowly it could scarcely be called a movement, Wizard

eased his lashes open. He bared the tiniest slit of eyeball, too narrow a gap to glitter in the darkness. In his swath and huddle of blankets, his chin tucked to his chest, his eyes were pits of darkness. His pupils adjusted to the room.

Horror clutched at his throat.

When he had pinched out his final candle, his cardboard and blanket screen had been perfectly adjusted across the window. The blanket was a recent addition, replacing three old sheets that had previously bolstered the cardboard's tattered morale. Wizard had stretched the blanket tight across the window frame and fastened it in place by silently pressing tacks gleaned from bulletin boards through the blanket and into the wooden sill. From outside the building, the cardboard appeared to be still wedged in place inside the cracked window where it had been taped many years before. Within, the blanket supported it firmly against the pigeon-streaked glass.

His heart foundered as he remembered the blanket had been a gift, freely given. Cassie had taught him how to be open to such gifts. He had been standing by the Goodwill drop box when the woman in the blue Chevy drove up. As she opened her car door and picked up the brown paper sack from the seat beside her, he had smilingly approached her, asking, "Would you like to give that to me?" She had nodded, pushed it into his hands, and driven away.

Within the bag he had found some infant clothing, a Johnny-Jump-Up infant swing, a worn pair of hunting boots too small for him, and the neatly folded blanket. It was dark blue, of thickly woven woolly stuff, with only two worn spots. But it *had* been a gift. Not all gifts were given to bring joy to the receiver. At the time, he had felt the blanket had been sent to him, but not for his bed. The stretched sheets, even layered three deep, still permitted a streaking of his candlelight to escape. The blanket would seal him in, protect both his light and his darkness, and shield him from the gray city-night outside. When he had put it up, it had baffled the light, sealing in every speck and ray. Not one fingering beam of the city-night seeped in. He had slept in safety.

And awakened to terror. His cardboard had been wrenched clear of his window to lie atop the clotting puddle of blanket on the gritty floor.

The cracked window was not transparent. Rising street dust and grime had given it a milky wash. Stalacities of pigeon droppings graced it *à la* Jack Frost. The recent pattering of rain against it had smeared it more, making it impossible to see out. But the ghostly back-gray that passes for night in the city seeped in, making shadows that oozed from the edges of his possessions and slunk from beneath the brick and board shelves.

A smear of harsher light in the lower left corner of the window was flung from the vulturing streetlamps of South Jackson. The light striated across the cracked window, destroying even his memories of the blessed empty darkness of true night. Sweet night of star-specked skies and tree-breathed air had been replaced by a crouching grayness that emanated from the city. It came as much from the gutters and dumpsters as from headlights and streetlamps. It was more than the fogging breath of huddled winos and the gray puffing of exhaust. It was not inanimate.

Wizard kept his breathing steady, but from the skin in he trembled. His heart longed to gallop, his lungs screamed for more oxygen, faster. He smothered them, choking on fear, and tried to think.

It was gray. And now that he so desperately needed to recall everything he had ever known about it, he could remember nothing. Nothing. Except . . . Mir. A name, he wondered, and chased the wonder away. No time for it. All he could do right now was to defend. But at least it thought he was sleeping. He reined his power back, risking no contact. It wanted him. He didn't move. If he trembled, if he flinched, if his power just brushed it, it would suck at him. It would drag him from his bed to the window. It believed he still slept; he felt its tenuous probings. It sought to find his dreams and slip in the unguarded back door of his mind. Not again. Like the shock of a bright flashlight in the eyes, an unbidden memory came to him. Once it had forced him to come to it. It had never forgotten its triumph over him. But Wizard had. He could not keep the memory, let the force of the recollection assault him. He couldn't let it weaken him. If he harked to that memory, it would sense his awareness. Without a reason to hover and sneak and wait, it would leap in and fasten itself to him. Right now, it hunted his dreams.

It pressed against the cracked window pane. He saw the glass bend with its weight, heard a slight scratch as the rough edges of the crack grated against each other. His first night in this room, he had pressed the edges of the glass back into smooth alignment. Now he saw lengthening cracks race across the glass to meet the dried putty in the frame with a final click. The tip of the broken wedge of glass began to veer slowly in. It separated from the window, swinging on the putty edge like a hinge, pointing at him like an accusing finger.

Wizard held himself in check. He had a chance, if he kept his defenses tight. Let it think he slept. Let it pray and peer for the easy way into him. He could wait it out. He poised his power, waiting for it to extend itself into the room. Let it think he was defenseless; he was ready for it.

Black Thomas betrayed him. Some questing tendrils of the Gray's power must have brushed his feline senses. From a curled ball of damp fur and warmth, the cat catapulted into panic. His hind legs and razor claws flashed down Wizard's bony back. The black tom bounded from the mattress to crouch in awful fury between Wizard and the thing at the window. Deep growls scraped from Black Thomas's throat as his tail lashed defensively. He did not know what threatened him, but he defied it.

"Thomas!" Wizard warned, too late. The thing outside the window bellied and gusted in its power, delighted at the cat's foolish bravery and Wizard's wakefulness. Wizard flung up his power as he heard the gathering forces race down the long alley beneath his window and bellow through the broken pane. Wizard held his position, but poor Thomas could not. It was too much for any cat. He broached Wizard's defenses, springing out from that protection into the heart of the oncoming malice. In terror he flung himself toward the connecting door and the other room. That way had always been escape, but now escape was the bait in the trap. Mir roared menacingly into the room. A wedge of glass leaped from the broken window. It sliced the foot off the fleeing tom's right hind leg as easily as a knife slices butter.

The moment was frozen and offered to Wizard. He stared at the slicing glass falling intact to the floor. The small black foot bounded and tumbled to a stop. It twitched on the floor like a witchery charm. Yowling terror and spraying blood, Black Thomas fled to the other room and down the fire escape. Impulsively Wizard reached after him. He sealed off the pumping veins in the stump of the leg as the cat ran. But gray Mir had known he would reach after the cat. With a roar of triumphant mirth, it fell on him.

It closed on him like a fist. Wizard balled himself into a

tiny hard nut in its grasp. It might hold him, but it would not have him.

The winds of eternity screamed past his soul. Wizard shivered, then shuddered in their chill. They forced his eyes open, though he had not closed them. Tears streamed from the corners of his eyes, streaking into his hairline. He was peering down through a hole in the sky. In a barnyard, three boys were killing chickens. He fell into them.

The dark-haired boy holding the chicken's feet did not look at what they were doing. He looked away from the bird, wincing each time the axe bit into the chopping block beneath the bird's outstretched neck. He flung the beheaded body from him, his lips pinched in a tight white line. Then he stooped down to the gunnysack he held shut with one foot. He reached into the struggling bag to extract another squawking victim. He drew out a black and gleaming rooster. He knew this one. He had been a multicolored chick, with dark stripes on his head and wings. The dark-haired boy remembered a morning when he went out to feed the stock, and discovered that this chick and one other had gone into the wrong nesting box at night. The mother hen had taken the other chicks into another nesting box and covered them. When he had found the two chicks, they were cold. Their little feet bent stiffly against his fingers. Their eyes were lidded with white covers. He had stuffed them inside his shirt so his little sister wouldn't see them and cry. The feel of their cold fuzziness and their scratchy little legs had given him the creeps. Dead chicks against his bare belly. He had three more pens of chickens to feed. By the time he was pouring the feed in the second pen, he thought he felt a twitch. When he finished the third pen, there was a definite stirring inside his shirt. He had crouched in the dung and straw to lift the chicks out of his shirt and breathe on them. They had revived in his hands, and soon their earsplitting peeps had their mother flying in a fury against the mesh of her pen. He returned them to her. The little hen chick blended right in with the rest of the flock, but the striped one was always easy to spot. The dark-haired boy placed the shining black rooster on the chopping block. He gripped the two yellow legs firmly, letting the young spurs dig into his palms. He turned away and clenched his jaws.

A rusty-haired boy with freckles was holding the heads. He had a method of pinching the heads firmly on the ear spots and drawing the necks long and straight until the neck feathers stretched flat. He had never killed chickens before; his speckled face glistening with excitement. Some chickens were silent as soon as he stretched them out on the block; others kept squawking even as the hatchet fell. Then, when they threw the bodies aside, it was the bodies that still gobbled and honked as they jigged about. The heads were voiceless as they lay on the block, their beaks opening and closing soundlessly, the eyelids still blinking as if to focus the vision of a bodiless brain. He wondered what they saw. The solitary heads reminded him of goldfish gaping on a table top. He brushed them from the block onto the short grass, and found it sort of a shame when specks of dust fell on the clear eyes that still blinked and puzzled. His hands and forearms were wet with chicken blood. No matter how fast he jerked his hands back, the jumping gout of blood splashed him. Then, when the bodies hit the ground, there was no telling where they'd stagger and run. Two had crashed right into him, and one had run right between his legs, squirting blood all over his socks and sneakers. Wait until the other kids saw it! Geez, he wished he could live on the farm with the cousins. They had only done four chickens, and already his ribs ached from laughing. His dad had once told him that chickens were the stupidest creature God ever invented, and now he knew why. He gripped the black rooster's head firmly and pulled its neck out straight. "I got dibs on the tail feathers!" The lush red comb flopped over his fingers; the bright yellow eye winked at the falling hatchet.

A stocky boy wielded the tool; its handle was slick with blood. As the eldest son, he was supposed to be careful enough to be trusted with it. A maniac smile sat his lips and he laughed at Red's gross jokes. Under his striped t-shirt, his stomach felt cold. At least this time he was doing it out under the sun, in the open where it all could disperse afterward. In winter, he had to do it alone, in the straw-shed, lit by a single bulb turned on with a pull string. No matter how he swept the floor afterwards, there was always the wash of dark blood across the old boards, the stray wet feather caught in the cracks in the floor or snagged around a loosened nail. It was never warm in there, even on the hottest days. In winter it was a dark and comfortless place, feeling more like a dank cave than a wooden shed. He did not like to go into the straw-shed, even in summer. He always left the wide door open, and hurried in and out again, fleeing with the heavy bale thumping against his legs.

Once he had tried to confide in his cousin. "Don't you feel it in there?" he had whispered to Red one night. "Like clusters of little spirits, little feathery ghosts wanting to know why you fed them and cared for them and then smacked their heads off one day? Can't you feel them?"

"Chicken ghosts?" his cousin had hooted, and must have spread the joke to the neighbor kids, for the next night he awoke to drawn-out moans outside his bedroom window: "Cluh-uh-uh-uh-cluck! Cluh-uh-uck!" But the mockery could not quell the fear or the guilt. He chopped their heads off because his dad was busy and he was old enough and his mom said that if she could do the dressing out, he could do the chopping and the plucking. Go free, Rooster Spirit, he thought, go up into the blue sky and spread out across the pasture. After he had finished killing this batch of chickens, he would split up the chopping stump into firewood and stack it to be burned. The rain would wash the blood down into the soil, the wind and wild birds would carry off the stray feathers. Nothing would be left for the forlorn little souls to congeal around. He lined up his hatchet carefully and brought it down so hard that it wedged firmly into the chopping stump, trapping a few bright feathers with it.

One of them was you, Mir accused, but Wizard still refused to answer. He had been trapped that way before. Past guilt was better forgotten, lest it be savored. He blinked his eyes and was three places at once.

The eldest son had just finished all the plucking. The bright blue sky of early afternoon had waned into a grayness that promised rain. He pulled the black plastic garbage sack full of feathers free of the plastic trash bin and dragged it around the chopping block. Kneeling, he searched through the grass for the discarded heads. Blood had smeared and spoiled the bright plumage. Some had eyes or beaks open; others were closed. He did not flinch from them, but he picked them up as delicately as sleeping butterflies and dropped them in the sack. Rural trash pick-up would take away the heads and the feathers. The rest could be cleansed by sun and rain. But he found only twelve heads. Scour as he might the grass, two heads were missing. He cursed softly to himself. If his little sister found one and screamed, there would be hell to pay. If the dog ate one and got sick, he would get a licking for it. A few stray drops of rain spattered on his back. He gave it up. He knotted the plastic sack tightly shut and toted it over to the gray metal cans.

The dark-haired boy slipped silently out of the kitchen. Deep in his denim jacket pocket were the bright tail feathers that Red had snatched from the dead rooster's body. In his other pocket was the rooster's head, wrapped in a paper napkin. He hurried from the yard before Red could notice the theft of the tail feathers. He'd have to hurry; it was going to rain soon. He crossed the pasture, avoiding the moist brown cow flops, slipped through a barbed wire fence, crossed a survey cut, and fled into the woods. He followed a rabbit trail that wound beneath the trees until he came to a stand of spruce trees. Dropping to his knees, he crawled under the low swoop of outer branches until he came to a place in the center of the thicket. He could see the sky, and a tiny patch of sunlight reached the ground. This was his best place, his sitting and thinking place. He used a stick to brush away a year's layer of spruce needles. He dug down into the rich humus, the ripe smell of summer earth rising past him. He dug until he could thrust his entire hand and wrist into the hole. That was deep enough. He took the head from his pocket and unwrapped it to look a last time into the golden-orange eyes. But death had spoiled their color; he could not bring himself to try and close the lids. Instead he rewrapped it carefully in the paper napkin and placed it in the bottom of the hole. He buried it, squishing the earth down firmly with a clenched fist. When the hole was packed full, he sprinkled a layer of spruce needles across the scar. The tail feathers he stuck up in a small circle around the tiny grave. They kept falling over, but he patiently stood them up again and again, until the circle was complete. He never spoke as he did it; he made no sound at all. He bowed his head gravely to the circle of feathers and backed out of the grove, the trailing branches scratching his back and neck. He never went there again.

Red got in trouble. The school suspended him for three days after it became known that he had wrapped a chicken head in tinfoil and slipped it into a girl's lunch bag. His father claimed the chicken feathers for tying flies, and his mother bleached the blood stains out of his sneakers. His whole weekend at the farm, flushed! He wished he lived on the farm and killed chickens every day. He imagined setting their heads up on a little row of stakes by the driveway, or giving foil-wrapped chicken heads to trick-or-treaters, or stringing heads and feet on thread and trimming the Christmas tree with them. Some kids had all the luck.

You were one of them, Mir insisted. *Which one were you?*

Wizard would not answer. He would not wonder if it were true. He made himself as hard and solid as a macadamia nut. He made his soul so dense that it could not be compressed any further. He huddled within, knowing that it could not hold him prisoner forever. A pang echoed through his heart as he thought of Black Thomas, but he stilled it quickly. No avenue of vulnerability could be left unguarded.

Come, it demanded and seduced. *Look some more.*

Wizard refused; he would not look. But he could not stop feeling, and he felt the damp, clinging walls of the tunnel. He wanted to howl. It had put him back in the tunnel. He was not a big man, but he was too big for the tunnel. It had been made for ones smaller than he. It gripped him like a child's sticky fist grips a bar of candy. He was wedged in it, with blackness and danger before him, and no way to wriggle backward. He worked his toes in his heavy boots, but they were laced too tightly. His ankles cramped with the effort.

He tried not to think that the tunnel might have to end, that there might not be a path back to the hot sunlight. He steeled himself. He could not go back, so he would go on. He felt for his hands and arms. They were trapped under him. His arms were stretched flat under him, his full weight pressing them against the damp floor of the tunnel. He had no idea how it could have happened. He flexed his fingers of his hands helplessly, felt the tunnel soil grate into the rawness of knuckles and joints and wrists. His neck was cramped from the exertion of holding his head up. But if he relaxed, he knew that his face would go into the mud floor of the tunnel. He'd suffocate. Panic swelled inside him like a balloon being blown up inside his rib cage. He couldn't breathe; his inflated chest was too big for the tunnel, but his lungs weren't getting any air. He couldn't get his breath.

Wizard surrendered. He opened his eyes, but nothing changed. Blackness before him and the grip of the tunnel around him. He had no breath left to scream, but he wept, his tears choking his throat and his nose swelling shut with mucus. No air. This had never happened, he told himself, and it wasn't happening now. It was just a sham and a cheat, a corruption of all he had struggled to become. He couldn't let it drag him back to a past he had never had. He wouldn't. He would not.

With an effort of will, he ceased to struggle against it. He let his neck go limp and his face fell into the mud of the tunnel floor.

Wizard's forehead hit the floor with a resounding thump. As suddenly as it had possessed him, it had left him. He remained motionless, savoring the mildewy smell of the peeling linoleum. His face felt stiff as a mask and his head ached with the sensation of having cried for a very long time. At last he peeled his reluctant eyes open.

A thin dawn was seeping in the window through the shattered pane. Cautiously he turned his head to put his cheek against the floor. Inches from his face, his eyes barely able to focus on it, was the star of blood Black Thomas had left. Dread rose in his heart as he peered beyond it for the severed foot. But it was gone. Gone. Taken as a trophy, he didn't doubt. Wizard felt sick. He started to rise, but found part of his dream carried over into waking; something constricted his body, binding his arms to his torso. He rolled cautiously over, bending his neck to look at himself. It was the window blanket. He was swaddled in it like a cocoon. And dawn was already seeping in the window.

Working in silence, he wriggled free of the blanket. He must be out of here, down on the streets, before people began to open up the shops two floors below him. He never remained in his den during the day, never entered or left it during the hours of light. The upper floors of this building had been abandoned for years. The floor below him was mostly storage. He did not want anyone to hear a suspicious noise or see him on the fire escape and decide to investigate. The first thing Cassie had taught him was never to take chances, at all, at all. Gray Mir had forced him into this foolishness.

The floor was cold beneath his socks. First, the shard of glass. He glanced quickly out into his alley. No one yet. Working quickly but carefully, he pushed the wedge of glass back into its putty nest and then tapped his finger against it until it was nearly flush with the rest of the pane. Surely no one would notice that the cracked window now had new and larger cracks in it. Now the cardboard. It was soft with age and would not stand alone. It needed support. After a moment's hesitation, Wizard picked up the blanket. Surely it had done him all the harm it could. And he had nothing else to use. The thumbtacks were still wedged through it, save a few rolling on the floor.

He got the two upper corners, then the lower ones. It was while he was securing the side tacks that he noticed it.

He did not remember a closet being there. He did not remember it at all. The rest of the room was his, as it had always been. No item was changed. There were his few books on his crude shelves, his mattress, the two cardboard boxes that held his wardrobe. A sturdier wooden crate held his few food supplies and sundries. High on the walls were the pigeons' shelves, where they nested and roosted. All of that he remembered, and it was exactly as he recalled it. But he did not recall the closet whose open door now gaped at him. He closed his eyes and tried to picture that section of smooth wall, the painted surface pocked with careless nail holes and scuffed and stained. He was sure of it, until he opened his eyes again and the closet yawned at him laughingly.

A murky daylight filled his room, seeping in from the next chamber. He tried to remember opening the door to that room, as he did every pre-dawn, to allow his pigeons to exit. He was sure he had not. It should have been closed still, shut tight as he shut it every night before he slept. But it, too, gaped at him, allowing in the light that delineated the horrors of the closet.

Wizard's heart felt like it was beating naked on a bed of gravel. A footlocker crouched inside the closet. Its hasp was still in place, but the padlock to secure it was closed on the floor before it. Only two metal buckles kept the footlocker shut. It was finished in dull olive drab paint, scratched and gouged from use and miles of travel. Three letters were stenciled on the front in white paint. Whoever had done it had made a poor job of it. The letters were uneven and a white haze outside their outlines showed where the spray paint had drifted. Wizard stared at them. MIR. Mir. It made no sense, but a far death bell sounded in his brain.

He swallowed queasily. The footlocker seemed to swell to fill his room, muttering its ugly secrets to itself. He wiped his sweating palms down the front of his longjohns. Dust was heavy on the top of the footlocker. Whatever was inside, it had been sealed in for a very long time. Why should he fear that it could get out now? But such arguments did not comfort him. It seemed to him that the only thing more important than getting away from it was making sure that no one else ever got near it. Just touching the closet door made his flesh crawl. It swung a few inches before it screeched against its warped doorjamb. Push as he might, lift up or press down on the handle, the door would not shut. He had to content himself with wedging it as tightly as its twisted wood permitted.

The next part was the most dangerous and foolish of all. The sun was half up. He knew that his wisest course would be to lie back on his bed and be still for the day. He could abide his hunger and aching bladder until the sun had left the skies and the darkness cleared the streets. But he wouldn't. He needed to talk to Cassie. Even more strongly, he yearned to be away from the unclosed closet and the crouching secrets within.

He dressed hastily. Carrying his shoes, he slipped into the next room. He longed to shut the connecting door to his den, but knew he had to leave it ajar so the pigeons could come and go. The window in this room has intact but heavily streaked with pigeon droppings. It was also jammed open about six inches from the bottom. Through this opening the cats and pigeons came and went. Wizard slid it silently wider to permit his own departure. Fortune finally pitied him on this miserable day. The alley below was clear. He stepped out onto the fire escape, easing the window down to its usual stuck position.

He padded lightly down the fire escape, moving almost as silently as the cats did. At the bottom, there was a drop. He landed lightly on the old red bricks that paved his alley. As he stepped into his shoes he remembered, too late, that he had brought no change with him. True, his magic prohibited him from carrying more than a dollar's worth of change at any time, but he could at least have started the day with enough coins for coffee. Once he had found a fifty-dollar bill pinned inside the sleeve of a Goodwill coat. He had not squandered it, but had parceled it out, fifty-seven or sixty-two cents at a time, for coffee. He only drew from his hoard in gravest need. Today, he had surpassed gravest need. His battle last night had drained his power to the dregs. He needed coffee and warmth and a washroom with hot water and taps that stayed turned on. He was not ready for this day. Survival would be that much tougher.

But not impossible. Some days he flowed with his power. Today the current of the magic roared against him, and he was hard pressed to cling to a rock in the rapids. But he would survive, like a one-legged pigeon, by keeping a new balance. This was his city; it would feed him and shelter him and lead him to Cassie. The rock in the current.

4

WIZARD LEFT HIS ALLEY, hit Jackson Street and tried to put some purpose in his lagging stride. First of all, he had to stop looking like an urban blight resident. There was a public rest-room near the fire station, only a block and a half away now. But he dreaded its stainless steel walls and fixtures and the bizarre patrons it attracted. Instead he steered toward the Am-trak passenger station on Third and Jackson. Its tall tower and severe clock face reared up above the other buildings like a red brick daffodil. It had been months since he had last been there. It was an "emergencies only" stopping place, by his own rules. But today was a day for breaking rules it seemed, and he had saved the train station for plights such as this.

He pushed through the heavy doors. Within was a stale smell, like an unused car with full ashtrays. It was not busy right now. The inside of the building was as generic as the outside was distinctive. Nothing about it suggested trains and railroads. It was a faceless place, with vinyl covered chairs and metal ashtrays that could have come from any airport or bus station or hospital waiting room. The bright Amtrak posters were unconvincing. Wizard believed they were neither current nor real; the waiting passengers looked artificial, too.

The lavatory boasted a small sitting room. A weary janitor was mopping this area, swirling his mop strands around the legs of the stuffed chairs. He didn't spare a glance for Wizard. The room stank of bleach and disinfectant. Wizard skidded on the damp floor, then walked more carefully.

After relieving himself, Wizard stood before a mirror and eyed himself critically. It was not bad, he decided, considering his quick exit from his den, but it was scarcely professional. Taking off his overcoat, he folded it carefully and set it on the tiled counter. He adjusted his conservative tie over his pastel yellow shirt. Damping a paper towel, he sponged away a spot of mud on the cuff of his polyester jacket. The one thing an expert scavenger could not look like was a scavenger. Leave that for the dreary men in overcoats perched on their benches. Strange, how they looked like scavengers, but were not. They were not even survivors, except in the briefest sense of the term. Wizard was. He inspected his clothing. He could now pass for anything from a car salesman to a food service supervisor. Almost.

From the pocket of the tan overcoat he drew a small vinyl case. Once it had protected someone's pocket camera. Now it housed a straight razor, neatly folded; a small bar of hotel soap; a sample size bottle of Old Spice Lime cologne; a small toothbrush and a comb. He washed, brushed his teeth, and shaved quickly but carefully. Finished, he rinsed the straight razor and dried it carefully before folding it shut. He had found it long ago and cherished it because it never needed a new blade. There was the added bonus that while his shaving in public restrooms occasionally drew more than a passing glance, as long as he had used the straight razor, no one had ever bothered him about it. He used the cologne very sparingly; it was not easy to obtain, and was nearly as important a prop as the newspaper. On his way out of the terminal, he snagged yesterday's *Seattle Times* from one of the plastic chairs.

It took an effort of will to rein his mind away from last night's visitation. No sense in focusing on it. Not until he had seen Cassie and asked her advice. She would know all about it and what to do. He hurried down the street, looking as preoccupied as he was. His tan overcoat flapped convincingly against his polyester slacks. The November day was damply brisk, stinging his newly shaven cheeks. The city smelled almost clean.

On Second Avenue, a neon Keystone Kop beckoned to him

with an offer of coffee. He turned toward Duffy's. It was a little place, sandwiched between more prosaic businesses. It was not his ideal milieu, but he thought he could handle it, even on a day like this. He entered the narrow little shop.

It didn't offer much cover. It was set up as a cafeteria. One took a tray and pushed it along shining steel rails past displays of carrot cake and potato salad and weeping Jell-O and sandwiches, to where one could order a hot sandwich or a warmed sweet roll, if one wished to do so and one had money. Wizard didn't and hadn't. He wanted coffee. And here they refilled your cup for you. If you had a cup. He squinted his eyes and looked down the short row of small tables pushed up against the wall. They had red-checked table cloths, their tops weighted and protected by sheets of clear plexiglas. The scarred hardwood floors and aged red brick walls looked ashamed of the huge color TV mounted high in one corner of the café. At least today it was turned off. A sign near it proclaimed that Duffy's was OPEN FOR KING DOME EVENTS. Wizard hastily scanned the tables. He had to be settled before he was noticed.

There were no promising openings. For one thing, there weren't enough customers. It was the wrong time of day, and the help was busy restocking the shelves and cases. He was on the point of retreat when luck struck. As if in response to a mental command that Wizard hadn't sent, a man rose abruptly. He gulped his coffee down while standing, shrugged into his tan overcoat, and strode out, giving the door a shove it didn't deserve. Wizard instinctively stepped out of his way, then dodged in behind him. The coincidence of the overcoats was too much to resist. In two steps Wizard had the man's mug and half of a cinnamon roll he had left. One more step backed him up to the next table; he settled himself quietly. No one in the place glanced at him. Good. He was now established. He kept the overcoat on and concentrated on being unremarkable.

A girl came in from the back, bearing a hot pot of coffee. Smiling, she poured down the line of little tables. A frown divided her brows for a moment when she came to the table where Tan Overcoat had been sitting. She paused fractionally and glanced about. Then her head went up, her jaw firmed, and her waitress smile returned. She stepped to Wizard's table and poured for him.

The steaming coffee sloshed down, drowning the white interior of the brown mug. He breathed deeply of the aroma. As soon as she stepped away, he wrapped both his chilled hands around the mug and lifted it like a chalice. It was a bit hotter than drinking temperature, but this early in the day it didn't deter him. He took down half the mug, feeling it hit his empty stomach and spread its warmth. Setting the mug down with a sigh, he added sugar from the dispenser and turned to the cinnamon roll. It was poor fare, being too sweet, too stiff, and lacking in raisins. But it made a comfortable little cushion for the next draught of coffee.

Wizard had just lifted his mug in signal for a refill when disaster fell on him. The Tan Overcoat stepped back into the door. He did not have to turn to see him. His shadow fell on the floor beside him. Wizard drew his folded newspaper from his pocket and began to shake it out. He sheltered in the sports section as the man took another step and then another. The storm broke over the table he had vacated and Wizard had cleared.

"Can't wait to get me out of your life, can you?" Tan Overcoat's voice was like a bellowing bull as he slammed a set of keys onto the table. "Well, you can bring me another goddam cinnamon roll and a fresh cup of coffee. You can kick me out of your apartment, but you got no right to steal my breakfast!"

In two quick steps the waitress stood before him. Her eyes flashed, and she seemed to relish this confrontation rather than fear it. Small and steady she stood before him, clutching her coffee pot in front of her like the shield of Truth and Virtue. "I never touched your damn breakfast!" Her hand swooped down to snatch up the keys. "And that's another reason why I want you out; you never give anyone a chance to explain anything. You jump to conclusions and then you jump on me. I'm sick of it! Find a new patsy, Booth. I'm done with you!"

The older man behind the counter didn't even look up from the meat he was slicing. "Lynda. Can it. This is neither the time nor the place. Booth. I don't want no trouble in here. You can have a reorder or your money back. Take your pick."

"Screw you!" Booth snapped at the man, who never flinched. "And you too, bitch. I'm glad to be gone."

The glass door wheezed shut behind him. The stirring in the room simmered back to a near normal level.

"Lynda," the counter man said reasonably. "One more scene like that in here, and I'm letting you go. Get two more carrot cakes out of the freezer, would you?"

"Sure, Dan."

For an instant before she left, Wizard thought he felt her

eyes on him, touching and finding him. But when she came back to thunk the carrot cakes down on the back counter, she paid no attention to him. Her trim back was to the customers as she clattered out another order. He watched with admiration as she loaded one hand with three plates of food and deftly scooped up the coffee pot with the other. She moved gracefully down the line of tables, filling cups, landing two of the plates without disturbing the third, remembering the creamer for coffee for one and artificial sweetener for another. Then she was by his table, filling his cup from a freshly brewed pot. He kept his face behind the paper, carefully shielding himself, until he heard the incredible thunk of a loaded plate being placed on his table. He twitched the paper aside to see what was going on, to find himself impaled on her eyes.

He swallowed drily and tried to maintain his identity. "I didn't order—" he began, but she cut in.

"Eat while it's hot," she told him softly in a voice that knew everything. Then she moved on to the next table.

Steam was rising from a golden waffle. A scooped ball of butter was melting in the center, surrounded by a ring of gently warmed strawberries that were in turn ringed by an edging of whipped cream. His stomach leaped with hunger. He turned to look after the waitress, but she didn't look at him. I do not see you at all, her straight back told him as plainly as if she had spoken.

Such a thing had never happened to him before; he did not know what to feel or how to react. Ashamed, to have been caught? Humiliated, to be considered a charity case? Should he be too proud to accept it, should he rise and stalk from the café? But he was hungry, and the coffee was hot, and he could not remember when anything had ever smelled so good to him. Lynda disappeared behind the counter and his trembling hand picked up a fork. He tasted a tiny bit of the whipped cream and then began to eat as he had not eaten in days. Whole bites of sweet food, washed down with gulps of hot coffee. It was hard to restrain himself from gobbling. In a remarkably short time he was finished, and felt almost heavy with the unaccustomed weight of a full meal inside him. There was a mouthful of coffee left, just enough to finish on. He glanced shyly about, but there was no sign of Lynda. Some other waitress had come in and was clearing tables at the far end of the room. He hesitated before rising. He would have liked to leave her some sign of his appreciation, a tip or a note. But he had neither coins nor pencil, even if his natural wariness had not forbidden such contacts. So he rose, folding his newspaper in a leisurely manner, and stuffing it into his overcoat pocket. The door didn't even sigh as he passed through it. No one watched him go.

He shuddered out a sigh as he strode down Second. That had been a closer call than he liked to think about. Suppose she had pointed to him as the breakfast thief? Suppose someone had noticed him moving the roll and the mug? Even her giving him food had felt wrong; there was nothing of power or magic in her gesture toward him; only pity. He walked faster. Had he thought himself struggling against the current? No, it was more like being caught in a riptide. He had best beach himself before he made any more dangerous mistakes. He longed to feel safe, to have a sheltered spot in which to catch his breath. But there was an oppression in the air today, as if that thing called Mir was lurking overhead, watching and spoiling everything. He thought of getting on a Metro bus and cruising the Ride Free area all day. He knew it well. From Jackson Street on the south to Battery Street on the north, from Sixth Avenue on the east to the waterfront. He could ride the bus all day and watch the city from the window. But it could not take him out of danger. At every stop the grayness of Mir would be hovering, waiting for the moment when he would be alone with his guard down. He had to find Cassie, with no more stupid mistakes. He set out on his rounds.

Pioneer Square Historical District. Not because he expected to find her there, but because it was closest. Occidental Park was the name of this particular section of it, but no one in this part of town much cared. Wizard doubted if they even knew they were in Seattle. The "park" was a chunk of Occidental Avenue just above the King Dome area that had been closed off to all but pedestrian traffic. Now they called it a park. It was paved with rough gray bricks, gone uneven. Stubborn grass sprouted up between the gray bricks, and lichen and moss clung to their crumbling edges. The slightest amount of rain left the bricks damp and a frost turned them treacherous. There were trees, of course, sprouting from rings of bricks and looking as natural as mastodons in such a setting. In their shade, benches sprouted from the bricks like toadstools. Discarded humans and pigeons perched and loitered there.

Cassie was not on any of the benches. Men in dark-colored coats hunched on them, their chests huffed out against the chill. Pigeons perched on the wrought iron rails of the benches, their feathers fluffed against the cold. The pigeons looked more competent. Brick buildings fronted the park, offering small cafés, book stores, a Western Union office, a bank, and other shops even more unlikely. Wizard's favorite building was a four-story red brick one with tall arched doors and windows. Ivy climbed up the side of it. The tall glass and wrought iron doors opened into a mini-mall. One could descend a flight of steps for underground shopping after browsing the ground floor shops. The Bakery with its good hot coffee was right inside the door. There was even a gas fireplace with wooden tables near it. Inside the Arcade it was warm. Outside, the bench people were cold. And not too bright, Wizard thought, not harshly but not pityingly.

A tall, skinny black man wearing two pairs of pants moved in aimless despair from a shaded bench to one that soaked up the thin sunlight. Wizard shook his head. Now, any fool should have known that if you must wear two pants against the cold, you should wear the shorter ones on the inside where they didn't show. No animal would have flaunted such vulnerability. If only the man had attended to that detail, he could have passed for a starving grad student from the university. Didn't he know about the gas fireplace that burned by the wooden tables just beyond those tall doors? With an old text book salvaged from the dumpster behind the used book store, and the price of a cup of coffee, that man could have passed a warm morning. But if he had to be taught that, he'd never learn it.

Cassie had told him that, the first time they'd met. Wizard had been sitting on one of the sunnier benches here, but it hadn't taken the chill off him. The cold had soaked him, saturated his flesh. He remembered little of himself on that day, other than how cold he was, and the terrible sadness that welled from him like water from an inexhaustible spring. He could almost see the sadness puddling out around him, filling the cobblestoned park with his melancholy. The pigeons had come to him, and he had reached into his pocket and pulled out the crumpled bag of stale popcorn and fed them. They clustered at his feet, looking like small gray pilgrims seeking out his wisdom. They perched on the bench beside him and walked on his body, but soiled him not. One fat gray fellow with irridescent neck feathers had stood before him and puffed himself out, to bob and coo his ritual dance to his mate, which promised that life went on, always. He had fed them, never speaking, but feeling a tiny warmth come from the feathered bodies clustered so closely about him. A strange little hope was nourished by the sight of such successful scavengers surviving.

Suddenly, Cassie had stood before him. The pigeons had billowed up, fanning him with the cold air of their passage. "They know I'd eat 'em," she laughed, and had sat down beside him. She had been a stout lady, her feet laced up in white nurse's shoes. Her nylon uniform was too long for current styles; her nubbly black coat didn't reach to the hem of it. A sensible black kerchief imprisoned her steel wool hair. She had heaved the sigh of a heavy woman glad to be off her feet.

"That's a strange gift you have," she'd said. It was her way, to start a conversation in the middle. "Can't say as I've ever seen it before. Must be based on the old loaves and fishes routine." She had laughed softly, showing yellowed teeth. Wizard had not answered her. He remembered that about himself. He had known that small survival trait. Talk makes openings, and openings admit weapons. Given enough silence, anyone will go away. Unless she's Cassie.

"Been watching you," she'd said, when her laugh was done. "These last nine days. Every day you're here. Every day is the same bag of popcorn. Every day it holds enough to fill up these feathered pigs. But even when they're stuffed, they don't leave you. They know that you won't harm them. Can't harm them, without harming yourself. And if you know that much, you'd better know me. Because there aren't that many of us around. You either have it, or you don't. And if you have to be taught it, you can't learn it."

Ironically, that had been what she had taught him. That he had a gift, and that gift meant survival. That was what he could not teach to others, unless they already knew it. He was of the pigeons, and they were his flock. But it was a non-transferable bond. He couldn't teach anyone else to feed his pigeons, for he had never learned it himself. Nor would he ever know why that particular gift was the one bestowed on him. Cassie would only shrug and say, "Bound to be a reason for it, sooner or later."

Today there was a carelessly dressed woman standing beside a trash bin. Three winos were grouped respectfully around her. Wizard kept his distance as they each produced their small coins. Only then did the woman stoop, to drag out the hidden bottle from beneath the trash bin. She poured them each a measure into a much crumpled paper cup. When the last wino was drinking, and the two others were licking their lips, he approached them. They regarded him with hostile alarm. He was too well dressed to voluntarily speak to them. What did he want?

"Seen Cassie?" he asked gently. They stared at him uncomprehendingly. "If you see Cassie, tell her I'm looking for her."

"If yer lookin fer a woman, whasamatter with me?" the woman demanded boldly. She gave a waggle of her body that reminded Wizard of a labrador retriever shaking off water.

"Mononucleosis." He wished she had not asked him. Now Truth was on him and must be told. "You got it from a wino you served last week. But if you go to a clinic now, they can help you before you spread it to all Seattle. Tell Cassie I'm looking for her."

Wizard walked briskly away just as one wino got up the courage to hold out his hand, palm up. He wished the woman had not asked him, but once he was asked, he had to answer. All powers had balancing points, and all sticks were dirty on at least one end.

Down to First Avenue and the bus. A derelict accosted him at the bus stop. He was a heavy, jowly man dressed in a black overcoat, black slacks, and brown shoes. "I'm just trying to get something to eat. Can you help me?" The man held out a pink hand hopefully.

"No," Wizard answered truthfully. He could smell the Bread of Life Mission meal on the man's breath. The man stumped off down the sidewalk, blowing like a walrus on an ice floe. Wizard's bus came.

It took him north up First and farted him out at the intersection of Pine. The wind off the water wafted the sound and smell of the Pike Place Public Market to him. He strolled toward it, savoring anticipation. He never saw it with jaded eyes. The market bore her eighty-odd years as well as any eccentric grande dame. It never showed him the same face twice. Depending on how he approached, it was a bower of flowers, or a bouquet of fresh fish, or a tower of shining oranges. From Alaskan Way at the bottom of the Hillclimb, it was the magic castle rising up at the top of an impossible flight of stairs. He knew there were twelve buildings and seven levels, all interwoven with misleading ramps and stairs. He had taken care to never memorize the layout of the market; to him it was always an enchanted labyrinth of shops and vendors, a maze of produce, fish, and finery. In this part of

Seattle, he chose to be forever a tourist, sampling and charmed and overwhelmed. He strode gracefully through the maze like a dancer on the kaleidoscope's rim.

Fish from every U.S. coast sprawled in tubs and buckets of ice, inside glass counters, and in boxes lining the walkway. Their round eyes stared at him unblinking as he hurried past. The vendors in the low stalls begged him to taste a slice of orange, a piece of kiwi fruit, a bit of crisp apple. He did, and smiled and thanked them, but did not buy today. At a bakery, he helped himself to a sample of flaky croissant. Every little bit helped him, and the market lined up to feed and entertain him. He admired vintage comic books, magicians' accessories, a hat from the 'forties, stationery block printed this morning, and fresh ground spices in fat apothecary jars. In their own sweet wandering, the halls and tunnels of the market surprised him by spilling him out on a landing on the Hillclimb.

Euripides was already at work. Wizard approached respectfully. The small dark man had opened his fiddle case on the sidewalk before him and was playing merrily. Several landings below, a clarinet was completing with but not matching him. Euripides skipped and hopped his bow from one tune to the next. Wizard felt proud to have seen him and Known his gift without Cassie pointing him out. As Euripides fiddled, bright quarters would bounce off the worn blue lining of his instrument case. He had a knack for playing the tune that was running through your head even before you saw him. It was a subtle gift. Keep your quarter in your pocket, and the same tune might run through your head for weeks at a time. To those who walked by with no music in their souls, he gave a note or two, kindly. He was not a pure scavenger, but Wizard still admired him. Each man had his own calling, Cassie would say, yes, and every woman, too.

Wizard waited politely for Euripides to pause between tunes. He watched the passing folk, those who tossed a quarter and those who didn't. A little girl in Seattle Blues jeans and a Kliban cat sweatshirt was coming down the steps. Her mother was walking behind her, a rather annoyed look on her face, for the child was going very slowly. A second glance showed the mother's face to be more anxious than angry, irritated by some unseen threat. The girl was thin, and her dark skin seemed to be darkest in the wrong places. Euripides played for her. The girl gave two skips and stopped to listen.

She drew closer and closer to the fiddler, paying no attention to the mother who warned, "Sarah! Come on now, or I'll leave you." Her ears belonged to the fiddler as his bow danced through the Arkansas Traveller. Closer still she came, bobbing like a little bird to the music. When Euripides made his final flourish, she did not hesitate. From her pants pocket she tugged a crumpled one-dollar bill. Hastily she smoothed it, and stooped to place it in the fiddler's case. Euripides had put the bow to his fiddle again but, at the sight of the green paper, he paused.

"That's a lot of money to give a beggar," he said. His voice was not like his fiddle. It sawed and creaked.

"I liked your music," she said simply.

He played a few errant notes thoughtfully and gave a glance at the mother, whose face was not approving. "Well, I don't think I can take it. Not that much money."

"But I liked your music that much," the girl insisted.

"And I like you." Euripides looked at her deeply. "Tell you what. I gave you a tune, and you gave me a dollar. Let me give you one more thing. A wish."

She laughed. "I'm too big for that. Wishes aren't real."

Euripides was serious. "This one is. One of the very few real ones left in the world. And I'm giving it to you. One wish. For you alone to have and make. So you must promise me to use it wisely. Don't wish it today, for a ball of green yarn or a blue rose. Don't even wish it tomorrow. Because you must think it through carefully, and not be like all the foolish folk in the old tales. Think of all the consequences of the wish. And when you're sure you know what to wish for, wait three more days, just to be positive. Will you promise me that?"

The girl's face had changed as he spoke. From the laughing face of a little girl who is just a tiny bit annoyed to be mistaken for such a baby, her expression had changed to one of doubt, and then wonder. Euripides's earnestness had taken its effect. By the time he finished, there was belief and awe in her face. The crumpled dollar bill seemed a paltry thing indeed compared to what she had been given.

"He's given me a wish, Mommy," she exclaimed excitedly as she turned to her mother.

"So I heard." Mommy was not completely sold on the wish idea, but she did not look as annoyed as she had a few moments ago.

"One more thing!" Euripides's rusty voice stopped them as they turned away. He focused himself on the child. "A wish takes belief and heart. You have to believe you'll get your wish. That means being prepared for it, and working to help it grow. The wish is like a seed. I can give you a seed and tell you there's a tree inside it. But it won't come out unless you believe it, too, and believe it enough to plant it and water it and keep weeds and bugs away. So care for your wish."

"I will," she promised, eyes shining.

"Sarah," her mother prodded gently.

They left. Wizard moved closer to Euripides. "What was it?" he asked softly.

"Leukemia," he sighed. "I just hopes she remembers the wish. They don't know, yet. And when the chemo-therapy has taken away all your pretty curls, it's hard to remember a ragged old fiddler in Pike Place Market."

"Maybe you should have given it to her mother, to hold for her."

"Naw. She wouldn't . . . couldn't believe in it. She would have thrown it away, or forgotten it." He cleared his throat huskily. "You know, Wizard, that was the last one I had, too. God only knows when I'll be given more. I hate to think it might be wasted."

"She'll remember it," Wizard said comfortingly. "Kids remember the oddest things."

"Do you Know that?" Euripides demanded of him, eyeing Wizard keenly. "Or are you just talking?"

Wizard couldn't meet his eyes. "Just talking, this time. The Knowings are like your wishes, fiddler. When you've got a wish to give away, you feel it. And when I Know, I just know it. But not this time. I do hope it, though."

"Me, too."

"Hey, seen Cassie?"

The fiddler grinned. "Not today. Three, four days back, she was here. She was the Gypsy girl, in a flaming skirt that wouldn't stay down, and a white blouse that clung to her shoulders like mist. She started to dance, and I couldn't stop playing. Played tunes I didn't even know. My fingers are still sore. I had so much silver in my case, the coins were bouncing off each other and ringing with the music. Some old dude in a black suit and whiskers even joined in the dance, 'til his granddaughter hauled him away wheezing. And when Cassie was all done, she wouldn't take a dime. Let me buy her some potatoes and carrots, and a red rose to carry in one hand as she walked down the street, but that was all. That Cassie!"

Wizard grinned. "Sorry I missed it. But if you see her, tell her I'm looking for her."

"Will do. By the bye, my friend, the garbage truck broke down. It didn't get to the end of its rounds, and the replacement truck missed a dumpster. That green one, with 'not all men are rapists' spraypainted on it. You know the one. Some good stuff, from the look of it. Everyone cleaned out their Hallowe'en stock."

"Thanks."

The clacking of feet coming down the steps sounded. Euripides lifted his bow and set it dancing to the same rhythm. Wizard merged back into the flow of people and disappeared.

At the top of the Hillclimb, he stopped to survey his domain. The steps spilled down the open hillside amidst plantings and landings. In the summer, some landings had little white and yellow tables with people laughing and eating. But the chill wind off Elliott Bay had blown away such diners today. A shame, thought Wizard. The wind was juggling seagulls for an empty grandstand. Past the gray chute of Highway 99, there were the piers of the Aquarium and Waterfront Park. The waterfront Streetcar clanged past, elegant in green and gold. Wizard had ridden it once, for the extravagant sum of sixty cents. We had stayed on for the full ninety minutes allowed, touching the shining woodwork and gleaming brass, smelling the past in the vintage 1927 genuine Australian trolley car. They were a recent import to Seattle, but already he loved them as much as he loved Sylvester and the pigeons and the market itself.

At the bottom of the Pike Street stairs, he sauntered along past parked cars to the dumpster. Even from a distance, he could see it wouldn't yield much. Two men with green plastic trash sacks were working it for aluminum cans. He slowed his pace to allow them to finish. It was painful to watch their pitiful efforts. They had the basic idea of scavenging, but could not surrender their belief in money. There were too many steps to their survival. Find the cans, crush the cans, haul the cans, sell the cans, and go buy a cup of coffee. They wouldn't have too much luck; the dumpster looked as if it had already been worked several times that morning. Ironically, there would be more in there for a pure scavenger than for a can hunter.

He watched them plod off with their sacks over their shoulders before he approached the dumpster. He gave a snort at Euripides's idea of good stuff. Fish bones and stray socks, empty cans and crumpled newspapers. A ripped tutu. Seven squished tubes of Vampire Blood, complete with plastic fangs. Empty cardboard boxes and packing. A plastic fright wig. A box of brown lettuce. A brown paper sack labeled WIZARD.

It was cold, suddenly. Not that the wind came any swifter off the bay. The seagulls were still screaming as they wheeled, the traffic still rushed and rumbled. A breeze, half of power and half gray, stirred his hair. The cold began in the pit of Wizard's stomach and emanated outward. His ears rang and he cringed from the expected blow.

A pigeon swooped down suddenly to alight on the edge of the open dumpster. He eyed Wizard anxiously. He was very young, his beak still wide and pink. "I'm all right," Wizard reassured him. "Just give me a moment. I'll be fine." The pigeon fluttered closer, to peck at the fish bones, and reject them. A sudden jab of his beak rustled the paper sack. "Yes, yes, I see it. It just took me a bit by surprise, that's all. Go along now. Popcorn later, at the park. If you see Cassie, tell her I'm looking for her. No, on second thought, stay clear of her. You're still tender, and you aren't fast enough to get away from her. Just pass it on to anyone. I'm looking for Cassie."

The young bird was gone in a clap of wings. A lot of homer in that one, Wizard thought, watching his soaring, careless flight.

He flicked the fish bones away from the bag and extracted it from the dumpster. It was not heavy. He felt it cautiously. Cloth, perhaps. He walked slowly away with it. He was not ready to look inside the bag. Not yet. It swung ominously at the end of his arm and disturbed him. It didn't match his clothing. It betrayed him. No one in this suit and shoes would carry a dumpster-stained crumpled brown bag. He could get away with trash digging in a suit; people were always throwing things away by mistake and digging through dumpsters for them: lottery tickets and car registrations and phone numbers scribbled on the backs of envelopes. But men dressed as salesmen did not wander around the city carrying dirty paper bags labeled WIZARD. He felt the cold touch of the power on him again, both a threat and a consolation. If he could find the balancing point, he could use whatever force was working here. If he failed to find it, it would smash him.

Today he had had enough of shadows and the rumble of Highway 99 overhead. He needed sunlight. He crossed Alaskan Way recklessly and wandered out onto the pier of the Aquarium.

The sky was overcast, but he sensed the sun behind the clouds and took comfort from it. He sat down on the guard rail of the dock and looked down at the sloshing water. The bag leaned against his leg, rustling secrets whenever the wind touched it. People were slowing to stare at him. It would be a very stupid place to try to commit suicide, but he felt them wondering if he were going to jump. He rose and took up his bag.

Privacy, he reflected as he strolled down Alaskan Way, was in damned short supply in the city. Whatever was in this bag, it was not something to be poked through on a crowded sidewalk, or investigated in the closed stall of a men's room. No, it demanded solitude. And the only way to be alone in a city was to be where no one else wanted to be. Someplace cold and windy and smelly with nothing worth looking at. He hiked along Alaskan Way, past the fireboat station and the ferry terminal, past Ye Olde Curiosity Shop. Beyond it was a small grab-and-run diner in a sort of kiosk in a bare parking lot. There was a dumpster behind it, redolent of old grease and fish. Not even the cold wind off the bay could disperse the stink. Wizard stood in the lee of the dumpster and opened his bag.

It took his breath away. For a moment he forgot the stink and the cold and the traffic sounds. He touched with a cautious finger.

The long robe was dark blue, spangled with stars and crescent moons that sparkled silver when the cloth moved. It had long, loose sleeves and a high collar. There was no need to hold it up against himself. He knew it would fit. The cloak was the same blue, but unadorned except for silver trim at the collar and throat. It tied with little silver tassels.

Wizard looked into the bag again. The hat. It was blue, one shade short of black. It had a broad brim, floppier than he had supposed it would be, and a tall, pointed peak. But the tip of this lofty spire was bent. He reached into the bag and attempted to straighten it. The touch of the hat on his hand was like the touch of ice against teeth, like the unfelt slicing of a razor blade against callused skin. Slowly Wizard drew back his hand. The tip would not straighten. It was meant to be bent, and the power in it had let him know it. He felt it as a rebuke to him, some sort of subtle mockery that the tip of his wizard's hat should be bent at such a rakish angle. He remembered to breathe and took a long draw of air. Meticulously he refolded the robe and cloak and replaced them in the bag, packing them around the tall hat. He was carefully folding the mouth of the bag shut when the flutter of wings jarred him.

"Stupid!" Wizard rebuked him. "I warned you that you weren't fast enough for her."

The young homer's feathers were still ruffled, and two of his pinions were missing. In spite of his rakish appearance, he cocked his head at Wizard, fluffed his throat out and gave a bob and coo.

"I'm coming. Next time, don't be such a show-off. No, no popcorn until I get to my bench. Go on, now. I'll see you there."

The young homer soared off. Wizard watched the flick, flick, glide of his wings silhouetted against the lowering sky. Despite the chill of the day, he took off his tan overcoat and draped it over his arm, concealing the bag. That done, he headed for the bus stop.

5

HE STARED UNSEEING out the bus window, trying to still the small moth of excitement that always fluttered inside him when he knew he was going to rendezvous with Cassie. Rasputin's remarks of a few days ago came into his mind to haunt him. He pushed the ideas away angrily. As if he would ever endanger his relationship with Cassie that way, let alone the magic she had shown him how to unlock. That he had always had the ability to be a wizard he did not doubt; but without Cassie it would never have developed past the stages of odd hunches and strange turns of fortune. He had not been anxious to develop it either.

The second time Cassie had come to him, he had thought he was having a vision. He tried to remember the exact alley, but all his memories from that time were shadowed, like portrait proofs slowly darkening in his mind. It had been winter. That much was certain.

It had been snowing as it did in Seattle once or thrice a winter, with large wet white flakes that spiraled down from the sky. For the first hour, the flakes had melted as soon as they touched the gray streets or the red bricks that cobbled the alleys. Then the snow had begun to unite in ridges of gray slush in the streets, and in trackless white strips down the centers of the alleys. Soon even the edges of the streets turned white, and the snow filled in the black footprints of the few pedestrians as quickly as they passed. Tomorrow there would be school closures, and the buses would run on emergency schedules and refuse to stop in the middle of the steep streets. He had wiped a drop of moisture from the tip of his nose and slid his numbed hands back into the small warmth between his cramped thighs.

He had been crouching between the back of a dumpster and the brick wall of a building, where only the most persistent of the breezes could find him, and none of the snow. But the cold radiated from the bricks at his back and rose from the cobbled street beneath him. The earth was a cold fickle bitch that had turned her icy back on him. The seams of his old black boots were cracked and the faded denim of his pants was as stiff and rough as sandpaper against his chilled skin. His flannel shirt was not long enough to stay tucked in, and the denim jacket he wore was short, barely touching the top of his hips. The collar was turned up to chafe against his reddened ears whenever he turned his head.

He had been watching the snow as it fell past the glow of a streetlamp, trying to dream. There were two parts to the dream. The first was that if he sat still enough, crouched on his heels behind the dumpster, an envelope of body heat would form around his still body and protect him. Whenever the wind was still, he felt the warmth seeping out of his body and resting against his skin like a benign and transparent spirit. But then the wind would stir and rip his warmth away, and he would shiver again. The shivering made his spine ache and his muscles cramp. Every so often, his legs would give way beneath him and he would find himself sprawled flat on the damp, cold pavement. The bricks sucked greedily at his body heat until he raised himself to crouch on his heels again, his body in a shivering curl over his knees.

The other part of the dream was more frightening. When he stared at the swirl of flakes in front of the streetlamp, his perception of distance and speed changed. The flakes seemed to be originating in the lamp and zooming toward him in a dizzying rush. Stare a little longer, and he would feel that he was the one in motion, journeying to that far-off light, and the white bits of matter that rushed past him were the bright stars of a thousand galaxies. He could feel himself drawn to the light like a moth to the candle flame, could feel the pull as he was lifted from his aching crouch and rushed through a thousand nights. Then his body would fall with a crash, jarring him from both dreams, and he would have to begin again. Each time he felt he was getting closer to the light. He did not know what he would find when he arrived there, but he hoped it would be warm.

Without warning, his dream changed. He frowned to himself in annoyance. What business had this vision in coming between him and the brightness of his light? She floated toward him, white face and dark eyes, dark hair outlined and tipped with silver white, wearing a long dark garment that sparkled and shifted with the wind and whirling flakes. She seemed familiar, and yet he was equally certain he had never met her before. As she got closer to him, she became darker and darker, until she was a black shape between him and the light, nearly blocking out the glow of the street lamp. He blinked up at her.

"So here you are." There was relief in her voice, tinged with exasperation. "I was beginning to think it was a fool's errand to try and find you tonight. Rasputin told me not to waste my time. I told him there was a wizard lost in the city, and close to being dead. 'If he's a wizard, Cassie,' he told me, 'he'll find himself, and then come looking for us.' He can be so hard sometimes. But I told him no, I didn't think you would. I don't think you believe in yourself yet. Maybe because you don't want to. But it doesn't work that way, wanting or not wanting to be a wizard. You just are. Look at me!"

He had been trying to see past her, to focus on the streetlamp again. Her sharp nudge sent him sprawling to the cold damp pavement. Pins and needles shot through his cramped legs. He couldn't move, couldn't crawl away from her if he tried. She towered over him, darker than the night, and silver. He cowered, awaiting the finishing blow.

"You know who I am." It was an accusation.

He struggled with his mind, longing for his dream to come back, wishing that he were more stoned. But there was something about her that would have forced an answer from a rock.

"You're the woman from the park bench," he said, his words thick as settling snow. "The one who talked about popcorn."

"Damn right I am. But only a wizard could have known that."

She stooped beside him suddenly and he cringed away. "No. Please, no!" What was he denying? The charge of being a wizard, or the easy way she gripped him by the shoulders and lifted him to his feet? His knees, numb from his long inactivity and the cold, started to buckle under him. She slipped under one of his arms, bearing him up and taking charge of him. She staggered him along, he knew not where. The streets were silent, black and white and silver with snow and night and streetlights. Nothing else moved. No car passed, no other pedestrians struggled against the wind. Seattle was deathly silent, paused and poised between one moment and the next.

"Where are we going?" he managed. Their feet made tracks in the pristine white sidewalks, and the snow filled them up behind them, making their passage a fantasy. He wanted so badly to lie down in the soft clean snow and rest.

"To shelter," she told him, and in her voice he heard the telltale pant of effort. She was strong, but he was no easy burden for her.

"I don't want to go to a shelter," he half groaned. He had been to one of the shelters once. They had given him two pajama bottoms, one to sleep in and one to use as a towel after his shower. They had given him a box to put his own clothes in, and a piece of soap to wash himself. He had slept on a flat mattress on the floor with a rough blanket over him, listening to the coughs and rustlings and mutterings of a score of other men. The noises had brought back the old dreams and fears, so that he had sweated through his pajamas and blanket, soaking the mattress with sour fear stench. Never again. Better to freeze to death in the snow than to endure that long night again.

"To my shelter. This way."

The feeling came back to his legs and he supported his own weight, but she did not release his arm. He began to take note of the buildings they passed. Uneasiness sandpapered his nerves. This was no Seattle he knew. The patterns of brick in the buildings suggested vague faces, the fireplugs that hunched beneath snow caps were like cossack trolls. It was all alive and watching, awareness in the details like a Kay Nielsen illustration for a metropolitan fairytale. Cassie's grip was firm on his arm and he was suddenly grateful for it, sure she guided him past dangers and pitfalls. This was no place of dead stone and bare pavement, though thousands might walk its streets by day and believe so. This was an ecosystem, vital and aware, of interdependent life, of predators and prey and parasites. Wizard's heart nearly stopped as he thought how blindly he had wandered through these streets.

"This way. Down this way."

An alley mouth, and a wooden door in a brick wall. And then stairs. Stairs that barked his shins and cramped his cold calf muscles. He followed her up them, and through a door into a place that pressed him with silence and warmth. He noticed little more than that at first. He sank into the corner of a fat couch upholstered in cream cloth with large blue flowers on it. He let his head sag back against the cushioned support, feeling warmth and smelling dust. He heard her close the door, and then she moved into his field of vision again. She swirled a dark cloak free of her body, ridding it of snow with a snap. The *tack, tack* of her boots faded into another room, and was followed by the homey clatter of pans and cups. His cheeks and forehead tingled as his skin began to warm. Somewhere a kettle whistled, and a spoon stirred against ceramic mugs. A refrigerator opened and closed. Then he heard the soft tread of bare feet on carpeting and suddenly smelled rich chocolate. He opened his eyes, wondering when he had closed them. She was placing a tray on a low coffee table before the wide couch. "Hungry?" she asked.

He dragged himself upright. The smell of the food beckoned him, but he hesitated, wary as the wolf lured to the trap. He stared at the woman.

She was dressed in a long soft robe as white as the snow they had come from. It fell to her bare feet and then puddled around them as she suddenly sank down to sit gracefully on the floor by the table. Her long dark hair, dampened by the snow, hung straight past her shoulders, but short tendrils of it wisped around her face. And her face was classic, oval, with a straight nose and chiseled mouth such as one might expect to find stamped on ancient coins. Her eyes were darker than brown but not black, and the chill of the night had flushed her cheeks. He suddenly felt dirty and uncouth.

Behind her was a jungle. Plants lined and banked the wall, plants that trailed or climbed or stood upright on their stalks. Some bore blossoms in a rainbow of colors and some were innocently green. He recognized none of them. Turning his head, he discovered more plants, in tubs and pots and basins. Yet the room did not feel crowded. There was a harmony to this interior garden that he had never sensed before. They took in tension and breathed out peace.

"Aren't you hungry?" she asked, and he realized she was repeating herself. He nodded dumbly and took the mug she offered.

It was a most unorthodox meal. There was hot chocolate topped with dollops of cream, small rich biscuits swirled through with cinnamon and brown sugar, and little oranges she peeled for him because his hands were still too cold to manage them. He watched the long curls of rind, more green than gold, trail from her graceful fingers. The oranges were sweet and tart, and strangely right with the chocolate. He had not realized how cold he had been until he abruptly stopped shivering, and breathed a deep sigh as his body relaxed.

"Warmer now?" she asked, and when he nodded, smiled and said, "A quick shot of sugar will do that for you. Helps the body chase off the chill."

"You're gentler this time," he said suddenly, and then wondered what had prompted it from him.

"Am I? Sometimes I am. It depends on my mood more than on my form. Why, did I scare you before?"

"A little. I guess I'm just not that used to dealing with people anymore. I still don't understand what's happening, or who you are, or why I'm here. I'm just glad to be warm."

"For now, that's probably enough. But I'll give you a little more than that to think on tonight. I'm Cassie. And you're here because you have a lot to find out, and you won't find out what you already know by crouching behind a dumpster and freezing to death."

He nodded as if that made sense. "And where are we?"

"In my place. One of my favorite Seattles. We're in the one that would have been if the great fire hadn't happened at the turn of the century."

"Right. Bring on the rabbits with pocket watches."

"Not quite. More like bring on the wizards and wicked witches."

"Toto, I don't think we're in Kansas anymore."

"Precisely!" and she laughed delightedly. He laughed with her, uneasily, and rose as he did so.

"I think I'd better be going."

She shook her head with bemused tolerance. "I think you'd better stay. You need dry clothes, a haircut and a shave, and another meal or two before you're fit to try your wings. It's going to be a different world for you out there. Most of all, you need to understand who you are."

Her amusement stung him. "Listen, lady, I already understand myself just fine. Maybe if you understood me a little better, you wouldn't feel so cosy about what you've just dragged up to your apartment in the middle of the night. Picking up someone like me off the streets isn't a smart way to get your kicks."

"Maybe if you understood a little better just who had picked you up, you wouldn't feel so comfortable about being here, either. Now sit down and stop ruffling your feathers at me. No one has to feel threatened. Does the idea of dry clothes and a bath hurt your feelings?"

"No. But then what?"

"Then whatever. We'll take each step as it presents itself. Look, uh . . . what is your name?"

She had him there. He just stared at her, knowing he knew it, knowing he could remember it if he had to, if he wanted to. Then he tried to remember it, even wanted to remember it, and couldn't. And remembered that this had happened to him before.

"You see?" she said softly, and he suddenly felt the trap he had fallen into. She didn't push it. "The bathroom's down that hall, to the left. We'll talk later."

He stared at her for a long moment, thinking of a dozen possible courses. He could walk out the door, or insist that they talk right now, or throw the coffee table against the wall, or. . . . She didn't break away from his stare, but held him steady until it had all passed. He felt suddenly hollow and old. "To the left?"

She nodded.

He had been terrified that it would be all pinks and posies, with tiny bars of soap and ice white towels and delicate crystal soap dishes and figurines. It wasn't. The hot water steamed the big mirror in its wooden frame. The soap filled his hand, white and unscented. The towels were huge, brown, and mildly scratchy. But even shaved and washed he looked something of a wild man. Rough brown hair straggled over his ears and forehead. His eyes were rimmed with pink. He broke a toothbrush from an envelope of plastic and scrubbed at his teeth until his gums bled. He dug grime from under his fingernails, paying attention to each minute detail of cleansing himself so he wouldn't have to think.

His clothing had disappeared while he showered. Fresh jeans and a soft blue sweatshirt supported white underwear and socks. Eventually he had to emerge, feeling strangely vulnerable and light-headed in his cleanliness.

She was not in the living room, nor in the kitchen when he

peered around the door. He stood still, wondering whether he should sit down quietly on the couch and await her return, or call to her. He sat, but no sooner had he sunk into the couch's soft embrace than he felt he had to find the woman. Cassie. There were too many unanswered questions, and in the silence they were ganging up on him. He peered into the kitchen again, and saw a second door. He went to it, tapped and called softly, "Cassie?" There was no reply. He turned the knob and pushed it open.

A black wind was blowing past it, its whistle rising and falling in pitch. All beyond the door was dark, with a total darkness deeper than any he had ever glimpsed before. He stared out into it, petrified and fascinated. He felt neither cold nor warm in the wind that passed him, but neutrally at peace. Breathing took a little more effort, but somehow he didn't really mind that. His lungs pumped deep and steady, and he finally saw, infinitely far in the darkness, a pinprick of light. He gripped the edges of the doorjamb and leaned out, trying to see it better. It reminded him of the snowflakes in front of the streetlamp. There was that feeling again, of journeying rapidly to a place so far away that despite one's dizzying speed, one might never get there. Or was the pinprick of light actually getting smaller? He leaned further out.

She gripped him, not by the collar of his shirt, but by the back of his neck. Her hand was cold and strong, her nails sharp. He felt himself drawn firmly back from the pinhole of light, pulled back into light and kitchen fragrances and warmth on his skin. She jerked the door shut as soon as he was completely within it. Then she turned to him, shaking her head.

"Is there any kind of trouble you don't get into?" she asked with some asperity.

"I was looking for you. What was that?"

Cassie shrugged. "The part of the Seattle we're in has gaps like that. No one understands them, but we all know they're dangerous. If we open a door or a window and there's nothing there, we shut it. That's all."

"I know," he said, and then stopped suddenly.

"That's right. And I know that you know, too. You probably really knew it before you even turned the knob. So back to question one. Is there any kind of trouble you don't get into?"

He felt suddenly foggy again, lost and confused as he had felt for so many days—or was it weeks? "I was only looking for you," he said, trying not to make it sound like an apology.

She looked disappointed. "You're going to fight it all the way, aren't you? I can tell you there's no going back, but you aren't going to believe me. Look, Wizard. Nothing is going to get any easier until you start accepting things, and being who you are now. It's natural to be a bit confused at first, when your potential starts making you aware of it. Hiding from it and denying it won't make it go away; it will only make it take longer for you to reach your capacity, and possibly cause you a lot of pain in the process."

"I don't understand. I don't understand what the hell is going on at all. Who are you, anyway, and why did you bring me here?"

She shook her head and turned away from him. He trailed behind her into the living room. She dropped onto one corner of the couch and sat looking up at him. He started to sit down on the other end, but then retreated to the far side of the room, to lean on a mantelpiece and return her stare. He felt he had scored a small victory when she finally gave a sigh and then spoke.

"We'll do it one more time. I'm Cassie. And you are Wizard. And I went out tonight, through a hell of a lot of dangers that you refuse to recognize, and dragged you back here in the hopes that you'd live long enough to be worth something. It could be so simple, if you'd only let it. Just relax, man, and be yourself. The city will take care of you. And you take care of the city. That's all Seattle wants of you. That's all any of us want from you. Why are you being so damn stubborn?"

"I don't know what the hell you're talking about. Frankly, lady, I think you are almost as crazy as I think I am."

"How crazy is that?"

"I don't know!" he roared, exasperated with the conversation.

"Is there anything you do know?"

"I don't know!" The screech tore his throat. A rush of fear engulfed him, followed by the adrenalin strength that knotted his muscles and made him capable of anything. He took two steps toward her, knowing he could spindle that fragile body, smash the delicate skull that housed the pulpy gray brain, put an end to her and to her questions and statements that made no sense.

She looked up at him, eyes wide with curiosity, not fear. A

twitch was jumping in his cheek and there was the sound of roaring wind in his ears. "Harness that, and you'd have something," she said at last.

Her voice wrapped itself around his chafed nerves, soothed and calmed him. As quickly as his anger had risen, it drained from him. "Can't you start at the beginning, and go slowly?" he found himself asking.

"There are no beginnings," she said, almost sadly. "It happened the same way to all of us. Perhaps that's the only universal thing about it. You wake up the day after, and know that nothing will ever be the same. Some hear voices, and some are suddenly aware of the total silence of the world. Some of us are filled with awesome purpose, and some of us are emptied of ambition and opened to time. I can tell you a story, if you like. That was one of the things given to me. Sometimes they help. Listen. Once upon a time there was a young girl who lived in a crude hut on the edge of a great forest. Her parents were dead, and though she was not quite old enough to live by herself, she was too old for anyone in the village to feel they had to take her in. So she lived alone. She made a marginal living with her small flock of chickens and the herb garden that she tended. Her mother had possessed a gift for herbs, so the girl had plants there that were quite rare, with virtues unknown to many more learned folk. So not only the folk of the village came to her for herbs and spices, but also the Great Folk that could afford to travel afield for such luxuries.

"One day a great company of the folk, with some of the men dressed in rich robes, and some dressed in shining metal, and the women clad in rich dresses that near trailed the ground, even from the backs of their horses, rode past. They were talking and jesting among themselves, and three minstrels were singing, so that they made a fine noise and dust as they passed the little hut. None noticed the little maid in her garden, until at the very end of the company there came an old man, dressed in robe and mantle of blue. His hair and beard were as gray as sword metal, but he carried no such weapon. He stopped at the gate and sat his horse, looking down at her, while the rest of the Great Folk followed the King's Road into the forest. He was so quiet that at first she didn't even notice him. When he spoke, she started, and nearly uprooted the tiny plant she was weeding around. 'So you've been chosen, and I see you'll do very well indeed,' he said. He came down from his tall horse and entered the maid's garden and life. No harm did he offer her, but taught her much of herbs and all that grows, things beyond the teachings of any other mortal. Rules he gave her that she recognized as her own. 'You can offer,' he told her, 'but not with words, and until what you offer is accepted, you cannot give it. You must tend the plants wherever they may grow, and what you must ask of others is the most they can give. You can take all, except for the things you desire most, and those you must not touch until they are given freely.' These were the sort of things he taught her. For five years and a day he stayed with her, and neither of them ever regretted a day. Then one day they both knew that he had to go, for there were portentous events brewing, and a place in them for him. And so he left her, and never again was she the same person."

He had shifted impatiently all through the story, not wanting to be touched by it, not wanting to hear any of the silliness. She was so solemn as she told it, as if she were revealing the secrets of the universe. The mood she had created stretched like a bubble around them both, and he felt a compulsion to pop it.

"And the old man was Merlin, and the little girl was Cassie. The End."

But his mocking words did not shatter the bubble, nor even dent it. Cassie sat looking at him with cat-green eyes (hadn't they been brown a moment ago?) and smiling to herself. He had missed something, and his smart-ass remark hadn't made him seem any the wiser to it. He had only embarrassed himself and would have called his words back into his mouth if he could.

"You need a haircut," was all she said. "Shall I get the scissors?"

He nodded, and later sat on a straight-backed chair in the kitchen, looking at the newspapers on the floor that told the news of a Seattle that never existed. He felt the cold of the shears against the back of his neck and the tickling brush of his own hair as it fell.

And still later, he stood awkwardly by the couch as she unfolded it into a bed and brought out a stack of clean white linens and soft blue blankets. "I want to thank you. But there's no way I can ever repay you for any of this."

"There are many coins to repay kindness."

"I don't have any money," he told her, momentarily taken aback by her words. She had smiled and shook her head over him, and left him to sink into warmth and sleep. He had dreamed that in the night she came to lie beside him and watch over him while he slept. He had dreamed that he felt her warm breath on his skin, felt her eyes touch his face.

And he had awakened shivering in the melting snow behind a blue dumpster in an alley.

6

THE HOMER was already perched on the back of his bench when
Wizard arrived. He saw no sign of Cassie, but then he hadn't
expected to. She would come when she was ready. The pigeons
rose in a gray cloud to greet him. They wheeled once over the
park and settled around his usual bench. His flock awaited him.

He waded through his congregation to set his bag and overcoat on the bench and seat himself beside them. He took the
crumpled bag of stale popcorn from the overcoat pocket. The
pigeons surged forward in anticipation. But he was not to be
rushed. He pushed his hand into the soft wrinkled bag and
pulled out a handful of popcorn fragments. Leaning down, he
sprinkled them in a wide swath before his feet. The multitude
came to feed. The cocky young homer fluttered into his lap
and tried to stuff his head into the bag. Wizard gently restrained
him, but did allow him a small pile on the seat beside him.

About every five minutes he scattered another handful of
feed. The flock surged and retreated around his feet like a
feather ocean. As individual birds became sated, they came to
perch sleepily on the bench beside him. Several young ones
pushed under the fold of his overcoat and huddled there, enjoying the warmth and security. Their immature beaks were

pink and too wide for their heads. Tiny yellow hairs stuck out from the unfinished plumage on their necks.

Wizard gazed over his flock, at the majority of gray pigeons with black striped wings and irridescent blue neck feathers, and at the minority of escapees whose selective breeding showed. Darwin had concluded that if any naturalist had come across these results of controlled selection in the wild, he would not even classify them as pigeons. There was a black fan-tail strutting his peacock-span tail, and here a brown King pigeon, twice the size of any other bird there. There was an owl pigeon with a stubby black beak, yellow eyes, and half its feathers on backwards. There were three helmets, brown caps and tails looking like uniforms on their white bodies. And there were a number of renegade homers, drop-outs from some city race. A few showed feathered feet and legs, and one wore a tiny metal band around one leg. Given a generation or two of non-selective breeding, and their offspring would return to the gray and black uniforms of sidewalk pigeons everywhere.

Time dissipated. Wizard felt no chill as the gray afternoon wheeled overhead and dipped slowly away. A break in the cloud cover let in the slanting light of a setting sun. Like ancient lovers, the gray light touched the cobbled face of the park. One sensed rather than saw the beauty between them. They took one another on faith.

The pigeons rose suddenly, gusting cold wind past him and disappearing into the sky. Slowly Wizard folded his popcorn bag and stuffed it back into his coat pocket. Leaning back on the bench, he surveyed the square leisurely. It was all but deserted. Those who still hunched on the benches were as gray as the cobblestones. It only seemed fitting to leave them out all night. Then he became aware of Cassie.

Down the gray park strip she came like the last ray of daylight. Her gray sweatsuit was trimmed in yellow; a yellow sweatband held her mahogany hair back from her gray-blue eyes and high cheekbones. The bright flush on her cheeks showed that she was ending, not beginning, her run. Her pace became a jog as she passed his bench. She paid him no attention. He rose and gathered his things. He saw her vanish through the tall wrought iron doors of the Grand Arcade. He followed, and as the doors closed behind him, he glimpsed her going down the stairs to the underground shopping. She strode quickly away, her sneakers making no sound as she fled.

Sighing at this whim of hers, he gave chase. Where was

she going? He needed to talk to her. The footlocker leaped into his mind, submerging him in panic. Cassie gleamed before him like a lifeline. He bit down on his tongue to keep from calling her name aloud. Clutching his bag and overcoat, he went down the steps two at a time.

She threaded her way through the maze of underground shops and he gave chase. Past the Fireworks Art Gallery she strode, not even tarrying for a glance at the pottery. Wizard sidestepped a couple strolling arm in arm. She was hurrying up the stairs that led back to street level. That particular staircase would let her out in the cobbled square, scarcely a block from where she had entered the mall. Mystified, he raced up the steps after her. He reached the street level landing and stood panting as he stared about.

A door to his left was just closing. He tucked his bag more securely under his arm as he watched it swing toward him. It could not be there. The glass door in front of him revealed the cobbled square. The stairway emerged in the square, well clear of any buildings. There was nowhere for this door to lead. He caught it just before the catch snicked.

It opened onto a staircase, wooden and very dusty. The walls were white, lit by a single bulb that glared down at him. He thought he caught a whisper of her sneakers far above him. He panted up the steps, dust coating his mouth and throat. The steps went straight on, and on, with no windings or turns, lit at intervals by identical bare lightbulbs. The steps became steeper with every light he passed; there were no landings or hand rails to rest on. Wizard tried to calculate how far he had climbed, and failed miserably. He heard a far laugh. Shifting his coat and bag to his other arm, he hurried on. The light changed subtly. The next fixture he passed was a gas lamp in a glass chimney. Six of these he passed, and then he came to a sconce with white beeswax tapers. Wizard's face throbbed; he hoped his nose wouldn't bleed. His shirt stuck to him.

The stairs began to be in poor repair. He slipped twice on their worn edges, barking his shins. The wood creaked ominously, and once he snatched his foot up just as a rotting riser gave way beneath him. He passed bare windows, curtainless, with glass shattered away. Outside was blackness and stars; nothing else. He hurried past their empty stares. The lights were farther apart now; he climbed in a dusky twilight.

The walls of the staircase began to show cracks. Some were as wide as his fist. He caught glimpses of cold stars through them and felt the icy breath of night. He no longer dared to rest his hand against the wall. Once a whole step was missing. In the semi-darkness, he nearly didn't notice. His heart clutched at his throat as he stepped over a black eternity. He glanced back the way he had come. Behind him the lights were snuffed; the staircase down was a black tunnel.

He climbed on. Just as his calves hopelessly cramped, he reached a tiny landing. A door upholstered in red velvet was lit by a small bayberry candle guttering in a yellow glass globe. Wizard took a deep breath and lifted an ornate brass knocker. He let it fall twice. The door was opened instantly, and he stumbled in to sink onto low fat cushions.

"No wind," Cassie chided him. "I keep telling you to get more exercise. You could be a Sunday jogger."

"I don't have the wardrobe," he panted. Slowly his breathing steadied. He looked around an unfamiliar chamber furnished with a multitude of red and yellow cushions. Tall windows framed in sumptuous drapes let in the night and the constellations. The ceiling rose in a dome whose interior was calligraphied with gilt characters. Light came from various choirs of candles grouped around the chamber, and from a small bright fire in a squat brazier in the center of the room.

He took the tall glass she handed him and sipped from it. Clear, cold spring water, icy as a glacier, revived him. He smiled at her gratefully, beseechingly. "Cassie," he ventured. "I think I'm in terrible trouble."

"I know you are," she replied succinctly. She parted some draperies and disappeared. He stared at the banked candles until she returned, clad now in a white gown kirtled with green, and bearing a large tray. Tray and woman sank down gracefully beside Wizard. The tray had short legs that put it at kneeling height. The brazier warmed them both. She did not wait for him, but plunged ravenously into the meal.

Wizard picked up a thick meat sandwich on homemade bread and eyed it suspiciously. "You attacked one of my pigeons today," he accused her gravely.

"So what?" Cassie asked around a mouthful. "We all have to eat. Besides, I just rumpled his feathers. This meat isn't squab, if that's what you're worried about. Eat now, talk later. You're as skinny as a pile of kindling."

Wizard ate. He never asked her where she got things from. Beside the sandwiches were slivers of smoked salmon poked into cream cheese balls, crisp sour tiny pickles, cashews and almonds, and small pastry rolls with a mysterious spicy filling. As he ate, he felt his strength and calmness expanding to fill him. His fear had hidden inside him all day, nibbling away at his power. But at Cassie's he was safe, and the food she fed him gave him back his mind. With a sigh, he finished and leaned back to look at her.

Tonight she was young, perhaps in her early twenties. Her hair was caught back in a loose roll at the nape of her neck, but tendrils of it had pulled free to soften her grave features. She lapped cream cheese off a fingertip, and caught his eyes on her. "So?" she asked, wrinkling her nose at him.

"So," he agreed. The weight of his worry pressed down on him again. "I had a visitor last night, Cassie. An unpleasant one. It calls itself Mir."

"I know." She stopped his voice with a look. "I overheard it. Anyone with a shred of Power must have felt it last night. I imagine people had nightmares for blocks around here."

"Sorry," he murmured, feeling guilty about the overflow.

"Don't be. They should consider it fair warning. If you fall to it, not a street in the Ride Free Area will be safe. So it concerns them as much as it does you. What you are going to do about it?"

He shook his head slowly, having no answer. The Pimp entered, slipping between the drapes like perfume, strolling across the room with his orange tail held high. He glanced with green eyes at the ravaged tray and leaped to Wizard's lap, purring loudly. Wizard stroked his sleek sides, and the big cat stood up against him to rub cheeks with him. Sitting down fat on his lap, The Pimp gave a quick scrub at his face with one paw and uttered a questioning meow.

"Sorry," Wizard laughed gently. "We ate it all."

The Pimp was not slow. He sank his claws into Wizard's thighs and burned out across his chest, leaving clawmarks instead of smoking rubber. Wizard gave a yell and fell away from him as the angry cat vanished. Cassie only laughed. "You see where he got his name. Bring him something home and he's your sugar man. But greet him empty-handed. . . . That's The Pimp."

"Black Thomas lost a paw last night."

Cassie flinched. "I didn't pick up on that. Do you think he'll be all right?"

"I did what I could for him. That's how Mir got me. I reached after Thomas past my own shield, and couldn't pull back fast enough."

"I had wondered what made you go out there naked. Well. I suppose you want me to look into it?"

"Would you?"

"Why do you think I changed? I wasn't about to play seer in a sweatsuit. It would be akin to a priest granting absolution without a stole. I guess there's no sense in putting it off. Come on, then."

Cassie wiped her fingertips and mouth with a napkin and dropped it on the tray. Wizard rose slowly to follow her. As he picked up the bag and his coat, she focused on the bag.

"What's that?"

"I found it in a dumpster, with my name on it." He held it out to her. As quickly as she had put out her hand, she drew it back. Wonder and dread mingled in her voice.

"There's power there, but not for me to touch, nor use. It's harmless right now, but the right spark . . ."

"Just like plastic explosive."

"If I were one to give advice on things that aren't in my realm, I'd tell you to leave it in that bag until the moment comes. Don't touch it until then. Don't mantle yourself with its power until you are ready to pick up the gauntlet."

"Is this a Seeing?"

"Don't tease. No, it's just my opinion."

"If I didn't know better, I'd say you knew what was in the bag."

"Well, I don't. And I don't want to. Not any more than I want to ask you this. But I don't dare do a Seeing without knowing. Have you broken faith with the magic?"

Wizard stared at her, feeling slashed that she would even ask him such a thing. Did she suppose that he had forgotten the rules, unique to himself, that he must obey to retain his own special powers? He shook his head numbly.

"Are you sure? Not even by accident? Have you spoken the Truth when it was on you? When people ask, and you Know, have you always answered? Have you kept your pigeons safe and secure?"

He bobbed a nod at each question, but as she pressed on, he felt his control break. When she paused, he asked in a cold, uncertain voice, "Aren't you going to ask me if I've carried more than a dollar in change? If I've turned my strength loose upon others? If I've been with a woman?"

An abyss of dread opened in Cassie's eyes and was as quickly masked. "Do I need to ask those things?" she inquired evenly.

"No! Because you know I haven't. Can't we get on with this? That damn thing up in my den . . . I know it's from gray Mir. I Know it."

Cassie's calm held. "Then if you Know it, it must be so. Tell me: What do you remember of this Mir, from before?"

He shrugged heavily. "Nothing, I guess. Sometimes I feel like my life rolls itself up behind me as I live it. I try to look back, but it's all hidden inside itself. I see my yesterdays, but only so many at a time. Before that, there's nothing."

Cassie nodded quickly, seeming eager to stop his words. "Let's find out the worst, then. Come on."

"Cassie?" His anxious tone swung her eyes back to him. "It was a while back. Estrella the Gypsy gave me a tarot card. It said 'A Warning' and showed a man dangling upside down by one heel. But then it was gone, so I—"

"The Hanged Man." The silence that followed her words had a chilling eloquence. She swept across the room.

Wizard tucked the bag securely under his arm and followed. She parted the hanging drapes and waved him through. The next room was in darkness. Wizard smelled dust and mildew and heard the chitter and scuttling of mice alarmed by his approach. Cassie came behind him, bearing a candelabra. The flames of the candles didn't waver with her movement; they didn't light much more than her path, either. He trailed along behind her through a maze of rooms and corridors. Most of the chambers they passed through were dusty and abandoned, but some were strangely and sumptuously furnished, twined and draped with Cassie's ever-present plants, and lit by a pale yellow light that blinded Wizard until he passed into the darkened chambers beyond.

When they entered a carpeted room with many gilt-framed portraits on the wall, Cassie set her candles down on a low table. Wizard put his bag and coat on a loveseat beside it. Cassie was silent, so he watched her quietly as she went to a scarred roll-top desk. She wound her hair into a black scarf. A black cloak from a peg by the desk quenched her white robe. She began to take objects from the drawers. Stepping a little closer, he watched her arrange them on a little lacquered tray. There was a round mirror in a red frame with no handle; a thin ring of shining silver; four cats-eye marbles; a little pile of popcorn; five pennies polished copper bright; and white tail feathers from a pigeon.

"One never knows what they'll fancy," she murmured without looking at him. Taking the tray, she crossed the room to slide open a heavy wooden door on tracks. Beyond was a dizzying view. The lights of Seattle were impossibly small and spread out below them. But tree limbs reached up past the tiny rickety balcony which Cassie stepped onto. Wizard crept to the door and peered out. He longed to go to the edge and catch some glimpse of what supported them up here, but dared not. The gray wood of the railing was splintering and twisting away from its supports. The deck creaked under Cassie's weight. He followed her gaze up to the full moon and felt his heart squeeze. The moon had been only a quarter full last night; Wizard was sure of it. He swallowed drily.

Cassie's hair and body had vanished, dark cloth into dark night. Her pale face was full and shining as the moon herself. She set the tray down at her feet and straightened with the mirror cupped in her hand. Slowly she twisted and angled the mirror until the white moonlight filled it. She stared into it and began:

> *"Light of the sun, reflected in the moon's face;*
> *Light of the moon, reflected in my hand;*
> *Hear me now, and bring to me at this place*
> *Those I would consult, those I would command."*

As simple as a jump rope song, but Wizard's knees shook. The whole front of his body tingled as if painted with a sudden frost. He backed stealthily away from the open door and fled back to the candelabra. He put on his coat and held his bag on his lap before him like a shield. The brush of woman's power left his skin, but he seated himself firmly on the small couch to wait.

He sat watching the candle flames. He longed suddenly for coffee with an unsurpassed desire, but knew that Cassie never kept any. He shifted restlessly. Any company, even The Pimp's, would have been welcome, but he was alone. Cassie was singing softly on the balcony; he resisted hearing her. He passed the time by making the candle flames flare up tall and thin, until the tips of the flames broke off and winked out in the dark room. When he noticed the tapers melting low, he calmed the flames, reducing them to tiny tongues on the tips of the wicks.

"Mental masturbation," she scoffed.

He turned to find Cassie unwinding the cloth from her hair. Her hair fell in damp tendrils past her shoulders. As she swung the cloak free of herself and onto the hook, he caught the musk of her efforts. There was a hint of a tremble in her iron control as she sank onto the loveseat beside him.

"There are more candles in the lefthand cubbyhole of the desk," she told him.

As he fetched them, he glanced at her tray. The mirror was blackened as if by fire. The pigeon feathers were gone. He took the candles to her, and she kindled them to replace the softening stumps in the holder. Her lips looked chapped, her face windburned. "Give me space," she requested gently. Hastily he cleared his bag from the seat and moved to sit on the floor near her feet. She looked down at him almost fondly.

"Why did you have to come to Seattle?" she wondered in soft rebuke.

"Was I someplace else before I was here?" he asked in reply.

"Never mind. You are in Seattle, and it is here you will face it. Your battles with this grayness go back past your memories. In some, you have done well. From others, you bear the scars. We won't prod them now. I have only paltry things that I may tell you outright. There will be a final confrontation. Very soon. You must guard the weapons you have forged. If you guard them well, they may be just enough to defeat this Mir. Your edge will be a small one; if you do win, it will be by a tiny margin. This grayness is too clever to let you hone your weapons long. It will come for you soon. If it wins, it keeps you. If it loses, it leaves you alone."

"Can I not vanquish it completely, destroy it all?"

"Listen to him!" Cassie hooted. "Vanquish it! Have you any idea what you ask to do? No man may do that for any other. You can win yourself free, and no more than that."

"Then, if I lose, I will be the only loser."

"You know better." Cassie's voice went deadly soft. "Through you, the grayness could rout us all, as easily as shoving a hose down a molehill. There'd be no escaping for any of us. But if it comes to that, it would no longer be you, nor any of your doing. You'd only be the tool. Let's see." She sighed heavily. "What else was there?"

"Cassie, you're not telling me anything new."

"I know that. I'm telling you what you knew and were afraid to admit to yourself. Listen. I can give you a story. Would you like a story?"

"Go ahead," Wizard said grumpily. Cassie's stories usually obscured more than they illuminated.

"Good. Because I have a good one for you. No, two. This is the first. Once upon a time, a long, long time ago, in France during World War Two, not that it matters, there were some people being shelled. Among them were a young French woman and her two small children. The two children were very, very frightened. So the mother, to distract them from their terror, began to make silly faces for them, and funny noises. It worked. The children paid attention to her and were no longer afraid. But suddenly a shell exploded very near them, and a tiny fragment of shrapnel struck the woman in the throat. She choked and gurgled in her own blood, making terrible grimaces of pain, but unable to call aloud for help. How the children laughed to see the funny faces Mama made, and hear the silly noises! She died to the sound of her children's laughter."

Cassie paused expectantly. Wizard just stared, his face gone white. "I didn't say the stories wouldn't hurt," she said softly. "But they may help, too. Once upon a time, in England, during World War Two, a bomb fell on an old folks' home. After the raid was over, rescuers came to dig them out and see if there were any survivors. They found one old man sitting on a toilet, still holding the pull chain in his hand, and laughing uproariously. 'I pulled the chain,' he said, 'And the 'ole bloody building came down on me 'ead.'

"There's one more I'll throw in for free," Cassie added quickly before Wizard could speak. "It was the first bombing raid over Norwich in World War Two. We were all running for the shelters, when I saw one man come dashing up with an armload of white lilies. 'Well,' I said to him, 'If they get you, at least you'll have your lilies ready.' He threw down the flowers with a look of horror and dashed down the shelter steps."

Cassie stopped and looked at Wizard expectantly.

"Were you really there? In Norwich, the first time it was bombed?"

She looked disgusted. "That story is always told in the first person. Well. Do you understand now?"

"Understand what?"

"Everything. Why the grayness came to you to test you last night, and what weapons you must keep safe and keen."

"I'm afraid I'll have to ponder your stories a bit more before it all comes clear," he extemporized. Never call Cassie obscure to her face. "But there is one more thing that I have to ask. Something that has troubled me. Cassie, do you know what Mir showed me? About the boys and the chickens, I mean?"

Cassie nodded, turning her head away. "I couldn't help but overhear, my friend. I'm sorry to intrude."

"I don't mind. Perhaps I would mind more if I understood more. It seemed so monstrous a task for young boys to do."

"Some say it's the root of all domestic violence."

Wizard looked befuddled, so she continued.

"Don't you see? Teach a child that it's fine, even necessary, to gently raise an animal, seeing to its every need, protecting its well-being. Of course, along the way, you cut off the end of the chicken's beak, so it can't peck other chickens. The same for the rooster's spurs. Then you make a couple of incisions, and reach in and cut his balls out so he'll get nice and fat. Then, after he's nice and fat, you whack off his head and devour him. Now, how far is it from that logic to loving your wife, but beating her into submission if she goes against your wishes. Or feed, clothe, and shelter your kids, but kick the crap out of them for their own good when it suits you? Answer me that."

Wizard considered the connection a bit far-fetched. "I've never heard that theory before. Who did you say advanced it?"

"Well." Cassie shifted. "Me. But I'm someone, and it makes sense to me."

"I'd have to think it through, thoroughly. But there is still something I'd like to ask you. Mir said I was one of them, that I was there. Was it true?"

Cassie had to nod.

"Which one, then? I remembered being all those boys, as soon as the grayness showed them to me. But surely I could have been only one of them. Yet having seen them from the inside, I would not choose to have been any of them."

"Poor Wizard." Cassie put a hand to her face to scratch the bridge of her nose and then rub at her eyes. "Don't you see? You were there, yes. But you were the Black Rooster."

7

WIZARD SHIFTED IRRITABLY in his sleep. The room was cooling off. He had been comfortable enough when he had dozed off, even though he had scrunched himself to fit onto the loveseat. He had stared at the tracing of tree branches against the moon's face until she had blinded him and he closed his eyes. How long had he slept? He opened his eyes a slit. The branches still twined before the moon's round face, but even as he stared at her, she winked out.

He struggled to rise but felt the world tilt; he fell. Cold cobblestones slammed up against his hands and knees. After a shocked moment, he clambered back up to a seat on the park bench and sat rubbing his scraped palms against his trouser legs. He glanced once more at the globe light fixture at the top of the pole. Tree limbs did twine between it and him, and he would have sworn they were in the same pattern as the ones seen from Cassie's chamber. But he was here, in the cold pre-dawn of Occidental Square. He found that he had been using his bag for a pillow. He picked it up and stood yawning in the chill air. Such were the awakenings after an evening with Cassie. They always left him wondering where reality and sanity touched.

He walked slowly through the square, easing the stiffness of cold muscles, and groaned softly to himself as he realized just how awful this day was to be. He could not return to his den to get clean clothes and stash his bag. Daylight was too close. So here he was; no change, his overcoat wrinkled from a night on the bench (or wherever), his suit beneath it showing a day and a night of wear, and a crumpled paper sack for a companion. He tried to weigh his alternatives. Most places with public restrooms were not open yet. There was the train station, but he had been there only yesterday, and his present attire would not make him welcome. He considered trying it anyway, but sternly rejected his impulse. He had to live strictly by his rules now; Cassie had said as much. He could not cut any more corners.

In an alley between buildings, he stopped to run his comb through his hair. He took off his overcoat and shook it zealously to remove as many wrinkles as possible. He brushed at his jacket and slacks as best he could. He didn't need a mirror to know how inadequate it was. He took a deep breath and firmed himself against the day. He was a scavenger and a survivor, he told himself firmly. He must either seize the day and accept what it offered him, or go join the other bench squatters.

He spent the first hour walking the alleys, inspecting the dumpsters the trucks had not emptied yet. They didn't have what he was looking for. He needed a raincoat or an overcoat of some sort, in reasonably decent condition, to replace the crumpled one he wore. He found assorted small items of marginal usefulness, but took few of them, only what could fit in a pocket. He didn't want to crowd anything else into his wizard bag. As the sky shifted from gray of dawn to gray of overcast, he found a plastic Pay N Save shopping bag. He dumped out its load of tissue paper and cellophane shirt wrapping. This was how it was to be today, he mused as he fit his brown paper sack inside it. A day of coping, of imperfect camouflage, of minimal surviving.

As soon as his bag was protected, he fell better. In the next dumpster, he found an unstained, unrumpled newspaper. He rolled it casually, and stuck it out the top of the bag. He strolled on, eating half an orange and throwing the moldy part into the next dumpster. He would make it, he cheered himself on. He just had to keep moving today, had to flow with the day as it presented itself to him. With a little faith, a little work and a touch of imagination, Seattle would take care of him.

He was at Pike Place Market at nine when it opened, having scavenged all the alleys between it and Occidental Square. He had precious little to show for his efforts, other than a bit of food in his belly and a plastic sack. His head was starting to ache; he needed a shot of coffee. But he wouldn't get it looking as he did right now.

He had never liked the bathrooms at the market. For one thing, too many people passed through them; they were never truly clean or in the best repair. Although they were not dim, they were scarcely lit for shaving, even if they had boasted mirrors. He had to do a quick job by touch. He shook out his jacket, tucked his shirt in tightly, straightened his tie, and wiped his shoes over with a damp paper towel. Frantically, he tried to decide who he could be today. He looked, he decided, like a salesperson whose wife kicked him out of the house last night. No. The Pay N Save bag didn't fit. Perhaps he worked in a slightly sleazy pawn shop, or adult book store. So what would he be doing in Pike Place Market in the middle of the day?

It didn't work. He couldn't get into it. The day had begun badly and would run badly. He ran over his mental list of sanctuaries and decided on the Klondike Gold Rush Memorial Park. That strange designation meant a storefront building on South Main where a bored man in a ranger suit presided over memorabilia of the Gold Rush. But Wizard could spend time there, sitting in a darkened room while the park ranger ran educational films about the Gold Rush era, or perhaps about the Great Seattle Fire of 1889. It didn't matter which today, for he wouldn't be watching. He'd only be marking time until evening when he could make a run for his den.

He boarded the bus and sat staring out the window. Depression stuck to him like old gum on a shoe. Hiding would not make him less vulnerable. One had to blend, to be unnoticed. The bus paused to let two more people board. Both of them walked past the empty seat beside Wizard to stand in the aisle at the back of the bus. When he realized it, he tried to keep the anger and panic out of his eyes. So he wasn't passing today. So I'm a derelict, he thought savagely. Well, then I'll damn well be one today. There's camouflage, and there's camouflage. So today he'd be a bum on a park bench, looking just as defeated and incompetent as the rest of them. He could tough it out until nightfall. He discarded the shopping bag and paper on the bus, wedging them down between the seats. When he stepped off at his stop with his wadded paper bag and wrinkled suit, he scowled at the people boarding. No beggar asked him for money today.

Resentment seethed through him as he stumped back to Occidental Square, and he didn't try to resist it. A sense of being wronged by everyone fit well with this new character. He'd enjoy it. So why hadn't Cassie put him out last night so he could have headed for his own den? Why hadn't he thought of it himself? She warned him to conserve his strength and guard his weapons, then kept him at her place with small talk until he dozed off, and had to awaken and face this day. If only he had dressed a little more casually yesterday, in jeans and a sweater, it wouldn't have mattered today. But no, he had followed Cassie's idea for him. "Always dress up, never down. A little bit of class implies authority and intimidates. Besides, dressy clothes are discarded before they are worn out, and a truly classic style varies little from year to year. Take the blazer, for example, or a man's black raincoat. How much have they changed in the last ten years? Now, if you went to the second-hand store and looked for jeans, you'd only find worn ones with the knees and crotch gone, and new ones in improbable sizes. But dress slacks are given away because hubby got a bit too chubby, or they don't go with the new jacket. It's the same for dress shoes. You'll never find decent sneakers in a dumpster, but one out of every ten dumpsters will yield a perfectly good pair of loafers or oxfords. Keep looking and you'll find a size close to yours."

He could almost hear her. She was right, usually, he grudgingly admitted. He had once spent an entire day in the Elliott Bay Bookstore, looking at the shelves, and no one had asked him to leave. He'd had a tie on.

His pigeons dipped and wheeled to meet him; his black mood lifted slightly. Then he noticed the heaviness of the clouds that made up their backdrop. It was going to rain today, rain as only Seattle knew how. "Like a cow pissing on a flat rock," someone had bitched to him once. He tried to catch the fleeting memory and got a confusing image of a triple-canopy jungle and a sweating black man with rain dripping off his chin. He blinked away the non sequitur and sat on his bench to begin his methodical scattering of popcorn.

Lost in thought, he watched the feathered backs before him as the birds pecked and scrabbled for the feed. Their tidy industriousness sank him further into bleakness. He was failing today, defeated by himself before he had even confronted the grayness of Mir. If only he had a cup of coffee.

He was unaware of the woman until the pigeons swirled up in alarm. He shot her a quick scowl as she seated herself on the end of his bench with her own sack of popcorn. It wasn't so unusual for this to happen, but usually it was a kid who didn't have the patience to dole out feed a bit at a time and acquire his own following of birds to feed. He didn't mind it when kids horned in on his flock; kids weren't supposed to have patience. But this woman was a grown adult and should have had more courtesy, if not patience. She was almost as rude as those who walked right through the middle of a flock of feeding birds.

He glared at her again and felt the bottom of his stomach tilt. He knew her. He scrabbled frantically through memories, his alarm building. He had no business knowing her; she wasn't even a street person. It was as dangerous for him to know a regular person like her as it was for him to be known to one. He turned slightly away from her and tried to calm himself. He was being foolish. Maybe he had sat next to her on the bus last week, or stood behind her in line at some coffee shop. Maybe. But he didn't think so. She was danger.

"Bet you thought you were cute yesterday," she said.

Wizard stiffened. Carefully he took another handful of popcorn from his bag and scattered it for his pigeons. He had not heard her.

"You coulda cost me my job, you know that? I don't know why I didn't give the whole thing away. Yes, I do. It was because I was so pissed at Booth for right away assuming it was me. And because I knew he woulda knocked you right outa your chair. He loves to show his muscles when he gets mad. Showed them to me once too often. So I showed him mine." The quaver in her voice belied the toughness of her words.

"He came home from the night shift, and found his junk piled up on the staircase. So he comes down to where I'm working and tries to raise a fuss. So I tell him to leave my key, 'cause the lease is in my name, and if he doesn't, I'm calling the cops. Booth knows he can't afford to talk to the cops about nothing. He's got a bunch of speeding tickets in the glove compartment of his car. Oh, he still thinks he's tough. He phoned me last night and threatened to come by and 'see' me.

But I told him I had told Mrs. McWhirter to call the cops if she even seen him come in the lobby. And I did, too, and she will, too. So he can blow it out his ass for all I care."

Worse and worse. Wizard's hands shook slightly as he scattered popcorn. Should he stand up, gather his bag, and leave? That was admitting too much. Silence and the back of his shoulder for her. He wasn't even listening to her monologue. The pigeons pecked at his feet.

"I'm sposed to be working afternoon shift today. But I forgot and got here early, so I thought, what the hell, I'll go feed the pigeons and kill a little time. Then I seen you out here already feeding them, and figured I'd let you know that I knew what went down. Waitresses aren't as dumb as most people think. You gotta really know people to be a waitress. And you gotta have a good memory, especially for matching up faces and orders. That black one sure has a funny tail, don't he?"

The black pigeon's mother had been a full fan-tail, but Wizard wasn't going to chat about it. She was a talker. So let her talk as much as she liked, and when she ran down, she'd leave. She'd have to go to her job soon, anyway. He'd never set foot in Duffy's again, and that would be the end of this whole sorry mess.

She had already fallen silent. He saw, from the corner of one eye, a handful of popcorn pelt the ground with more than necessary force. A short moment later he heard a light gasp, as if someone had poked her with a pin. She took a husky breath and was silent again. Now she would go away. But she didn't. He wished he could stop thinking about the waffle and the strawberries and whipped cream. It wasn't as if he had asked for it. She had given it to him, of her own free will, and there was no reason for him to feel guilty or obliged to her. He intended to take only a quick peek at her, to see if she showed signs of leaving. But when he turned his head for a glimpse of her, she was already staring at him. Her eyes were too shiny; he saw her stuff a tissue back into her pocket.

"So go ahead and stare," she said bitterly. "Stare at a stupid woman who sits on a bench and talks to some bum like he's listening and then starts to fall apart. Go ahead and stare. See if I give a damn."

He had snatched his eyes away as soon as their gazes met, but that was already too late. She had seen him look at her and knew she had his attention. Now she would talk until the clock made her go to work. It was through his own fault, his most grievous fault, and his penance would be to listen to it. He threw more popcorn.

"I don't know why I keep going. Why the hell should I keep going? I get up, I go to work, I get my pay, I eat, and I sleep. What the hell kind of a life is that? You know how bad it is? It's so bad that when some shit like Booth treats me so lousy that I throw him out, after he's gone, I cry. You know what my sister says when I'm like this? She tells people, 'Don't mind Lynda, she's just between men now.' She says it in this bitchy, whiney voice, like someone else would say, 'She's on the rag.' And she's my own sister. She thinks it's just terrible that I'm not married. So is that my fault? I like men. It's not my fault I haven't found the right one just yet. Does that mean I've got to live like a nun to keep her happy? Women have needs. We're not supposed to, but we do, you know. When Booth welted on me and I called her up, do you know what she said? You know what she said to me? She said, 'You sure can pick 'em, Lynda, can't you? You got yourself into it with that creep, so you get yourself out of it.' And she hung up on me. Well, I did get myself out of it. I wasn't asking for her goddamn help anyway. I just wanted someone to talk to. C'mere, birdie."

He felt more than saw her abrupt movement. He kept his eyes on the ground before him, hoping she had missed. For a moment all was silence and he started to relax. Then he heard the frantic flapping of wings. It was the crisp sound of wing pinions beating against hands, of delicate flight feathers bending against a relentless grip. Wizard's stomach turned over.

"Let him go." He spoke before he knew he was going to, turning to confront her. She held his gaze, their knees nearly touching as they shared the bench. The pigeon she held was a young one; its beak was shell pink and looked too large for its head. Its feathers were white with gray splotches and an even shading of black across the end of its tail. It was frantic. It struggled with all its strength against Lynda's hands, panic in its round orange eyes. Lynda had one wing pinned neatly to its body. She had partially trapped the other wing with her hand and was trying to fold it back down. But the struggling pigeon was still trying to open it. Lynda was pushing on it, not roughly, but relentlessly. It folded beneath her strength, but not naturally. Lynda's face was calmly preoccupied.

"Oh, so you can talk? I thought you were part of the bench."

"Let the bird go. Its wing doesn't fold like that."

"I just want to hold it for a minute. Come on, little bird, quiet down, put your wing down."

"You're going to hurt it. Its heart will burst from terror. That's no way to handle a bird. Give it to me."

"I'm not hurting it."

Wizard reached, not swiftly, but efficiently, and took her right wrist between the thumb and forefinger of his right hand. He caught it right at the soft spot between the wrist and the hand itself, just past the knobby little bones. Before she knew what he was up to, he squeezed firmly. "Hey!" she exclaimed, but she had already released the pigeon. It floundered away from her in wobbly flight to the top of a tree. The rest of the flock had fled as soon as the flap had begun.

"Why'd you do that?" she demanded angrily. He dropped her wrist hastily and leaned back on the bench. He found he was breathing heavily. Terrified. He had come so close to giving the twist and jerk that would have disabled the hand completely. He stared at her, looking deeply at himself and what he had just done. He felt sick and his hands were gray. For a long moment the world was tilting and sliding past him. His stomach squeezed acid up into the back of his throat.

"You would have killed him," he whispered hoarsely.

"I would not. Now look what you done. Now I got to start all over again. Here, birdies!" Lynda threw more popcorn that bounced off the cobblestones and threw a penetrating look that struck deeply into him. "You don't look so good. You eaten today?"

Having spoken to her once, nothing was to be gained by silence. "Not much."

"I didn't think so. You look worse than these pigeons. Oh, look, here they come. Not too bright, are they?"

"No, they're not," Wizard admitted sadly. She was right. They were coming, the hungriest ones dropping from the trees like leaves, dipping down to peck at the farthest outreaches of the popcorn she had scattered. They were stupid, but they were his. He knew what would happen. They would come, a few at first and wary, to nip up the pieces of popcorn. Then they would get greedy, and more would come, and in the competition for the feed, they would forget the danger from the feeder. They would jostle and push, crowding ever closer to her, until some unwary one was under her squeezing, gripping hand.

He shuddered. He picked up his own bag of popcorn and

reached deep into it for a large handful. He flung it with a snap of his wrist that sent the seeds and popped corn scattering far beyond Lynda's tossed food. His flock swooped to it, feeding well outside her perimeter. Lynda dropped plump kernels right at her feet and sat perfectly still. He felt a sweat break out on the back of his neck as the birds ventured closer. He took another handful and threw it, deliberately pelting the birds that were daringly close to her. They started back, raising reproving eyes to him. He kept his face stony. Back! he thought at them. Back, you fools!

"You're doing that on purpose!" Lynda accused him, but she laughed as she said it. She was very pretty when she laughed, all her sulkiness turning to softness. Like a different woman. She smiled at him looking at her, and gave her head a toss that sent her hair dancing. "Look. I give up, okay? You win. If you won't let me feed your birds, how about you? Why don't you let me buy you some breakfast?"

"No. Thank you. I'm not that type of person."

She didn't understand him and laughed at what she thought a joke. "Yeah, me neither. Let's just go grab a sandwich and some coffee or something. I was so upset this morning, I hardly ate a thing myself. I hate to eat alone. Look, we can go right inside to the Bakery. Ever been there? Right inside the doors? Good coffee." She tilted her head toward the tall glass and metal doors. Her eyes had brightened, and in her red jacket she looked like a bright bird perched on the end of the bench.

"I've been there," he admitted grudgingly.

"You are such a stone-face. It wasn't so hard to get you to eat yesterday. Look, don't feel awkward about it. It's just the way I am with people. I like you. I don't even know why I say that, but it's true. Even not knowing you much, I can tell we could be friends. Guess I knew it when I came to sit down over here. Rats!" She threw a handful of popcorn. "That's the last of mine. Share with me, okay?"

She tweaked the bag of popcorn from his grip and put her small hand into it. His heart tried to burst from his chest. She pulled out a fistful of fragments and threw them on the ground. "Hey, look, yours was all gone, too." She shook the little bag upside down over the cobblestones. An errant wind carried away a few fragments of popcorn from it. Wizard stared with uncomprehending eyes. He reached numbly to take the empty bag from her fingers, but she wadded it up nimbly and stuffed it into her own empty bag. She thrust both into her pocket.

"So, that's that! No more popcorn, so no more birds. Really, you might as well come and eat with me."

He stared at her pocket. His throat was closed tight, too tight for any words to pass.

"Oh, come on," she begged impatiently. "Don't be so shy. Look, I know about guys like you. I'm not a kid. You don't stink like a drunk, but you don't shake like a junkie. I think you're just temporarily down. Lady dumped you, maybe, or your job ran out. I mean, look at how you're dressed. You're not really a bum. All you need is to get thinking straight again and get back on the tracks. Just have a cup of coffee and keep me company while I eat; it's no big deal. What do you say?"

He dragged his eyes away from her pocket and up to her face. Her front teeth nibbled appealingly at her lower lip, but he scarcely noticed. He mustn't stare at her pocket. If he agreed and went with her, he might have a chance to get his bag back. He could offer to take her coat, to hang it on a chair or something. A quick stab of his hand into her pocket and . . . No. He didn't want to feel it for himself, didn't want to stick his hand into an empty bag with a wrinkled paper bottom. Most of all he didn't want to pull his hand out with nothing in it for the flock. He agonized again over how it could have happened. But it was gone, his gift taken as abruptly as it had been bestowed. He had never known how he could feed the pigeons, and now he would never understand how he could not.

"Lunch, then?" Her cool fingers touched his wrist, numbing it. She snatched them back with a cry of dismay and gripped her own wrist. "Oh, look at the time! I hate it when I'm on afternoon shift. Just about the time I start to enjoy the day, I have to rush off to work. Look, I'm sorry. I have to go now if I'm going to be on time, so I can't take you to lunch."

He stared up at her miserably as she rose. She looked deep into his eyes and misread them. "Hey, look. It's not that way! I wasn't teasing you. Look, take this," she dug in a bottomless purse and came up with a folded green bill. "Take this, I mean it, and get a bite to eat. You really look like you need it. And meet me here, tomorrow, early, and we'll talk and have breakfast. You can tell me all about yourself. Now, don't shake your head at me. You take this." Boldly she tucked it into the chest pocket of his jacket. Wizard felt strangely powerless before her insistence. "You eat something, you'll feel better, and I'll see you tomorrow. Don't look so surprised. That's how I am. I can never turn away from someone who really needs help.

And I can tell a lot about people just by looking at them, maybe 'cause I been waiting tables for so long. Now you get something to eat. I mean it, now. See you later."

She left him buried in the avalanche of her words. She looked back once as she hurried away to give him a friendly little wave and an admonishing shake of her finger that cautioned him to obey. It was all he could do to stare after her, totally unmanned.

When he looked away from her diminishing figure, the square looked unfamiliar. The light seemed dimmed, and his eyes would not focus as sharply as he wanted them to. Like waking from a nap you hadn't known you'd taken. He blinked and felt the wetness of his lashes. Rain. It was raining very tiny drops, millions of them, like a determined mist condensing on him. Wizard sat in it for a long time, feeling the money in his breast pocket where she had jabbed it in, feeling the emptiness in his coat pocket where the popcorn bag had been. His birds were gone, abandoning him to seek shelter in treetops and on window ledges. He was alone in the gray rain, caught between numbness and a creeping cold. Just like bleeding to death, he thought to himself; once the shock takes away the pain, you just get colder and sleepier and dimmer. He turned his eyes down. His coat and slacks were dark and wet, but this time it was only rain. Only rain.

He dragged himself to his feet, forced himself to move. The square boasted a concrete monstrosity that passed for a rain shelter and benches. It was very big and stark, with the roof so high that the rain blew in under it. Even in summer, its shade was too cool. The cleverly designed brass drinking fountain beside it squirted everyone in the face. The designer who had envisioned mothers and small children relaxing there was mistaken. Only street people did. Different clichés claimed different benches, sprawling or hunching on them as decreed by the weather. Hostile stares greeted intruders. Wizard walked past it. On one of the unsheltered benches a lone boy sat, trying to make fifteen years look like twenty. His black hair had been greased into spikes that were wilting in the rain. He reminded Wizard of a forlorn Statue of Liberty. He had scratched lightning strikes into his cheeks and etched fear behind his eyes. He sat very still as Wizard walked up behind him. When he leaned over the back of his bench, the boy neither moved nor spoke.

"Go home, kid." Wizard lifted the money from his pocket

with the tips of his fingers and dropped it in the boy's lap. "Your mom threw out that guy that hurt you. She doesn't show it by day, but at night she cries, and she lets your cat sleep on the pillow by her head. She keeps the porch light on, and there's a box of chocolate mints in the freezer compartment of the fridge for you. She's not such a bad old broad; besides, she loves you. Bus can take you as far as Auburn. You can hike the rest of the way. Go for it, kid."

Wizard stepped away. The boy never looked at him. He just nodded, as if to himself, and picked up the money in his lap. He rose a second later and headed for the bus stop. Wizard nodded after him, relieved. At least he had managed to get rid of the money. He tucked his bag more firmly under his arm.

He walked, through streets and weather too wet for walking, ignoring the buses. He walked away from his home and his territory, out past the King Dome, walked right out of the Ride Free Area and into the uncharted lands beyond. Restless and rootless, he drifted, turning aimlessly down any street that presented itself, wandering through areas of warehouses, offices, and old residential sections, wandering much farther than he would have imagined he could.

He stopped in a Thriftway grocery to ask if his wife had forgotten her spare keys there, on a keychain with a green-dyed rabbit's foot on it. She hadn't, but while they looked, he had a free sample of Brim Decaffeinated Coffee and a heated Jeno's Pizza Roll served by a smiling lady from a tin-foil-lined tray. There was a dime on the floor of a phone booth outside a convenience store. In the drugstore, they didn't have his daughter's asthma prescription on file, but they let him use the bathroom while they checked. He looked at the man in their mirror. The rain had helped, actually. He did look like a harrassed father sent on a wild goose chase on a rainy day. Darn kid had left her prescription in her gym locker and someone had stolen it. Probably thought they could get high on it; you know kids these days. Well, he'd have to get the nurse to track the doctor down and phone it in again. Thanks, anyway, and back into the rain. Outside the Langendorf Bakery thrift store, a man with a farm pickup full of rotten produce and brown lettuce dropped two packets of tiger-tails as he was loading in three boxes of outdated baked goods. After he drove away, Wizard salvaged them and ate them as he walked. They were squished and stale; their sweetness made him long for rich black coffee, hot enough to burn their cloying taste away. He thought longingly of Starbucks Coffee, Tea, and Spice, down on Virginia across from the market. Or better still, the Elliott Bay Café just under the book store; there was something about the old books on their shelves gazing down benignly on him as he sipped from a steaming mug. He wanted coffee and he needed home. He circled the block and turned his steps back.

The day was cooling and the rain had finally managed to soak through his clothes. He shivered. Walking was no longer enough to warm him, not even fast walking. The paper sack under his arm had started softening. Now he wished he had folded up the plastic shopping bag and stuffed it in his pocket. He didn't know what he would do if the tired seams of the bag gave way and the wizard things dropped out on the wet sidewalk. He snuggled it protectively against him and walked a little faster. Streetlamps began to come on, blossoming overhead against the gathering darkness.

He almost made it safely home. As the darkness and rain intensified, he broke into a wolf-trot, trusting to the night to keep him anonymous. His feet ate up the blocks, carrying him up Alaskan Way under the length of the viaduct. The highway and traffic overhead could not keep the rain off him, nor could their noise keep the thoughts from pelting down on his mind. There was a hypnotic effect to the regular beat of his feet against the ground, the *whoosh* of traffic overhead and beside him, and the totally miserable weather. He could move himself doggedly along and keep his consciousness alway from how acutely miserable he was. But he could not keep his thoughts from chewing at the edges of his mind, shredding his calm with a threat of gray Mir out there somewhere in the night, stabbing his soul with the loss of his popcorn bag. It was almost a relief when his quick ears picked up the sounds of a scuffle and a single, sharp cry.

Under the viaduct it was dark, making a jest of the lights that lined Alaskan Way. This time of night, it should have been deserted. The noises were coming from the shadows behind a dumpster. Wizard felt the familiar unwelcome surge and was running the zigzag path before he was aware of it, his bag tucked tightly to him. As he passed the corner of the dumpster, he gave the bag a toss that carried it safely under it. His feet made no sound as he approached the struggle, and he gave no cry of warning.

He hit the tangled knot like a striking eagle. The boy dropped and skidded on the pavement, but the narrow man snaked away into the darkness. The old man on the ground gave another cry and tried to crawl away. Wizard ignored him. Damn, but he wished that the adult one had not escaped. Now he would have to worry about him coming from behind. But for now. . . .

"Let me go, please, mister!" the boy wailed suddenly as the dead-faced man towered over him. He tried to scrabble away, but he was on his back, and his arms and legs refused to work properly when glowing blue eyes stared down at him.

Three kicks. To throat and belly and armpit, and then he could pursue the other black-clad man melting into the night. Or he could push his fingers down fast as a snap against the soft hollow of the boy's throat, to crush the tiny fishlike bones within and flood blood all through the secret caverns of his flesh. Wizard smelled the pungent odor of urine as the scrabbling boy wet himself. Snatches of gray fog were drifting in off Elliott Bay and floating through the night. There was no solution so simple and beautiful as death. He could put him out and be done with him, never have to worry about this particular one again. No one would ever see what was going to happen here. The boy was like a cake waiting to be cut. "O god o god o god," he was praying, sobbing and sniffling already, before Wizard had ever touched him. But now he touched and the boy squealed long. Wizard looked at the rag of shirt in his hand, marveling at how easily the cloth had torn. A tendril of fog passed between the boy and himself, drifting like blood in water. The gray fog stank in his nostrils, worse than the urine, and he shook it from his nose.

For the first time he heard the old man's repeated words. "I'm all right. Let him go and help me. Please." Wizard stared down at the boy. His eyes were squeezed shut and water from them was leaking down his cheeks. He felt suddenly and intensely sick.

"Get out of here, kid. Go!"

Wizard stood up, but the boy was gone even before he stepped back. He stared after his vanishing prey.

"Please. Please help me."

The gray sheaf of hair that was supposed to be combed to cover the old man's bald spot had draggled down one side of his head. His old brown sweater was muddied at the elbow and one knee of his gray pants was torn. Wizard raised him gently, smelling the unmistakable odor of fried chicken and fish clinging to him. "Are you hurt?"

"No. God be thanked, I'm not hurt. Boys today. Only a boy

that was, did you see? I told them I didn't have any money. But they said they had watched me carrying a bag home every night, and they wanted the deposit. Deposit! Leftover chicken and fish from the restaurant for my cat. For that they put a knife to my throat."

"So why did you tell me to let him go?" Wizard spoke softly, his voice a deeper rumble than the traffic overhead.

"So maybe it's not that different, if he kills me over leftover chicken, or you kill him. Or maybe it's the delicate ecological balance I was worrying about." A quavery laugh shook the old man's voice. "Look at it this way. I've just had the rare opportunity of seeing a fullgrown Mugger in its natural surroundings as it taught its young to stalk and attack its natural prey. Think of what might have happened if you had killed it. Why, there might be a mother Mugger, and a whole litter of little baby Muggers at home in the den, waiting for those two to bring home their kill. Oh, God!"

The old man started shaking suddenly. Wizard helped him to the dumpster and he leaned against it until the belated adrenalin shudders had passed. He tried for another laugh, but it failed. "Or think what it could have done to you, if you had killed him. Or to me."

"Would it be worse than what's been done to you?" Wizard asked. He didn't want to be speaking to him like this, especially not in this chilly soulless voice, but the words were swelling out of him like blood from a wound.

"I'm not hurt. Well, not much. It would be nothing to a man your age. Oh, I've bruises that won't heal for a week, and a scrape that's going to keep me awake all night. But if it hadn't been for you, I might be headed for the hospital. Or the morgue. But you came along and stopped it. I'll be fine."

"Will you? And will you walk home with your kitchen scraps tomorrow night?"

For a moment the only sound other than the roar of traffic overhead was the labored pumping of the old man's lungs. "No. I guess I won't be doing that anymore," he admitted slowly. "I guess I'll call a cab, or get the cook to drop me off on his way. No, I don't suppose I'll be walking home after work anymore."

"Then that's what they took from you tonight, old man. Not your money nor your life, not even your cold chicken. They took your private walk home of an evening, through the streets that should belong to you. You've been robbed and you don't even know it."

With a trembling hand the old man flipped his hair back into place and patted it down. He was over the worst of his fright now, and dignity was coming back to his voice.

"I know it, young man. I knew it before they had even knocked me down. But do you think it would be different if you had killed that boy? Then on the walk home at night I could look at this dumpster and say to myself, 'That's where that young bastard died for trying to rob me.' I saw you. You weren't going to rough him up or hold him for the cops. You were on the killing edge. Do you think I'd be thinking of punks and muggers as I walked up this street alone at night? No. I'd be thinking of you. Good evening."

There was strength in the old man. Rebuked, Wizard stepped back to let him pass. He didn't even look back at Wizard as he continued his interrupted walk home. Shame, weariness, and cold flooded up through Wizard, rising like a cold tide from the pavement. He wished no one had seen him tonight. He stooped to retrieve his bag from under the dumpster. From there his nose led him to the crumpled sack of cold chicken and fish fillets. The muggers had tossed it aside, untouched. He claimed it and took a cold fillet to nibble as he walked. Dark cold pressed against the back of his neck as he headed up South Jackson. Strips and rags of fog drifted past him and tried to surround him. Gray as Mir. Wizard walked faster. His heart was beating hard in his chest when he reached the mouth of his alley. He glanced furtively about, but he was alone.

A light toss of the wizard bag took it to the landing of the old fire escape. The chicken bag followed it. He bounced once or twice on the balls of his feet, trying to limber up muscles chilled stiff. He sprang, caught the old pipe, braced a foot lightly against the bricks, and pushed up until his hands could shift suddenly to the edge of the fire escape. He hauled himself up silently. Moments later he was sliding open the propped window, and then he was inside the outer chamber of his den. He stumbled into the inner room where he slept. He was tired.

Too tired. Too tired to light his can of sterno and brew a hot cup of tea. Too tired to do anything but put his sodden wizard bag safely into his wardrobe box. He let his clothing fall to the floor around him. It was too wet and dirty to use again. Tomorrow he would redonate it to the Salvation Army.

He shivered as he pulled on his quilted long-johns and a dry pair of socks. Black Thomas was nowhere to be seen or felt. He wished he were here to share the cold chicken. Wizard burrowed into his bedding, shivered himself into a warm ball, and then felt the growlings of an unappeased stomach. He reached out into the darkness to the chicken bag and found a thigh piece. His nose and ears were cold, but he didn't want to pull the blankets over his head. He dropped the greasy bone beside the mattress for the cat and sat up to reach for a woolen cap from his wardrobe box.

It watched him. It gloated. Wizard stared back, but it didn't go away. Because it was real. A cold separate from night slunk through his bones. Who was the prisoner and who was the guard? It had nearly had him tonight; it knew it, too. They both knew and sat staring at one another, knowing it together. Wizard's hand found the cap. Slowly he drew it to him and dragged it on over his ears. Ever so slowly he eased himself down, never taking his eyes from it. The closet door hung broken on one hinge. It would not be shut in again. It glowed faintly in the dark with a rotten, mildewed light. The accusing letters never blinked. MIR.

8

NINJA WOKE HIM an hour before dawn grayed the skies. Wizard never heard her light steps. What shocked him out of sleep was the thunderous clapping of wings as the pigeons fled for their lives. They thudded blindly into the walls of the dark room, calling pathetically to one another. He rolled from his mattress and leaped at a darker patch of moving night. Ninja gave a howl of dismay and released a flapping bird. Wizard gripped the big black cat by the scruff of her neck. "How did you get in here?" he demanded of her, but she only growled murderously in her throat. Tucking her under his arm, he gathered up last night's chicken bones. He took Ninja into the next room and then dumped her unceremoniously outside the window of the fire escape. The bones followed. A piece of old plywood kept for just such occasions blocked the window and her re-entry. Wizard went back to his den.

In the blackness he groped for his can of Sterno. Ninja growled and crunched bones outside the window. Inside, the pigeons rustled on their high shelves and cooed reassuringly to their mates. He set the Sterno inside the punctured coffee can that served as a light shield and stove. He stared through the dimness at the Sterno surface and focused his mind. Flames.

93

He sat still, recalling the perfect flickering details of a tongue of fire. He was still sleepy and it took longer than usual to bring the magic to bear. It came as dancing sparks that finally and suddenly coalesced into a single fat flame.

He shivered as he set the pan of rainwater over the mouth of the can. Little bits of light escaped from the holes in the can's sides, spattering dots of light on the wall but not illuminating the room. He was grateful. He didn't need light to sense the hulking presence of the footlocker in its closet. It crouched beside the half-fallen door like a gray predator awaiting unwariness. He herded his eyes and mind away from it and immersed himself in his routine.

As his tea brewed, he dug out a pair of corduroy pants and a Pendleton shirt. Mandarin Orange Spice was an herbal tea with no caffeine, but he spiked it heavily with pilfered sugar packets. The sweetness warmed him and calmed his shivering. The last piece of cold chicken became his breakfast. A quick check of the fire escape revealed that Ninja had eaten and left. He set his boots down by the window and opened the connecting door between the rooms for the pigeons. By ones and twos they fluttered past him and sought the dawn sky. Returning to his own room, he kindled a candle from his hoard and extinguished his precious supply of Sterno. Time to tidy up the den, he admonished himself as he slipped ninety-nine cents into his pants pocket.

Yesterday's clothing went into a bag to be disposed of today. He smoothed the crumpled sides of the wizard bag and set it carefully atop his wardrobe box. He shook and respread his blankets atop his thin mattress. He tidied his books, bringing their spines even with the front of the shelf and carefully wiped out his tea mug. The crumpled wrappings from the cold fish and chicken were placed beside his boots for disposal in the dumpster. A glance out his window showed him that his darkness was still holding. He dug out his pocket mirror and shaved with the warm water from the kettle. He detested shaving without running water, but today he resolved to be fully prepared before he set foot out the window. He finished his cleanup with time to spare and extinguished the candle. The skies were just beginning to lighten.

Secure and satisfied, he looked around his room. His gaze ran aground on the footlocker's stark grayness. Its foreign presence mocked him, blowing away the homey comfort of his small den and meager possessions like an icy gale through a broken window. It turned his departure into a rout. He tied his boots, glanced back over his shoulder at it, and left laden with items to dispose of. As he exited, he propped the window for the pigeons.

He walked briskly, propelled by dread of the thing in his room. His mind sought refuge in a detailed schedule for his day. Everything would be planned, each step completed carefully, so that nothing might derail this day and make it a repeat of yesterday's disaster. First, he would dispose of the soiled clothing. Then, coffee and food; he had eaten only sparsely yesterday, and his stomach was a growling burden. Then Cassie. He set his teeth tightly together as he imagined admitting to her the loss of the popcorn bag. Well, it couldn't be helped. The sooner he faced up to it, the sooner it would be remedied. He refused to wonder if Cassie would be able to help him with it. Of course she could, he told himself firmly. Of course she could.

On Second Avenue, he left the bag of soiled clothes leaned up against the door of the Salvation Army Thrift Store. Someone else had left a bag there also, but it held only baby clothes. He neatly refolded its top and placed it against the door.

The trash went into the next dumpster. He walked another brisk two blocks, pumping his blood to dispel the last traces of sleepiness and apprehension. Coffee. That was what he needed to burn the night fears from his mind. The hot tea had warmed him, but it lacked caffeine and the rich brown taste with the bitter edge that let him know it was morning. He jingled the emergency coins in his pocket and toyed with temptation. Elliott Bay Café. It should be open by now. The spirit of hot espresso plucked at his sleeve. With a sigh, he denied it. The coins would only cover coffee there, and it was a difficult place to cadge a meal. No, today was not a day for a fling. Today was a day to be very conscientious, to obey every rule and take every step with absolute correctness. Wizard wanted no part of days like yesterday.

He waited alone at the bus stop, taking comfort from his surroundings. It was his favorite bus stop, under an iron and glass Victorian pergola at First and Yesler. The Pergola, in Seattle. Since 1909, it had sheltered folk, first for trollies and cable cars, now for the bus. A Tlingit totem pole shared its sidewalk island, and a bronze bust of Chief Sealth presided over the area. The drinking fountain offered facilities for people, horses, and dogs. When Wizard stood in this small triangular plot of history, he felt as if the spirit of Seattle flowed through him, backwards and forwards in time, with him as a sort of intelligent filter. This was his city, and he knew it as well as any. Much of his knowledge had been gained by following city tours at a discreet distance, or eavesdropping on the benches here as the guides went through their spiels. The details amused him. The totem pole was the second one to stand here. The first had been stolen from a tribal burial ground in 1899, but was lost to fire in 1938. When the city sent a five-thousand-dollar check to pay for the carving of a new pole, the Tlingits had served their revenge cold and sweet. "Thanks for finally paying for the first one," the cancelled check was endorsed. "A new pole will cost you another five thousand." Wizard grinned softly to himself at the thought of it. The bus thundered up in front of him in a belch of heat. The doors hissed open and the driver scowled down on him.

"This ain't a flophouse," he commented sourly as Wizard came up the steps. "So don't even think about going to sleep in here."

Wizard kept his aplomb. No bus driver had ever dared speak to him like that before, though he had heard similar comments made to derelicts on stormy days. He tried a jaunty smile. "The night was late, but not that late."

"Surprised you knew it was daytime." The driver didn't wait for him to be seated, but jerked the bus back into traffic. Wizard kept his balance and made for a seat near the back. As he stared out the window, he mentally reviewed his appearance. He was shaven, washed, and tidily, if casually, attired. So why had the driver been able to pick him out as a resident of the streets? No matter how he puzzled over it, he could find no loophole, no crevice in his protective armor. He should have been immune to such hassles. He stooped to retie his bootlaces and to force himself to calmness. He refused to heed a little voice that warned of impending disaster. No doubt the driver had simply had a rough night of his own and had unerringly assumed that Wizard was a safe target. No matter. He would not let it ruffle him. He sat up straight. A wave of illness swept over him.

Perhaps he had straightened up too fast, driving the blood from his brain. He closed his eyes to let it pass. A blacker darkness closed on him and Mir laughed. His mind was flooded with images, stark, terrifying, and disgusting. Like a series of slides, the women appeared and disappeared before him.

Knowing came, filled with sadness. They were real. Each slashed face, each savaged body had led a life and been part of a whole. Mothers, sisters, friends, and lovers. Their deaths went on forever in the gaping holes left by their passing. Each a precious gear snatched from the clockwork of a family. Wizard forced his bile back down and tried to study them. The backdrops were not western Washington. He saw the red banks of a wide muddy river and trees he had no names for. Wizard lost count of how many faces passed before him. He wondered desperately what was happening to him. Had Mir trapped him forever in this dreadful Seeing? Would his comatose body be taken from the bus and placed on a narrow bed somewhere, so his mind could sink into the nightmares and never return? He set his teeth stubbornly as his magic took him deeper into horror.

No. The knife. He was suddenly aware of the knife. He jerked his eyes open to the daily reality of the bus, to men in overcoats and women chatting together. But the knife did not go away. This knife was a thing to be felt, not seen. The women had felt it with their bodies; he touched its cutting edge with his mind, felt with horror the traces of blood and skin worn into its wooden handle. Someone on the bus had it and was dreaming of using it again. Wizard started to rise, then forced himself to sit still and feel. He groped about in the swaying bus, and finally focused on a man three seats in front of him. He was a swarthy, heavyset man who flinched suddenly as if a pin had jabbed him. As the bus eased into its next stop, Wizard located the knife. It was suspended by a leather thong around his neck. Beneath the man's faded shirt, it nestled by his heart.

At the stop the man rose hastily, glancing about. Wizard suppressed a groan and stood up to follow him. What now? he asked of his magic, but, having shown him, it was silent. It was not, Wizard reflected, the same as a stranger pouring out his heart and the magic giving him the words of comfort to speak. The swarthy man hit the sidewalk and strode off with Wizard a timid shadow.

For two blocks he followed, debating a course of action. The man glanced back once and Wizard cringed, but he was only checking a street sign. He sensed how secure the killer was, content in his invulnerability. A new territory and unalerted victims by the score. He slowed to watch a high school girl hurry past and Wizard felt ill.

Anger flared suddenly in him, searing him to determination.

The hot pain of it felt good. The knife. It had been given to him for a reason; he was suddenly sure the magic had shown it to him for a purpose. In some far place, Mir chuckled gleefully, but Wizard blocked him. He zoomed in on the knife, feeling the oiled grain of the hickory handle and the sleek steel of the blade. Steel. He felt deeper, sensing molecules in sleepy motion. He lost them when, in his concentration, he walked into a parking meter. The swarthy man glanced back again at his involuntary exclamation. Wizard felt himself noticed. Well, there was no help for it. He matched the man's increased stride and went back to the knife. Little tiny molecules, drifting like particles of sand in lake water. Wizard stirred them. Faster they swirled. The temperature of the steel crept up a fraction of a degree. Wizard's face hardened in a tight smile. So that was how. He set his mind on the metal and stirred frantically.

Sweat sprang out on his face and back. A headache crept up from the base of his skull and spread like a net over his head. He followed the dark killer through a red mist. Never had he felt such a strain as this magic demanded. He fueled it with his anger. The killer increased his pace and Wizard stumbled after him, narrowly dodging other pedestrians and always focused on the knife, the knife. He imagined it molten hot, dripping and scalding the man's chest. His breath was coming dry in his throat and now the man was definitely fleeing. He glanced back frequently at Wizard's set face, but was unwilling as yet to break into a full run.

Wizard felt a sudden drop in ability. He groped after the magic like a receiver seeking after a fading FM signal. Everything dimmed and slowed. He found it again, but thinner. He locked himself into it and fed it to the molecules in the knife. Just a little more now and the killer would become aware of the knife's heat against his skin. His own blade would sear his chest, the hot metal eating through his skin.

But the knife was cooling. The thread of the magic was too finely spun and Wizard was suddenly weary. Mir laughed. He would have to get closer to once again hasten the perpetual dance of the molecules in the steel. Wizard stepped up his pace. Hot and blind as a hound on the scent, he trailed the man into the deadend alley. The man and the magic stopped at the same instant. Wizard stood alone.

"Are you following me?" The man's voice was low, almost melodic. His smile was ethereal as a blessing.

"Yes. I am." Wizard spoke distractedly. He could see the

swarthy man edging closer to him in the narrow alley, but he
felt blinded. Bereft of his magic, the edges of the world dimmed
and the colors all ran together in muddiness. He groped after
the magic and the knife, but it was like trying to reach without
arms. There was only an emptiness he scrabbled in, as gut-
wrenching as a missing step on a dark staircase. "The Knife!"
Wizard suddenly cried aloud, imploring the magic's return. But
it was deaf to him, the abandonment total. He sensed the loss
fully in that instant, and it was so tearing a thing he could not
focus on the more immediate problem of the smiling man lifting
the loop of leather over his head.

As the man reached inside his shirt for the knife, Wizard
moved. A training older than the magic took over, lessons
learned more harshly and thoroughly. The man stepped into it.
Three fast kicks while Wizard's upper body leaned away, beyond the knife's leap. The first kick went to the man's knee
cap, the second two to his torso as he staggered in pain. His
thick hands never ceased tearing at his shirt, trying to bring
free the knife that would solidify his courage. Wizard gave him
no time. His boot connected with the man's floating ribs, pushing them in solidly against softer organs and wringing a gasping
grunt from the man. "Never hit a man when he's down; it's
always easier to kick him." Was the quote Mir's? There was
no time to wonder.

"Drop it!" Wizard commanded in the same voice he might
tell a dog to sit. "Drop it!"

But the swarthy man believed in the knife too strongly to
surrender it. He gripped its hilt firmly, the blade pointed toward
Wizard as he began a desperate roll that would take him back
to his feet. But Wizard did not cringe from that shining point
as all his other victims had. Nor did he try to fight the blade
as a few desperate ones had. His attention was focused on the
man behind the weapon. He stepped into the man's range and
shot out a kick that smashed into his shoulder, numbing his
arm and sending the knife clattering onto the worn paving
stones.

With an incoherent roar halfway between outrage and terror,
the man staggered to his feet. Cold-eyed and gaunt as Death,
Wizard stepped over the knife, ready to close with him again.
Expert eyes searched for openings. The man's eyes flickered
from the fallen blade to his opponent, making a swift evalu-
ation. He feinted at Wizard, then spun on his heel and fled
from the alley, cradling his injured arm as he ran.

Two strides Wizard took after him and then halted, swaying
on his feet. The winds of Mir's triumphant laughter blasted
him. Knifing realization ripped through him, disemboweling
his strength so that he would have gone to his knees but for
his frantic clutch at a dumpster. He leaned against its sticky
side, breathing its foulness and trying to come to terms with
his loss. He was emptied. What magic he had left after his loss
of his popcorn bag had been burned away. He was a stick man
now, flimsy and impotent. Gutted by his own anger. He stared
at the fallen knife on the pavement, trying to tell himself that
it was a fair trade. But the knife was nothing, and he knew it
now. The knife was just an ordinary knife, such as could be
found in the kitchen-ware section of any supermarket. The killer
could replace it in less than an hour. Would replace it. For an
instant he Knew it, but then that power faded, too. All systems
down, he told himself, feeling the blackout in his soul. It was
only half a step short of dying.

He rubbed at his eyes, and the terrible ache behind them
was worse than any tears. "I've lived through this before," he
told himself sternly. "And I can do it again." But he could not
quite recall what loss had ever so grieved him. There was only
the hopeless sense of déjà vu, and the press of the Now, cold
against his back. There were things he had to do. Best do them.
He drew closer to the knife and stared at it.

Evil had soaked into its wood and honed its metal. It was
a fearsome thing, possessed of its own wicked lusts. He had
sensed that on the bus. He knew it was true, he could remember
the loathsome touch of its nastiness against his bare mind. But
now he stooped and picked it up by its thong without a shudder.
Like a photograph in the hands of a blind man, its secrets were
safe from him. Best give it to others less blind than he.

The alley dumpster yielded all he needed. He tore free a
section of brown paper sack and wrapped the knife securely,
folding in the ends of the paper to make a package. With a
broken bit of crayon, he wrote POLICE as firmly as his shaking
hands could manage. Composing himself, he ventured out upon
the sidewalk once more. He dropped the package into the first
mailbox he came to. There. It was gone, on its way to tattle
on the killer, if he had left more prosaic traces of himself upon
it. Wizard walked quickly on.

The sidewalks and streets were busier now, with the cafés
and restaurants in the throes of the breakfast rush. He should
have felt confident and brash; this was the best time of day to

cadge a meal. But that other emptiness inside him had engulfed his hunger and made it trivial. Coffee, he tried to lure himself. There was always coffee to think of; his shaking hands would feel steadier wrapped around a steaming mug. Waves of giddiness assailed him. He touched his own face and throat surreptitiously, trying to remember if he had taken the fever pills today. The thought swirled away from him, and he was annoyed to find himself patting at his face. What had he been needing? Coffee.

At the door of the next café, he composed himself, running his hands over his wind-tousled hair and tucking in his shirt a little tighter. He pushed the door open and strolled in. As he stood in line, he scanned tables hopefully, looking for someone with food on a plate and showing signs of leaving. Luckily it was crowded enough that people were already sharing tables. No one would fuss about a stranger sitting down. He fingered the coins in his pocket and studied the menu printed high on the wall.

"You." He felt a hand on his arm and someone eased him out of his place in line. Wizard looked up at the man in trepidation. He didn't know him. He was big and stern and determined.

"Sir?" Wizard managed with cold courtesy.

"Try one of the missions on Second. Or the Bread of Life on Main. They do a coffee and donut thing there at noon." Wizard found he was being walked to the door. He knew his mouth was open, but he couldn't get words out. He tried to pull the coins from his pocket, in a childish show of cash, but the man had too firm a grip on his arm. The grip tightened when he thought Wizard was trying to struggle. "Look. Don't make a scene. I can't have your kind in here, or I lose my regular trade. Here's some change. Go get yourself some wine or whatever. But don't come back here, and don't try to panhandle my customers. Next time there won't be a handout, just a cop. You'd better believe me."

The man gave him a firm pat on the back that propelled him out the door. Wizard found himself back on the morning streets with a handful of pennies and three nickels, but no coffee. Worse, no confidence. His hands shook worse than ever as he stuffed the telltale coins into his pockets.

Two cafés later, he was still coffeeless. In one a hostess had refused to seat him. In the other, the manager had come from behind the till and suggested they have a little chat outside.

He'd given Wizard another quarter. He was carrying more money now than he ever had before, and he still couldn't get a cup of coffee.

He dragged himself along the street. He felt colder and emptier than a lack of coffee could account for. Giddiness came and went, washing over him in surges. He hoped he wasn't coming down with something; what if last night's fish had been spoiled? His body had begun a headache to protest caffeine withdrawal. He ignored it and walked, his hands pushed deep into his pockets, his fist gripping the money there. Money. He had withdrawn from the major economic system of this country a long time ago. He didn't need their official federal confetti, or their Social Security, or their welfare, or their lousy Veteran's Administration. Hell, that screwed-up Vets Ad was strictly a place for old men to get their prostate glands fixed or their ingrown toenails dug out. Go to them with a real problem and they shit on you. They were just a part of the whole shitty system. Well, they'd had all they were going to get out of this boy. Six years of his life shot to hell, not to mention. Not to mention.

Wizard had lost his train of thought. He looked about himself in some alarm as he come out of his brown study. How had he gotten off the main drag? There were no bus stops on this street. No cafés, either, just business offices: lawyers, accountants, and brokers. He had even lost his orientation. He walked for three more blocks before he figured out where he was. At the next intersection, he turned and headed back toward Western Avenue. His headache throbbed. He had to stop it so he could think. There were things he had best admit to himself and accept, but not without a cup of coffee.

He found a diner that consisted of a long counter and a row of stools. The windows were dirty, with old tape marks on them. Inside it smelled of grease. As he approached the counter he dragged his money from his pocket and held it before him like a talisman. He made it to the counter and claimed a stool. A waitress grudgingly paused before him. She was forty and bursting from an aqua uniform with a line of greasy dirt at the collar. She looked at the money in his hand and demanded, "What do you want?"

"Coffee."

She nodded, clanked a saucer and empty cup onto the counter in front of him and hurried away. He stared after her, feeling old. So this was what he had come to. The magic had turned

its back on him. Here he sat, no character, no hopes of breakfast, just coins for a cup of coffee. He felt dirty.

On her next trip past, the waitress dumped coffee into his
cup, wrote his slip, took his money, gave him change and told
him, "You get three refills. And I do keep track." The whole
transaction took her less than a minute. He gave a defeated
nod. The coffee was old and black and acid. The cream in the
little tin dispenser came out stringy and yellow. The sugar
dispenser was stuck shut and she hadn't given him a spoon.
The magic was gone. The top of the cup tasted bitter and the
dregs were a sugary syrup in his mouth. She refilled his cup
with more of the same and didn't hear his request for a spoon.
A heavyset man on the stool next to him gave him a supercilious
smile. "Going to sober up, huh? Well, her coffee would sober
up Jack Daniels himself."

"I haven't been drunk." Wizard spoke softly but clearly.

"No, me neither. Haven't been sober, either." The man
laughed at his own witticism and went back to shoveling scrambled eggs. Wizard watched him fork a mound of egg onto a
piece of toast and bite the whole thing off at once. The smell
of the eggs and the sound of his mastication made Wizard's
stomach roll over. He took a deep drink of the bitter black
coffee.

By his fourth cup, his headache had changed to a standard
migraine. He drank down the last of the coffee, left a nickel
tip and headed for the restroom. No mirror. No hot water, and
the cold stayed on only if you held it. A blower instead of
paper towels. Wizard patted his face lightly with wet fingertips
and stared at the chipped plaster over the sink. On the wall
was a condom vending machine. Someone had written on it,
"Don't buy this gum, it tastes like rubber." He wanted to find
that funny, but couldn't dredge up a smile. The magic was
gone. He headed for the streets.

He didn't know where to go. The more he thought about
it, the more he hurt. He wandered into an alley and squatted
beside a dumpster, out of the wind. If he had no magic, he
wasn't Wizard. If he wasn't Wizard. . . . A terrible combination
of anger, bitter hurt, and bewilderment churned through his
guts on a tide of acid coffee. Like a man helplessly slapping
his pockets for a lost wallet, Wizard searched within himself
for the subtle signs of the magic.

But all was silent inside him. Nothing. It was gone. Stubbornly, frantically, he tried to think of ways to test it. Nothing

came to him. He stepped away from the dumpster, feeling a bit shaky in the legs. He was hollow now, light as a man made of straw. The wind off the bay nearly pushed him down. He hit Western Avenue and tromped down it, feeling the sidewalks slap back against his feet until his arches ached. He could hear the gulls crying on the bay like abandoned babies in bombed out places. The city stinks choked him. What the hell was he doing in a city anyway? He had always hated cities. He walked too fast, feeling his shirt stick to him with sweat even as his ears stung with cold. He didn't pause as he passed the market. He didn't want to face Euripides today. Cassie he could not even think of. He turned up Marion, driving himself on.

It was steep going. The first block or two didn't bother him. He distracted himself by watching the cars with manual shifts struggle to advance through the changing lights without rolling backwards into the cars behind them. There were stoplights at the lip of each rise, and the cars clung there, snorting and then roaring forward when the lights changed. Wizard was glad he was on foot. The buildings along here were old, with ornate decorations, some weathered to near obscurity, but some preserved proudly. Past Third, past Fourth, past Fifth he climbed, his calves aching. On Sixth he was stopped by the great gash of Interstate 5. He leaned against a building, panting. For a moment he closed his eyes and let his head loll back against the wall. His throat was dry, his legs ached. He had to stop fleeing. He needed shelter, quiet, and a moment of thought without fear. He twitched his eyes open and stared around.

Across the roaring interstate in its bed, towers rose tall in the leaden sky. They were tipped with blue one shade deeper than aqua. He shivered in their grip, feeling their attraction. Then he turned left and jogged down a block to the overpass on Madison. He turned right on Ninth, trotting on, unmindful of the stares of the passing drivers. His throat and mouth were parched from panting. The buildings here emanated cold pride. He ignored them and moved on, drawn without thought.

On the sidewalk before the fortress he stopped. His breath cracked in his dry throat. The blue towers soared above him. Concrete steps draped in trailing ivy rose before him. His eyes ascended first. On the front of the building, gold branches twined on a shining black backdrop around a benign figure. I AM THE VINE it said, AND YOU ARE THE BRANCHES. St. James Cathedral. He crept up the steps, heart thundering. The cathedral doors were of plain brown wood. Sanctuary. For him?

They looked locked. He dared himself to push one, and it yielded to his cautious touch. He went in, out of the wind.

Silence and warmth filled the foyer, but it was a barren place. Posted notices of scheduled meetings said nothing to him. This was but a limbo between the outside world and that which lay beyond the inner doors. They were upholstered in leather with brass studs and prophesied wonders beyond. He coughed and pushed his way in.

It took his breath away. Had he been some European peasant viewing for the first time Christopher Wren's cathedral the impact could not have been greater. There was too much to behold and all of it shimmered with majesty. He groped his way to the back pew and found himself genuflecting in a re-action that went beyond his memories. He entered the pew and knelt, too humbled to sit. Before and beside and above him the cathedral opened out in swelling glory. Fat pillars of red marble held up the lofty ceiling. The green carpet and brown wood of the pews yet managed to give a sylvan air to the vastness. Marching forward on either side of him were stained glass windows set high in the walls, and below them small shrines to individual saints. Little votive candles burned before the saints in many-hued holders like shining gems offered to God's holy ones for their aid. His eyes followed the line of shrines forward to the front of the cathedral, where angels decked the main altar and hovered over it.

Slowly he became aware that the church was not empty. There were folk gathered here and there for silent devotions, but what was their puniness to this immense repository of godliness? They paid him no attention, and, encouraged by this, he rose and began to cautiously explore. Each stained glass window was dedicated to someone. The brilliance of the day-light when it reached through the purple or yellow of the glass brought tears to his eyes. "In Memory of James and Mary Gorman," he read, and wondered if they knew their window still scattered bits of colored light upon his upturned face.

He paused at the shrine dedicated to St. Frances Xavier Cabrini. Facts surged to the surface of his mind from some forgotten reservoir, broke like bubbles upon his thoughts. Mother Cabrini. A saint for Washington. In Seattle she had become a citizen in 1909, and worshiped in this very place. Canonized in 1949, she was the first United States citizen to be so honored. From his pocket he drew coins and pushed them into the do-nation slot. The book of paper matches was tucked behind one

of the candle holders. He lit a candle in a blue glass and knelt
to watch it burn before the image of the homely woman in
simple garb. He felt consoled by its light and let himself sink
into a dream.

First Communion Day. His stiff collar chafed the back of
his neck raw. He approached the altar beside a little girl in a
white dress with crackling petticoats. She wore a veil over her
shining hair and her eyes glowed as she turned them up to the
crucifix. He had knelt beside her at the altar railing, the gold
and white fence that separated the priest and the holy place
from the commoners. He had put out his tongue and received
on it the round Host. It was white and stiff and dry, tasting of
sanctity. It stuck to the roof of his mouth as he rose and carefully
walked back to his pew with the other First Communicants.
He knew it was unseemly to chew it, so he waited patiently
until it dissolved into a soggy mass he could swallow whole.
And as it went down, an interior Goodness so real that it
warmed him flooded his whole body, making a shiver up his
back and tears in his eyes. Never had he felt so Chosen. Jesus
Christ was in him and his soul burned with a white flame of
purity.

He had tried to play it at home, to recapture that elusive
feeling for himself. In the game he was the priest, with a roll
of Necco Wafers, and two small sisters who would do anything
to get them. They knelt before him, wildflower crowned, and
responded "amen" as he set the candy on their pink outstretched
tongues. It was good, but it was not the same. Only in the
church did that feeling touch him, and he longed for a white
surplice and vestments of green and gold and purple, and people
kneeling before him to be nurtured. The mystical chanting of
the choir, the high Sanctus, Sanctus, Sanctus, like a joyous
bird rising to heaven. He knew that someday he would stand
before that altar, elevating the Host high, his sleeves falling
back to bare his arms as the masses behind him bowed their
heads and murmured, "my Lord and my God."

He had become an altar boy, memorizing the mystical Latin
responses with ease. He could still remember the tingle on his
skin the first time he slipped the black and white robes of his
office over his head. He had poured the water over the priest's
fingers from the tiny glass carafe trimmed in gold, had seen
him shake the shining drops from his fingertips as he mimicked
Pilate's denial. The white cloth for the priest to dry his fingers
on was always folded precisely over his arms, waiting to be

used. And, at exactly the right moment, he had rung the four golden bells fastened to a single handle, let their metal voices cry out in sweet precision at the elevation of the Host. That moment had always closed his throat and made his eyes sting with tears.

He felt a tap against his foot, heard a woman's murmured "Excuse me." Like a diver rising from deep water, Wizard took a deep breath of air and looked around him with fogged eyes. The church was filling with people. There were small family groups, easily identified as they filled half a pew, mothers holding small babies, fathers trying to maintain manners among older children. There were old women, their white heads draped in lacy scarves, and older men who sat, eyes lowered and shoulders rounded as they spoke to God. Wizard rose from kneeling at the shrine. The Mass was about to begin.

He left. He looked back as the heavy doors swung closed behind him. The tall pipe organ in the back of the cathedral had begun to sound, and the people rose as one. He watched them sail away from him on a sea of peace, and then the doors closed between them. He pushed through the outer doors into the cold and wind. He stumbled going down the steps and nearly fell. He glanced back once at the golden vines on the front of the cathedral. Once, he had been a branch. Now he was defoliated.

He sniffed as he strode down the street, and then surprised himself by coughing. Once he had begun to cough, he couldn't stop, as if he had loosened some sickness in the bottom of his lungs. He felt his face grow red and hot with the strain of it, and for long moments he couldn't draw in enough air to fill his lungs. He leaned against a building until his chest quit heaving, and then took in short, cautious breaths of the chill air. It had gotten colder while he was in the church. The brief November day was drawing to a close. He was glad of it, glad it was nearly done with. He was tired and suddenly weary. Sleepy was too gentle a word for what he felt. He wished he could just curl up on the sidewalk and sleep. Or in a doorway. There were those who did that, he knew, but he had never been one of them.

Or had he? He coughed again, not as strenuously this time, but a racking cough nonetheless. He had walked in the cold rain yesterday, and then slept damp and chill. It was no wonder he had a cough. The only strange thing was that he hadn't gotten it long before this. He brushed his hair back from his damp forehead, feeling the tenderness of old scar tissue just back of his hairline. He took his hand away from it and shoved it deep into his jacket pocket. He hunched his shoulders against the evening and began the cold trek to a bus stop.

9

THE BUS RIDE did not warm him. When he disembarked in the general area of home, he was still deeply chilled. The city seesawed around him. His feet knew where to take him, but nothing looked familiar. He focused himself on the streets determinedly. He belonged here. He had worked a long time to belong here. He knew this place, knew every damn square foot of it. He knew more about Seattle than people that had lived here fifty years. It couldn't turn its back on him now. He willed it to be alive, in the frightening and invigorating way Cassie had opened him to. But the buildings remained faceless, mere stone and mortar and wood and glass. When his magic had fled, it had taken all magic with it.

He stamped his feet a little harder on the sidewalks, to waken his numbed toes and stir the city beneath him. These sidewalks were hollow. He knew that. How many residents of Seattle knew that the sidewalks were hollow, with enough space beneath them for folk to walk around? Well, it was true. The hollow sidewalks came into being after the fire of 1889, as a very indirect result of it.

After the great fire, when the whole damned downtown area burned in less than seven hours, the city decided to rebuild

109

itself in brick. No more wood buildings to invite another tragedy like that. And shortly after that, the city decided to raise the streets and suspend the plumbing mains under them. It was all the fault of those new-fangled flush toilets. They had worked fine, on an individual basis. Folks just piped the stuff out into the garden patch or over the property lines. But when there got to be a lot of them, and folks joined up to funnel the stuff into big pipes that went out into the bay, problems cropped up. The system worked just fine, as long as the tide was going out. But when the tide came in, the sea paid back a dividend to all the residents in the lower parts of town. The easy solution was to raise the streets and put the plumbing mains under the new, higher streets. The sewage backup would be solved! But by the time the city got around to raising the streets, a lot of businesses had already constructed new buildings. So you had buildings that had their ground-floor store front windows eight to forty feet below street level. People had to climb up ladders to cross the streets. Horses fell from the streets onto the sidewalks below. In 1891 alone, there were seventeen deaths due to falls from the street to the sidewalks. It was not a good town to get drunk in.

So, of course, the city finally had to raise the sidewalks as well. This changed a lot of ground floor space into cellars. That's how the underground shopping began. For years the people of Seattle strolled along on the original sidewalks, their way lit by bottle-glass skylights set into the new sidewalks above. At first, the city had tried skylights made of thick clear glass. But young apprentices soon took to spending their lunch hours gazing up through the skylights at the passing ladies. Some of the more obliging hookers wrote their prices on the bottoms of their shoes. Morality demanded that the skylights be made opaque.

"I ain't interested!" The man walking in front of Wizard turned around and growled at him.

Wizard halted on the sidewalk in confusion. He had been wandering, not watching where he was going, and talking out loud about the history of Seattle like a weirdo. He shut his jaws firmly, clenching his teeth shut. They wanted to chatter against each other. He pulled his jacket closer around himself and hurried on, passing the man who had snarled at him. First and Yesler. Home was only a few blocks away.

As he entered Occidental Square, the pigeons rose and swirled over his head. A pang of loss jarred him. He had nothing for the hungry ones. He bowed his head and tried to hurry past them, but they refused to be ignored. Down they came like huge, dirty snowflakes, eddying around him, obscuring his vision with their flicking wings. The snap of pinions stung his face as they fought for the privilege of alighting on him. They settled on his shoulders, a feathered yoke of responsibility. He shook them off, gently at first, then more violently, like a dog trying to shake off water. Their questioning coos became alarmed. One tried to land on his head, missed his perch, and Wizard felt small cold feet and claws scrabble down his cheek.

"Leave me alone!" he cried out, and as swiftly as the storm had come, it dispersed. He watched them scatter up to black tree limbs and desolation filled his soul.

Ashamed, he fled them, scurrying across the square to the Grand Central Arcade and the gas fireplace. He rattled facts in his head to hold his despair at bay. It dated from 1889, this ivy clad building, and it had been the Squire Latimer Building. It boasted access to the old underground shopping. He squeezed his lips shut to keep from muttering to himself, but his wayward mind clutched at the distraction, hooking his identity to the city. He was losing his grip on both.

The sudden warmth of the mall made his nose start to drip. He hurried to the men's room for tissue. He plucked a handful of stiff leaves from the dispenser and scoured his nose with them. He stared blearily into the mirror. He looked like hell. Like he had died and someone had reheated the body in a microwave. He smiled mirthlessly at himself, a death's head grin. As he stuffed extra tissues into his pocket, his hand encountered coins. He fished them out and looked at them. A quarter, a dime, and a nickel. Forty cents. Worth virtually nothing in terms of food. Coffee was up to fifty cents a cup, and the ten-cent donut was a fragment of the past. But the coins were something to clutch as he strolled through the mall stores, seeking some sort of sustenance.

He made three circuits of the shops. He ventured up the stairs that had once led him to Cassie and safety. They stopped at street level and looked at him blankly. He pushed gently at the bare wall, feeling weak, tired, and sick. It turned him away and he returned to the underground stores.

He found a blacksmith working his forge and selling coat-hooks. He found greeting cards with cats on them, and crystals for sale, and jewelry, flowers, and an art gallery and rare books. He found nothing edible for forty cents. And he felt no warmer.

The chill that swept through him in waves seemed to come from his bones, flowing from the chill ashes of his magic. It was an exhausting, shivering cold that wearied him into an icy sweat. He stumbled back up the stairs to the street level of the arcade and the gas fireplace. He had no trouble finding a seat near the flames; the shoppers were thinning as the stores began to close for the night.

Numbly he sat, trying to absorb warmth. His eyes fixed on a woman tending a vendor's cart. It was a red popcorn stand, selling salted or caramel popcorn. The woman was scooping up her cooling wares with a shiny metal scoop and packing the popcorn into big plastic bags. Wizard stared at the placard on her cart until the words burned into his senses. Popcorn, eighty cents. Carmel Corn, sixty cents. Small, forty cents. The misspelling of caramel vexed him unreasonably. He wanted to demand that they change the sign immediately. Then the final line hit him. Forty cents. Salt beckoned him.

The woman looked up at him in a bored but guarded way as she went on shoveling popcorn. "Can I help you?" she asked in a voice that indicated she didn't want to.

"Popcorn." Wizard was amazed at his croak. He tried to clear his throat and coughed instead as he brought the change out of his pocket and proffered it to her.

"It's cold, you know. I'm just cleaning out the machine."

"That's okay. It'll be fine."

"I already counted out for the night."

He tried to reply, but a chill hit him. He pulled his jacket closed across his chest. Her eyes narrowed, then relaxed into a guarded pity. Poor junkie. She snapped open a small bag and packed popcorn into it. She pushed it into his hand and dropped his coins in the till without counting them.

Wizard took the bag awkwardly. She had stuffed it over full and, as he put his fingers in, a few kernels leaped out onto the floor. A man who had walked up beside him glared down at the popcorn on the floor as he commented loudly, "Arcade stores are getting ready to close now." Wizard nodded without looking at him and headed toward the tall doors.

Outside, a gust of wind carried off the top layer of popcorn. The darkening skies had banished the pigeons. No one would salvage the fluffy white puffs until they were sodden and gray beneath the dawn. He was just as glad there were no birds to greet him. There wasn't enough here for a tenth of his flock. He stuffed a few kernels into his own mouth and immediately

lost his appetite for more. A fit of shivering rattled him. He
twisted the top of the bag to seal it and stuffed it into his pocket.

"So here you are," she said.

He turned, needing Cassie. She smiled up at him and the
depth of his misfortune engulfed him. He could only stare at
her. Her face was turned up to his and raindrops misted her
lashes. He realized belatedly that it was raining. Drops were
darkening her blond hair. She was giving him a strange look,
half-smile, half-frown.

"Don't look so blank, honey. Lynda, remember? I told you
to meet me here this morning, for breakfast. But I was late
and I guess you gave up on me. So I felt just awful. But I
figured, well, maybe he'll be around there when I get off work
tonight. So I came by here, and sure enough, there you are
coming out of the arcade."

Her chatter went too fast for him. By the time he absorbed
the meaning of one sentence, she was two sentences away. He
groped to reply. "I wasn't here this morning." The words dragged
past the rawness of his throat. Lynda didn't appear to hear
them. At the sound of his croak, her eyes went wide. She
pressed her cold hand to his forehead and then the side of his
neck.

"You're burning up! Let's get you out of this rain. Hey—
I know just the place; it's a great little place, lots of really
healthy food, you know, fiber and vitamins and stuff that's
good for you. Come on, now."

Her arm was through his and her hand gripped his jacket
right above his elbow. She hurried him along with short quick
steps that put his long legs off stride. She appeared not to notice
as she chattered on about a customer who had left her tip in
the bottom of his water glass, and another who had wanted her
to go out with him after work. "He smelled just awful, like
mildewed cheese, you know what I mean."

Her words pattered and splashed against him like the rain,
drowning his thoughts. The streets were shiny, their wet pavement reflecting the streetlights. She hurried him across south
Main and into the Union Trust Annex and down some stairs.
She paused for breath on the stairs and he murmured, "Back
into underground Seattle." Lynda frowned up at his non sequitur. He felt a tiny triumph. "Notice the rough brick work
of the building fronts down here. These all used to be ground
floors, and now they're basements. Did I ever tell you the story
of the fire of 1889? A carpenter's apprentice let a pot of hot

glue boil over. I learned all about it at the Klondike Gold Rush Memorial National Park. Just down the street."

"You don't make any sense," she told him earnestly. "Come on."

She tugged at him and he followed her into City Picnics. She didn't pause to order at the counter, but took him straight to a table and parked him on a bench with her shopping bag and raincoat. Then she left him. He looked around dully. The tables were inlaid with genuine artificial wood. He didn't like it, but had to admit it was well done. He put his hand against the honest brick of the wall, feeling its integrity.

Someone loomed over the table. He turned to look up at her. But it was a stranger who bent down to put her face close to his as she whispered.

"You dummy! If you had listened, you would understand. War," she hissed, her breath vile, "is a sin, and it has to be atoned for. Penance. That's the only way out of it."

That old accusation. Someone had beaten her recently. Her features were swollen and blue, her ragged hair caught back in a ratty old scarf. Her words accused and snagged on old scars. "I didn't start the war," he tried to explain. "I didn't want the war."

"That doesn't matter," she snapped. "Listen to me. It's not a sin you commit, fool. It's a sin that happens to you. Passed on, like heredity and original sin. Like your mother's dimples or syphilis. It might not have been yours to start with, but once you've got it, it's yours. Are you going to let it infect you and eat up your whole life?"

"It wasn't my war," he insisted, begging her to say it was true. But she only smiled evilly.

"No? Then whose was it? Are you going to tell me it wasn't a hell of a lot of fun, when it wasn't just plain hell? Are you going to tell me that you'll ever feel that alive again? Isn't your life all the same now, day after day, beset by problems you're not allowed to solve? Wasn't it all simpler with a rifle in your hands?"

"What do you want of me?" he groaned.

"Get up. Come on. This one is your war, and yours alone. Don't run away from it. You have to fight."

He stared up at her, shaking, trickles of sweat or rain funneling down his face. She was so ugly and so close. She kept leaning closer, leering at him with her puffy eyes and squashed mouth. She was making him want to hit her, just so she would go away.

"Ex-cuse me!" Lynda's voice was politely venomous. "We're together." She shouldered past the woman with the professional grace and balance of a waitress, to land food on the table before him. A huge sandwich like a torpedo for Wizard, salad for herself, and two foaming mugs. "Michelob on tap!" she said with a flourish, and slid one over to him. She plumped down on the bench beside him, squeezing him up against the wall. The old woman wandered off muttering. Lynda glared after her. "Jee-sus H. They ought to lock up some of the crazies in this town, you know what I mean? What was she saying to you?"

"I don't remember." He stared down at the food in front of him. The smell had flooded his mouth with saliva. He could think of nothing else.

"So eat!" Lynda laughed, seeing his stare. "I got you a Gobbler on sourdough. Hope you like everything in a turkey sandwich, 'cause that's what you got."

Wizard ate ravenously, scarcely chewing, enjoying the scraping of large hunks of food moving down his throat. He washed it down with draughts of the cold beer whenever his mouth got too dry to chew. There was lettuce, tomatoes, onions, turkey and cheese, and the fragrant, chewy bread itself. He didn't see Lynda as he ate, only becoming aware of her when she replaced his mug with a full one. He didn't care for the beer, but drank it for the moisture. He recalled the taste, the slight bitterness. He seemed to remember that when he had been thirsty, they never let him have any, but there were too many times when there was too much of it and he had drunk beer until his belly sloshed. When that had been he could not be sure; there was only the unpleasant memory of thick cigarette smoke and too many people talking too loudly. His mind veered from the thought. He took a final swallow and stared in surprise at his empty plate.

"Hungry guy," Lynda observed with maternal pride. "Finish off your beer. Bet you feel better now."

Wizard checked. He was not sure himself that better was an accurate description. He felt heavy, logy as a sated wolf. His neck did not seem as strong as usual. It took a small portion of his concentration to keep his head upright; it wanted to sag onto the table. Setting down his empty mug, he leaned heavily

into the wall and sighed. The honesty of the bricks comforted
him. He looked at the woman beside him very carefully. This
was the second time she had fed him, yet she did not make
him feel that he owed her anything. She was smiling at him,
seeming glad of his attention. She had blue eyes and a straight
nose and abundant blond hair. Her mouth was too generous
for contemporary beauty, but he found he liked it. Her hands,
lying soft and empty on the table top, were small, but not well
cared for. Working hands.

"What?" she asked softly.

"I am trying to figure you out," he told her solemnly.

"There isn't much to figure out." She gave a deprecating
little laugh. "I'm just me. Just what you see. Maybe you think
I want something from you, because of the way I've, well,
almost picked you up. But that's not how it is, really. I don't
like to be alone. That's part of it. And I like helping people.
I know that sounds corny, but it really is true. When I saw you
sitting alone on the bench with only pigeons for company, my
heart just went out to you. I mean, at first I was really pissed
at you for the way you took Booth's breakfast, and let me get
the blame for it. But even right there in Duffy's, I looked at
you and couldn't stay mad. The way you peeked around your
newspaper, suddenly it just seemed so funny. Did you see
Booth's face when he tossed down my keys and his food was
gone? Did you see him?"

Lynda began to giggle. Wizard watched her face, studying
the sparkle that came into her eyes and made her girlish. There
was something here for him, something warm. He caught at
that thought and tried to find the sense in it, but he could no
longer follow it.

She had his hand. He looked down in some surprise, wondering why he hadn't noticed her touch before. Her hands were
white in contrast to his. His were browned and bony with little
gristly scars on his knuckles. The comparison made him feel
strong. She squeezed his hand gently, and the touch was good.

"You haven't told me a thing about yourself. And I've talked
and talked about me, and I suddenly realize that I just bought
dinner for a man, I don't even know his name. So what's your
name?"

The simple question stopped him cold. He had not realized
how much he had relaxed in her company until the iciness of
her querying tightened his muscles. He searched her face for
signs of treachery. Her blue eyes went wider at his grim

expression and her smile lost its confidence. He took a deep
breath to spill out some sort of an answer, but it came out as
a racking cough. It didn't stop. It tortured him, driving the air
from his lungs, reddening his face and making tears roll from
the corners of his eyes. He pushed against Lynda and then
staggered to his feet, his hands on his knees as he bent to try
and take in air. Other customers were looking up in dismay,
and one man rose to ask her if her friend were choking. Wizard
shook his head in an emphatic no. "Air," he gasped. "Cold
air."

He shook Lynda's grip from his sleeve and staggered out
the door of City Picnics. In the hallway he headed for the stairs
and clambered up them, still wheezing and hacking. The circle
of his vision was narrowing, darkness closing in from the pe-
riphery. He got the door open and staggered out onto the sidewalk, to lean up against the building. His chest did not feel so
compressed here. He began to take small, short breaths and
then longer, deeper ones. His face was still cooling when Lynda
dashed out the door, her head swiveling in all directions.

"There you are!" she exclaimed. She dropped her shopping
bag and shrugged into her raincoat, gripping her purse strap
with her teeth. "Are you all right?" she demanded as soon as
her mouth was empty. "That was just awful! Everyone was so
worried, but I said it was just a bronchial attack and grabbed
my stuff and followed you. I could tell you didn't want everyone making a big fuss over you. Now, are you okay?"

Wizard nodded slowly. He straightened from leaning on the
building, and she instantly had his arm. She was strong, taking
part of his weight whether he wanted her to or not. She began
to steer him slowly down the sidewalk, talking all the while.
That was one good thing about her. She talked so much that
he had to say almost nothing at all. Now, why was that good?
he wondered. He tuned into her monologue. ". . . Hot buttered
rum. Or a hot toddy or Irish coffee. Something hot. I bet I
know a good place for that. It'll cut that junk in your throat
and make you feel better. Warm you up inside. Come on, it's
only a few blocks from here."

Wizard found himself nodding as he leaned against her
support. She fit neatly under his arm. A hooker walked past
them, headed in the opposite direction. Her heels tacked clearly
against the pavement as she strode along, heading for more
heavily traveled streets. He had a brief impression of her short
bright dress, the elegantly casual coiling of her hair upon her

shoulders that was her only wrap against the cold November night, and her parted lips shining in the lamplight. Then her black empty eyes hit him with a bolt of sadness that staggered him back against the wall of the building. She turned her head as she passed, tearing him with the hooks of her smile. Her agony raced through him. For a second he felt sure that, had he been alone, she would have said something to him, and he would have Known something to tell her. But he wasn't alone, and he didn't Know, and she kept clipping along, her footsteps fading swiftly from his hearing. He rubbed his forehead and pushed the hair back from his face. Lynda was staring at him. He had almost forgotten her.

"What was that?" she demanded, little lights dancing angrily in her eyes.

"I don't know," he managed. Then more words pushed up out of him, words he hadn't consciously planned to say. "Lynda. I have to go home now. Thank you for treating me so kindly. But."

"Oh, no, you don't." She gripped his arm firmly and hauled him up beside her. "Some chippie walks past and gives you the eye, and you decide to drop me and give chase, huh?"

"No. No, not that way at all!"

"I know!" Her tone changed, and he stared at her, astonished. She had been joking with him, he realized giddily. Joking. "No, I knew you weren't going after her. But I also know where you were going. What are you worried about? That they'll run out of cots at the shelter? Forget that tonight. You're with me now, and I plan to take good care of you. We're going to take care of that cough and get you all straightened around. You just wait and see. And trust me. I mean it now. Trust me. Come on."

She dragged at him like a riptide. There was no resistance left in him. He pushed away his worries as she wrapped his arm around her. They walked, he paying no attention to where they were going.

Second Avenue South. It took a while for him to recognize it, lit up for the evening trade. Neon signs and streetlights and the headlights of passing cars gave more light to the barren streets than they got by day. The brightness of a beer advertisement in the night dazzled his eyes. But the place she chose for them was neither bright nor inviting. She trundled him past the Silver Dollar, Bogart's, and the Columbus Tavern to draw him into a place whose name he didn't notice.

The door was heavy, but she dragged him inside. Most of the interior space was devoted to pool tables with low, shaded lights dangling over the green felt. The men playing were working men. Regulars. It was obvious from a glance that he had entered their territory and they looked up from their games to stare at Wizard for longer than was polite. There was a long bar to the right, and to this Lynda steered him.

She hitched her tidy hips neatly onto a seat, but Wizard mounted the backless stool as if it were a strange animal. A confusion of odors assaulted him. He left his eyes rove over the back shelves of tall bottles. "Teddy!" Lynda called out. She was in command here, and enjoying it. "Let us have a couple of Irish coffees. In mugs; I hate those phony glass things. Seems quiet in here tonight."

It seemed anything but quiet to Wizard. There was the clack and rumble of the pool games and a large-pored man on television was excitedly relating the events of a ball game, backed by a chorus of male voices laughing and swearing and muttering. Above it all was the high-pitched whisper of the television tube, harmonizing with the special pitch of the fluorescent lights over the pool tables. Like tiny twin drills the high sounds bored into Wizard's ears and temples. And there was a third type of sound, for his ears only. Danger was screaming in here, pressing in all around him like a million tiny needles trying to pierce his flesh with their warnings. Danger and trap and an exposed back and an idiot on point and a coward on drag, they all screamed, all demanding his attention at once. His eyes roamed the room, trying to find the source of his uneasiness, but found nothing. Only people, the same sort of people he moved among every day. Teddy was setting mugs before them then.

"So where's Booth these days?" Teddy asked Lynda in a genially teasing voice.

"Not here, thank God!" she replied emphatically. Something whizzed past Wizard's mind, some very important clue. He went groping after it, but just as he nearly had it, Lynda shook his arm. "Come on, I want you to drink this. It'll do you good. Clear your chest so you can breathe. Try it, baby." She set an example, sipping from her mug as her eyes darted around the room. He wondered what she was watching for.

He picked up his own mug. The aroma of coffee rose like a benediction. He put it to his lips and drew in a mouthful. The cream was sweet, the coffee strong and the whiskey bit pleasantly. Somehow he had not expected it. As he set down the mug he observed to Lynda, "There's whiskey in my coffee."

"I hope to God there is, at the prices Teddy charges. Drink it up. Make you feel warmer."

Wizard nodded as he sipped again. A secret warmth was spreading out from his belly now.

"Listen," Lynda said suddenly, standing up. "I gotta visit the little girl's room. You sit tight and watch my stuff. Okay?"

Wizard nodded distractedly. He was experimenting with the coffee, sipping it and trying to sort out the electric shocks of the whiskey from the steady rush of the caffeine. He wrapped both hands around the mug, enjoying the heat against his chilled fingers. He glanced up to find Teddy watching him, a cruel smile hovering on his mouth. Then the smile went past Wizard and turned to a scowl. Wizard heard him growl softly to himself in puzzlement. He followed Teddy's stare.

She was a stout woman, dressed all in black. Her white hair was up in a severe bun at the back of her neck. Her disapproving mouth was buttoned over her double chin. She wore her heavy black good coat and sensible black lace-up shoes. Her eyes were black, too, and piercing. They bored into Wizard, and her second chin trembled with the strength of her indignation. She pushed past a pool player, spoiling his shot, and stepped up to within inches of Wizard. Her raspy voice cut through the noise of the bar like a radio signal cutting through static.

"I can't believe you're doing this to yourself! Adding booze on top of everything else. You're poisoning yourself! And what about the rest of us? After you go down, what happens to us? You've got to pull out of this tailspin."

"Stop bothering the customers, ma'am. This is no place for a lady like yourself. You could get into trouble here. Best you go home now." Teddy had come out from behind the bar. He didn't look as tall as he had when serving drinks. He tried to take the old woman's arm, but she jerked away from him angrily. She glared at the attention she was getting and lifted her voice high.

"Alcohol is a poison. Poison, plain and simple. You can dilute it, you can flavor it, you can age it in oak casks, but it is still poison. You are ingesting poison with every sip you take and asking your body to deal with it. Your body has enough to deal with just surviving in this day and age, without your deliberately poisoning it. Some of us," her eyes stabbed Wizard, "are less able to deal with the poisons of alcohol than others. Show yourself a man. Put down that evil drink and walk out of here. Take command of your life again!"

She shouted the last sentence as Teddy steered her toward the door, her head swiveling on her neck to fling the message at him. "A poison!" she called as the door swung shut. "Poisonous bait in a trap for the unwary!"

He felt relieved when she was gone, yet, again, the uneasiness nibbled at him. He had missed another clue. He was sure there was a hint at the reason for the nervousness that plagued him here. Yet it was not in the old woman's words, which he accepted as absolute truth, but in Teddy's. He knew he shouldn't be here. He sipped at his coffee, weighing his bits of clues. But just as they started to tumble into a pattern, he felt a bump of warm flesh and Lynda was back on the barstool behind him. "Did you miss me?" she asked in a silky voice.

"No," he replied distractedly, sipping at his drink.

"Oh, you!" Lynda gave him a friendly punch and took a healthy swallow of her drink. Her eyes flickered to Teddy, and then turned on her stool to face Wizard. Her knees were warm bumps against his thigh. She changed her face to a pout and her voice became childish as she complained, "I wish you'd talk to me more. Being out with you isn't much different from being out alone. You act like we're not even together. Is something wrong with me? Would you rather be alone?"

He looked at her very carefully. She sounded like a different woman than the Lynda who had fed him earlier. He wondered which question he was supposed to answer first. He had forgotten all about this kind of talking. It wasn't like talking to Cassie or Sylvester or Euripides or Rasputin. They had things to say, important things said in deceptively simple words. Lynda had something to say, but she said everything except what she was trying to tell him. Her message to him was lost in her words, and he had no idea of how to reply.

He stared at her over the rim of his mug. The renewed warmth of the drink hit the walls of his body like waves against a breakwater. He tried for an instant to find power and focus his magic on her so he could understand what was Truth here. But even as he groped in his darkened soul, he remembered the magic was gone. A wave of misery washed over him and he took a sip of coffee to counteract it. No wonder he could not find the right thing to say to her. He fell back on his old instincts, and picked through the bewildering array of things he could say to her for the most truthful one. She had stared

at him through his long silence. Teddy was smirking as he
polished a glass. Lynda's face was pinker than Wizard had ever
seen it.

"I have the feeling," he said carefully, "that this is not the
best place for us to be." That was better. Speaking his thoughts
did focus them, and she had gone from angry to rapt, leaning
closer to hear his soft voice. Teddy no longer looked so amused.
"I can't say what it is that bothers me, but this is not a good
place for us." Teddy's words leaped into his mind and he mouthed
them. "This is no place for a lady like yourself."

Lynda was glowing in his words, her smile gone soft and
gentle. Wizard felt very pleased with himself for an instant,
and then the impact of his own words broke on him like a
douse of cold water. This was no place for a lady. Not this bar.
This was a man's bar, with a constant edge in the air. A certain
type of man might bring his woman here, but not his lady. It
was not a place for quiet talking, for the sharing of thoughts
or companionable silences. It was a place for displays and
competitions, challenges and threats. It was a place where
misplaced men came to prod balls around a table, to drink and
mutter angrily and helplessly at one another, and then to fight
short, ugly fights. Not a place to bring a friend one valued. So
why had Lynda brought him here? And who had brought her
here before?

No answers to those questions, but a solution. Leave. He
rose from his stool, feeling a strange rubberiness in his knees.
It passed and he took Lynda's arm firmly. He was certain now
of the danger here. She had tempted it, but she had fed him.
The least he could do was take her to a safer place.

"What's wrong?" Her voice was a shade short of baby talk,
her mouth a plump little pout. Charades for Teddy.

"Nothing, yet. But if you want to sit and talk with me, we
have to find a place to talk where I don't feel exposed. I like
my back to a wall. When I'm with a lady, I like to concentrate
on the lady, not worry about someone behind me with a pool
cue." He listened to himself in surprise. So he did know how
to do that kind of talking. It came out of his mouth too smoothly,
too glibly, for it to be new talent. Even the words seemed
practiced in their sentences. It poured out of him almost like
a Knowing; almost.

"Well—but—let me finish my drink first, then." She pulled
gently away from him, and he saw her eyes dart to Teddy. She
wanted him to notice this exchange, to see how Wizard had

taken control and wanted to be alone with her. She wanted the other men in the room to see that she was desirable, that this man wanted her. He needed to follow that thought, but the sense of danger pressed against him, squeezing his mind to action. He coughed and, lifting the drink, drained it to clear his throat. The warmth spread through him anew.

"I think we should go someplace quieter, more private." These words came even more smoothly. Lynda turned in surprise and gave him a suddenly measuring look.

"Oh. I see. Well, keep your shirt on. The night is young; there's no rush. Besides, I want to finish my drink." She leaned to bump her shoulder gently against him, filling his nostrils with her scent. She was enjoying this. He wasn't.

"I want to leave here now, and I want you to come with me," he said bluntly. "I think you'd be stupid not to. You could get hurt."

"Are you threatening her?" Danger spoke from behind him. Wizard turned to it and found himself eye to eye with Booth. The final tumbler clicked into place. From the rosy flush on Lynda's face and the way she moistened her lips, he knew she had scored her hit. This was why she had brought him here, whether she knew it or not, to this place no man would bring a woman he cared about. Because this was Booth's place, and this was where he had brought her. She had come here to be seen with a new man. To lay a fresh little sting on Booth's pride in revenge for whatever he had done to her. Because she had known that Booth would come here, and the thought of their confrontation warmed her.

"I'm not threatening her." Wizard spoke the useless words. Lynda hitched closer on her barstool, and snugged her arm through his, keeping him on point. Perhaps she sensed he wanted to flee.

"Mind your own business, Booth," she snapped.

"I am. Just because we're not going together anymore doesn't mean I want to see you get hurt. Look at this guy, Lynda! Where the hell did you pick him up? I heard what he said to you. Don't do anything stupid like leaving with him."

Booth's words were like lines in a play. Wizard knew this scene by heart, had watched it played out in a thousand settings, but never before had he been a principal in it. He tried to step clear, but Lynda clung to his arm.

"Get lost, Booth. I'll go anywhere I want, with anyone I want." Her voice was clear and carrying, filling the tavern and interrupting pool games. She had her audience. "You don't own me. Not anymore. Mind your own business. You didn't want to treat me nice when you had me, so leave me alone now. What could he do to me worse than what you did? Answer me that?" Lynda blazed at him gloriously, letting her lips go full and her breasts heave, letting him see all he had so carelessly thrown away. "Baby." She had turned to Wizard now, changing her voice to intimacy, letting Booth see all he was shut away from. "Take me out of here. You were right. Let's go someplace more private." She leveled her eyes at Booth once more and fired with deadly accuracy as she observed in a clear voice, "It's been a long time since I was with a man who knew how to treat a lady. I'd almost forgotten what it was like."

Teddy the bartender had edged closer during the exchange. Wizard wondered if he was keeping himself handy to prevent trouble or just to witness it. His eyes had a hard, dead glint in them, the look of a man who expects to watch a fight. He wouldn't stop it. Wizard stiffened.

"If you're coming with me, we're leaving now," he said to Lynda. His voice was cold, its edge cutting through all other sounds in the room. He kept his eyes on Booth as he stepped away from the bar and was amazed to find how easily Lynda came along with him, floating on his arm. Her purse and bag were on her other arm, and he knew that she had been ready for this move, had planned it just this way. As Wizard moved toward the door, she rode on his arm as regally as any queen. Wizard didn't need to look back to know that Teddy was smirking and Booth was glowering. He heard the impact of Booth's fist on the bar, saw heads turning to watch their exit. It's not over yet, warned a voice in the back of his skull, and he felt a quickening of excitement in his body, surging like pleasure. It frightened him.

The woman was short and dark, with tightly curled hair and a nose like a Jewish elf. She was leaning against the wall of the building as Wizard and Lynda came out into the cool dark streets.

"Last chance to do anything smart tonight," she announced as he came out the door. "Run like hell, buddy. If you don't, forget it. Forget everything, because you are a babe in these woods and you are going to lose it all. Last chance." She hitched herself up off the wall and strode off into the darkness. Lynda was adjusting her coat. If she had heard or seen the other woman, she gave no sign of it.

She flashed a smile up to Wizard in the darkness. "Well, where do you want to go now?" There was a bit of a challenge in her smile. Did she know what came next as clearly as he did?

"You choose the place," he said, giving her a wolf-hard smile. He wondered if his teeth gleamed in the darkness. This was the part he had always loved best. Preparation. The rubberiness in his legs had been replaced with an old familiar springiness. Alertness coursed through his veins, making him more alive than his body could stand. Just like old times, someone whispered grayly. His readiness radiated off him, sending sparks of aggression into the night. "Lead the way," he commanded. To her puzzlement he let go of her arm and gave her a gentle push to set her going. She would be on point, but it didn't worry him, because he knew the attack would come from behind. He sauntered along, casual in the cold night. Waiting.

After a hesitant glance back, Lynda led off. Wizard followed her, smelling her perfume as it drifted back to him, listening for the inevitable.

Booth was good. Wizard gave him that. Anyone else would have been surprised when the hard hand fell on his shoulder and spun him around. Anyone else would have hit the wall and been off-balance, would have been struggling to come back to his feet as Booth's fist pinned him to the wall and the mocking words began. That was the scene Booth had planned. But when the hand spun Wizard, he went with it, not falling to one side but turning in a tight circle, using the momentum Booth had given him to plant his fist squarely in Booth's belly. Booth doubled over, pushing his face into Wizard's knee as it rose smartly to meet his nose. Wizard seized him by the ears and propelled him with vicious force into the side of the building. As Booth started to slide down the bricks, Wizard delivered a kick to the side of his knee. He was out of practice; no clean snap of joint followed it. There had been remarkably little sound since it had begun. Wizard's first blow had knocked the wind out of Booth, and his responses to what followed had been limited to piggish grunts, with the hint of a high squeal on each intake.

Only instants had passed. Now he lay on the ground and

Wizard stood over him, waiting for a movement or a sound. The sound came; the harsh noise of a man unused to tears but weeping with pain. Booth had not expected pain, had not been prepared to pay for his amusement. Wizard had felt him assessing him in the bar. Booth had not looked beyond the gaunt frame and cautious manner; he had read Wizard as a skinny and fearful target. He should have looked in my eyes, Wizard thought with satisfaction. Next time, he'll know better.

A disturbing thought. Far better to make sure there wasn't a next time. He knew of no more stupid mistake than to injure an enemy and leave him to brood and heal. When he came after Wizard the next time, he would be better prepared, with a knife or a small caliber pistol for luck. Better to eliminate next time now. Wizard glanced about as he considered quick, quiet ways. Lynda was standing like a stag at bay, her eyes huge but not disapproving. And if I had lost? he asked her silently. He could smell her excitement and the edges of her fear. It was happening so swiftly for them, and so slowly for him. He took a deep breath and tightened his guts for the finale.

"Didi mau!" A small slender shadow, blacker than the night, raced between him and Booth, shrieking the old warning. The urgency of it hit Wizard, moving him automatically. He gripped Lynda by the upper arm and rushed her off, almost lifting her off her feet to match his long-legged stride. She trotted beside him, not questioning him. They fled two blocks and then he abruptly jerked her to a walk. He put his arm hastily around her and they sauntered along, not speaking. Her eyes darted, their whites visible all around the edges. The patrol car rounded the corner as they waited to cross the intersection. It turned left, back the way they had come. Wizard watched it from the corner of his vision, saw it pass the crumpled man on the sidewalk, then back up. They'd cheated him of his prey this time, but the next time. . . .

"Let's go in here." Lynda's voice shook. Fear? No. Suppressed glee. They were scarcely in the door of Maudie's Corner before she began to shake. A titter of high laughter escaped her. She stilled it with her hand over her mouth, but her eyes were dancing as she looked up to Wizard. He met her look unsmiling and pushed his way into the bar.

It was a very narrow entryway. On his left were tiny two-person tables up against the windows. There was room for one person to walk between them and the row of barstools at the long red bar. It was noisy in here, and male. A TV was blasting in the corner, accompanied by the pinging of an Eight Ball pinball machine. A cigarette machine was crowded up beside that. The wall behind the bar was decorated with framed photos of teams, mostly baseball. Wizard had no doubt that this was another of Booth's hangouts. Well, he wouldn't be in tonight. It was as safe a place as any to hole up until the cops had finished with their assault victim.

He found a wall table with a cribbage board on it. He seated Lynda with a gesture and then sat down across from her. Even in the darkened atmosphere of the tavern, she shone with excitement. Men looked at her, at him, and then looked away. She shook off a shiver and leaned forward to cover his hands with hers.

"I never saw anything like that. Never! Well, on TV maybe, but never real like that. You know, so many times when Booth would rough me up, I'd dream about letting him know what it felt like. Tonight he knew it. Boy, he knew it good!" Her hands tightened on his; he felt her nails digging into his flesh. She released him and pawed through her purse to slap a five dollar bill on the table. "Order us some drinks, baby. I've got to go to the little girl's room again." She suppressed another little shiver. Wizard sat silently, looking up at her. As she rose to leave the table, she stepped closer to him. Taking his face in both her hands, she tipped his eyes up to hers. "You are some special kind of man. But I want you to know you didn't have to do that for me. I didn't expect you to protect me like that. No one ever did before."

Wizard's voice was hoarse. "I didn't do it for you," he croaked softly. Her eyes went puzzled. "I did it because I wanted to. Because it felt good to do it."

Her hands went warmer on his face. She leaned down to press her mouth against his. "You are some kind of man, aren't you? Don't go way, now. I'll be right back."

Her lips were cold on his mouth. They started a shiver that turned into a shaking as she walked away. A wave of heat followed it, and he coughed twice, achingly. He shook his head, feeling muffled, as if his brains were wrapped in a gray veil.

When he opened his eyes, his vision cleared, leaving him unshielded to the reality. His ribs and belly were sore from coughing. He rubbed his hands together, feeling the pain in his raw knuckles like an old, familiar sickness. He closed his eyes to it and saw Booth falling to the sidewalk. He opened them quickly, but the thud of full mugs on the bar was identical to the sound of his knee meeting Booth's nose. Vertigo swept through him, driving him to his feet. He surged from the table, pushing past a couple of men coming in the narrow door. They parted to let him through. Down the street he saw the steady blip-blip of the ambulance's lights. He leaned against the building, breathing in hard gasps of the cold air. "I've got to get home," he said aloud, the sickness in his voice.

He stuffed his hands in his pockets and stiffened his arms to keep his back straight. He wanted to curl up and around the hurt inside him and lie very still until it passed. But he couldn't. He had to get back to the den before he could rest. The alcohol was making the blood pound in his face, and he couldn't recapture his day. He tried to place himself in time. The cathedral seemed months ago. The incidents before that were ancient. Was it only this morning the magic had abandoned him? Why? The questions swirled about in his brain, eluding him. He had never been able to handle liquor; he should have left it alone. Cassie was right; it was poison. "I've poisoned myself," he muttered sadly and tottered on. He staggered toward the corner of a sidewalk that stretched eternally longer. "That woman was Cassie," he admitted when he teetered on the edge of the gutter. "And I knew it. But I didn't. I swear I didn't know her."

A thin gray fog was stringing through the streets. He tried to rub it from his eyes, but it hung before him like ratty curtains, coloring all he viewed. It opened and closed mockingly around him and whispered soundlessly and mockingly in his ears. Half a block more to go, he told himself and staggered on. On South Jackson he turned into his alley mouth. The fog massed there, defying him. He plunged into it, to crash into Wee Bit O'Ireland's trash and then rebound into Great Winds Kite Shop dumpster. The brick wall caught him roughly. His fire escape was a black shadow overhead.

He craned his head back to look up at it. He gave a testing bounce on his legs. A wave of dizziness and nausea washed up from his belly and drowned him. Wizard took a deeper breath. "You can do anything you have to do," he reminded himself sternly. He bent his knees deep, ignoring all the pain signals of his body. He concentrated only on the jump, and sprang. His hands caught like claws on the old pipe. Its rust bit into his palms. He braced his foot against the bricks and pushed up. But his knees had gone rubbery again, and the muscles in his arms were like limp strings. He tightened his arms, straining to pull himself closer to the fire escape. He braced his foot again and gave a kick that let him release the pipe and grab for the edge of the fire escape. His hands caught.

He dangled from the edge of the fire escape. He knew what he must do; he had done it a thousand times. He had to chin himself up to the edge of the fire escape platform and slither onto it. But instead he hung there, like a shirt on a clothesline. The cold black metal bit into his hands. His palms felt they must tear loose from the muscles and bones beneath them. He hung on doggedly, chewing pain. He could not make the quick hard pull that would jerk himself up to the edge. So he began the long slow tightening of muscles that would drag the full weight of his body up. His shoulder muscles creaked. Just a little farther, he promised himself, refusing to release his pent breath. A little more.

At the instant he knew that he must let go and drop to the pavement below, he felt two hands seize his ankles in a firm grip. Before he could kick free of them, they pushed up on his stiff legs, boosting him to the edge of the platform. He dragged himself up onto it and lay panting with his eyes shut. Waves of pastel light washed across the inside of his eyelids. His heart was slamming against his ribs and he couldn't remember how to calm it. He had to let it run down as the cold air of the night washed against his sweating face.

"Hey!" The voice came from below. "Aren't you going to give me a hand up?"

10

WIZARD ROLLED OUT of her way as she scrabbled up onto the platform. The aging iron landing groaned complainingly under the unaccustomed extra weight. Wizard sat up slowly to look at her. The climb had mussed her hair, but other than that she looked remarkably collected. She had clambered up the wall unaided. Now she brushed her hair back from her face and gave him a grin that was one part defiance to one part mischief.

"See? It's not that easy to get rid of me. I should have known better than to leave you alone. Why'd you run out on me?"

"I don't feel good." Wizard didn't want to talk, didn't want her up here, didn't want to do anything but crawl into an isolated place and curl up around the emptiness and sickness inside him. The magnitude of this disaster was such that he could not comprehend it. If only she would go away he could lie still and understand how awful it all was. Bent nearly double, he began his climb up the flight of metal steps. He heard her following. Well, let her. He couldn't stop her. Silently he raised his window wider and wriggled inside. It was dark, but not so dark that he couldn't make out his familiar path through the stacks of cardboard boxes stored in this room. He groped his way to the door of his den. There was a slight rustle from the roosting pigeons as he stepped through the door, but they settled again almost immediately. Behind him, Lynda had snagged her coat on the windowsill. She was muttering curses as she tugged at it, but he had no energy to hush her. He took four steps to his bed and dropped onto it. He could undress later.

Slowly he drew his knees up to his chest and tried to make his muscles go slack. His feet were horribly cold, but his fingers were too fuddled to manage the bootlaces. Best to just lie still for awhile. He heard a questioning mew; Black Thomas was on the pillow beside his head. He had narrowly missed him in the dark, and the big cat was not pleased with his carelessness. Wizard set one apologetic hand on his dark, damp fur. Thomas gave a growl of pain and moved carefully closer to the warmth of Wizard's body. He smelled like wet wool and clotted blood. The two huddled together, sharing misery.

"Jesus H!" Lynda blotted the faint light from the doorway. She seemed to fill the frame, looming over the room. He cringed deeper into his bed. "My God!" she went on. "I never imagined anything like this. What is that smell?"

She fumbled her way to the door and tried the light switch. Nothing happened. She clicked it a few times and began to dig in her purse. Black Thomas was growling low at the intruder. The pigeons huddled closer to one another on their shelves, cooing worriedly to one another. Wizard lay small and still, praying she would leave, praying this was just an evil dream. Then she blasted them all with the flame of her cigarette lighter.

Wizard rolled to his knees, heedless of the pains that lanced through him and the nausea that swelled inside him. "Turn it down!" he hissed at her. "We'll be seen!"

"Up here?" Lynda scoffed, but she whispered and adjusted the lighter to a smaller flame. "Look, don't you have candles or something? I can't see my way around in here."

"Sit down and be quiet!"

"Where?" she demanded. He gestured furiously and she clunked and fumbled her way across the room to his mattress. She lowered herself onto it with a snort of disgust and let the lighter go out. Wizard moved carefully through the darkness. He found his candle and holder and set it on the floor. In the darkness he slipped to his entry window to put the plywood in place, and to his second window to make sure the blanket was tight. Soundlessly he moved back to the candle and knelt before it. He began the slow concentration of self, stealing his attention bit by bit from his aching body and tortured mind, and putting it toward a flame. His hands clutched one another to still their trembling. He slowed his breathing to quiet the demands of his body. The flame. He could see it, he could smell it, he could feel it, could sense its warmth. It was coming now, about to blossom on the wick, the perfect orange and yellow flame.

With a click and a hiss the flame appeared, searing his eyes and exploding new pain in his head. The candle flared and Lynda leaned back, taking her thumb off the lever of her lighter. In the glare of the little flame, he watched her slip her lighter back into her purse. Her candle flame dazzled his eyes. The flame in his mind was still there, focused, with nowhere to go. It might be the last bit of magic left to him. Gradually it crumbled into bits inside him, falling like ash into the firepit of his soul. He sat on his heels, blinking away the black spots that danced before his eyes. Black Thomas moved up beside him to ask "Mrow?" Wizard put his hands on the cat's rough fur, feeling the ribs beneath the layer of tough meat and muscle and feeling the life beneath that. It was strangely comforting to feel how strongly life beat in the rickety little body.

Lynda stooped and took the candle. She moved slowly around his small room with it. "Jesus H." A few more steps. "My God!" She stooped to examine his small library on his home-made shelf. "I just don't believe it." She moved to the crate and inspected his slender stores of food. Then she rose and drifted back to him, exclaiming all the way. "I just don't believe it. I never suspected that anyone could live like this. I mean, I've seen bum's beds under the overpass and people living under bridges and stuff, but never like this. It's unreal!"

From her tone he knew she was not admiring his ingenuity at surviving, but disparaging his lack of success at it. He blinked and looked around his den. It had never seemed shabbier. The mattress and blankets beneath him felt dank. There were spots of mold on the spines of his books and pigeon droppings spattered on the floor. He had never noticed them before. The cardboard box that held his wardrobe was softening and sagging at the corners. Even Black Thomas looked like a battered stuffed toy. As Lynda sank down beside them on the mattress, the cat uttered a warning growl. He did not like her. Wizard put a soothing hand on him, but the tensed muscles didn't loosen. Thomas focused his great yellow eyes on her and wished her all the evils the depths of his fuzzy little soul could imagine. Wizard was shocked.

"You poor baby!" Lynda said sympathetically. Black Thomas increased slightly the pressure of his hand to hold him in place. and Thomas flattened his ears at her. "Is this your kitty?"

"No." Black Thomas belonged solely to himself. Wizard increased slightly the pressure of his hand to hold him in place.

"I wouldn't admit I owned him either. What a nasty looking animal. He doesn't smell so good, either. What's his name?"

"He had one of his paws cut off in an accident a few days ago," Wizard hedged. At the mention of names, Black Thomas had extended one of his front paws and sunk the claws into Wizard's thigh. He wanted no name-sharing with this intruder.

"What's your name, kitty-kitty?" Lynda pressed, reaching across Wizard to try and touch the cat. Wizard hastily blocked her hand and held it firmly away from the cat. Black Thomas squirmed from under his grip and gimped disgustedly from the room into the darkened entry chamber.

"Call him Tripod," Wizard suggested callously. If Thomas wanted to be rude, so could he. Lynda stared after the three-legged cat in a sort of frozen horror and then began to giggle. Wizard released his own rusty chuckle. Really, this wasn't so bad. He wondered why he had never before admitted anyone to his den. Not even Cassie had been here. Cassie.

The name was like a talisman against the realities Lynda brought. Wizard stiffened in its spell. He dropped her hand and put both his cold hands against his hot, dry face. The enormity of the day fell on him. He had broken the rules, his magic was gone, he was drunk and sick, his den was invaded, and he was helpless. He pressed his icy fingers against his temples and wished for a tourniquet he could bind around his temples and tighten and tighten until the pain went away. His head was so crowded with it, it was threatening to crack his skull and dribble down his face like blood.

"Headache, honey?" Lynda asked sympathetically. She began to dig yet again in her bottomless pit of a purse. Even in his pain, Wizard was tempted to make an outre request (Got a ham sandwich?) just to see what she could dredge up from in there. "I think I got some Tylenol or Bufferin or something in here. Dammit. No, I left it at work, in the bathroom. You got anything around here?"

Wizard shook his head in silent misery. It wasn't a hurt that pills could take away. You could take enough pills to kill yourself and it wouldn't touch this pain. Lynda had risen with the candle and was drifting around the room. She stopped by his food box, methodically shifted the items in it until she was certain it held only food, and then moved on. Wizard shut his eyes against the harshness of her candlelight. His own flames had always burned with a yellow softness and left a blessed dimness over the room. Hers burned white and harsh, showing every ball of dust, every cobweb and mouse dropping in every corner. It was searching and merciless as an illumination flare. A sudden fear that the light of the candle would find him seized Wizard. He opened his eyes and stood, ignoring the scream in his skull. Too late.

The scene remained forever fixed in his memory, like a tinted illustration from an old book. The light from the candle frame limned Lynda in gold, setting off her silhouette from the darkness that crouched before her. She knelt in the maw of the closet, her hands curled in front of her breasts, her mouth slightly ajar with intent interest. The lid of the footlocker gaped open before her.

Wizard's heart stopped. The pain inside his head became a roaring in his ears like a high wind rising. He expected to feel the air rush past his face, expected to be showered with dust and grit and bits of leaves. He sank to a crouch on his mattress. Her voice cut through his internal distress.

"Is this yours?"

The unanswerable question. Whatever truths he had known about the trunk were hidden from him now, lost with the magic. He heard himself evading. "It's in my room, isn't it?"

"Oh . . . yeah. Well, I thought someone else might have left it here. Well. Aspirin. Let's see."

It was apparent to Wizard that she was not really looking for aspirin. She began to lift items from the trunk and set them on the floor. The big manila envelope she raised looked nearly new, until he spotted a mildew stain on one corner. "Service Record. Mitchell Ignatius Reilly. Ignatius?" She raised a pitying eyebrow. "No wonder you didn't want to tell me your name. Just imagine hanging Ignatius on a newborn baby. But Mitchell isn't so bad. Do they call you Mitch?"

"No." He denied the name firmly, but Lynda was not listening. He thought for a moment that he heard evil gray laughter outside the window, but it was only the spattering of rain against the glass. It was falling in swift, large drops that rattled the old panes in their frames. Lynda ignored his denial. She was already opening the envelope and peering within.

"It's empty," she pouted, and set it on the floor. On top of it she set two olive drab t-shirts with the sleeves ripped off. They filled Wizard with a nameless disgust. Then came a tumble of paperbacks, the bright colors of their covers chafed away by long confinement. Then a handful of photos in a plastic sandwich bag. Lynda slipped them out as casually as if they were hers. The old polaroids stuck together. Even from his place on the mattress, he could see their crumpled corners. "Who are these?" she demanded, sorting through them.

"I don't know." He could scarcely be expected to know. He couldn't see them from here. They could be photos of anyone, of anything. Anything at all, he told himself firmly.

"Cute baby. Yours?"

"I don't know."

"Who's the girl on the bicycle?"

"I don't know."

"An Oriental woman holding up a six-pack of beer?"

"I don't know."

"You don't know much, do you?" Lynda teased gently. She set the pictures down on the pile. A pair of black-soled sandals joined them. "What's in here?" Lynda held up a locked document box. Wizard looked at the flat gray box with the inscrutable keyhole. She shook it at him and something slid around inside, whispering unmentionable secrets.

"Not aspirin," said Wizard briefly.

"Oh. Well, ex-cu-uuse me!" She laughed aloud at some joke he didn't know and set the box atop the pile on the floor. It teetered there and then slid drunkenly to the floor. Wizard stared at it, half-expecting it to scuttle off into the darkness, but it kept still.

"This looks gross! What's this?" Lynda held it out at arm's length for his inspection. The candle shone on it brightly with a merciless white light. A heavy piece of twine with something strung on it. Something small and brown and shriveled. Very far away, someone screamed out in the night.

"It's the cat's foot," Wizard admitted miserably.

Lynda gave an abbreviated shriek as she dropped it. Then, with a suspicious glance at him, she picked up the candle and leaned over to inspect the object more closely. "It is not!" she exclaimed indignantly. "It's got no fur and it's flat and wrinkly. That is not a cat's foot."

"It is," Wizard insisted, knowing it was true. She ignored him, digging into the footlocker again. "Hey! Look at this! Not aspirin, but good enough, I'll betcha. Kinda old, though. Maybe it's not good anymore. Geez! Look at the buds there. Not a stem or a seed anywhere. You got some papers?"

Wizard stared at her in mystification. She was holding a plastic sack of something. She shook it at him and it rattled like a shaman's charm. "You got any rolling papers?" she demanded again, a shade of irritation in her voice. "Geez, you're hard to talk to; you never say anything. Wait! Wait just a moment! Here's the pipe, down in a corner where the light didn't reach it. Okay, we are in mighty fine shape now."

She dug down into the footlocker and came up with an oddly carved little pipe. It was ivory and dirty orange, the color of old bones lying on red earth. The little face carved on the bowl had a pointy beard and squinchy little eyes. Wizard knew that face from somewhere. Somewhere nasty.

Lynda was carefully packing the herb into the pipe bowl. She had put the pipe completely inside the bag and was loading it there, loath to let any particle spill. There was a childish glee to her actions and the little sideways glances she kept shooting at Wizard. He felt acutely uncomfortable. Threatened. Every muscle in his body tensed as she crossed the room to him. She squatted and then sank onto the thin mattress beside him. Her thigh warmed his. Her perfume was stronger than the musk of frightened cat and sweat. Her presence pushed away the familiarity of the room.

Her lighter flared a third time, scalding his naked eyes. She drew the flame down into the bowl of the pipe. She sucked at it, making embers glow in the tiny bowl. She held her breath and then released a stream of gray smoke that coiled around them like incense. Wizard had a sudden flash of the cathedral with its vaulted ceilings and lofty ideas. The squinchy eyes of the pipeman winked at him.

"That's good," she breathed into his ear. She gave a sigh that was part groan. "I haven't done this in so long. Your turn, baby." She held the pipe in front of him. He stared into its mocking little face, making no move to take it. She shook it at him impatiently. "Hurry up, it'll go out." She set the stem to his lips and looked deep into his eyes. Her eyes were gray in the dim light and immensely large. They spun like luminous pinwheels as she stared down into his soul. A tiny alarm bell rang unheeded in the back of his mind.

His breath caught and he coughed, acrid smoke spilling from his nostrils and lips. Lynda laughed delightedly and compounded his difficulty by thumping his back. The room receded, fading into the darkness, then came back to press closely around him. He swung his eyes slowly, following the drifting walls. The pigeons were watching him. Their eyes were orange and gold and black as the candle flame touched them, tiny round eyes shining in the darkness. His flock. Their bills were sunk into their breast feathers, their wing plumes preened back smartly. Their little round orbs were carefully nonjudgmental. He would not find condemnation there.

His slow gaze wandered back to Lynda. She was breathing out, her warm breath and the smoke condensing in the chill air of the room. She leaned against him heavily with a throaty chuckle like the cooing of a fat gray pigeon. He looked down into her face, at her finely pored skin, the tiny individual hairs of her carefully groomed eyebrows, at the tiny lines in her lips where the color of her lipstick was trapped and brightest. She held the pipe up. He looked at her through a thin streamer of drifting gray smoke. A sudden gust of wind and rain rattled his windows and pushed at the blanket.

"No." The awareness was like a cold hand on the back of his neck. It hadn't been Booth at all. This ridiculous woman who talked so much she hardly noticed his silence, this foolish bit of fluff with her make-believe problems and her petty plottings; she was dangerous. Would she have stood by while Booth beat him to a pulp, and then left with the victor? He didn't know. Worse, she probably didn't know herself. She had set every stage this evening. He had drifted along with her plans like a canoe in the current. Now he heard the laughing whisper of the rapids ahead. She could dash him to pieces with her smile. He hitched himself away from her touch, heedless that she fell back onto his mattress. "No!" he repeated to the hand that reached up to wave the pipe lazily before him.

"Whatsa matter, baby?" Lynda sat up languorously. She unbuttoned her raincoat and shrugged out of it so that it fell onto the mattress behind her. She smiled, her generous mouth opening too far, showing too many teeth. "This is good stuff. Not the best I've ever had, but not average. Too good to waste. Come on, it's just burning itself up. Take a hit before it goes out."

The pipe came back to his lips. He pushed her hand away. "No. I want you to leave now. I'm tired and I'm sick. You'd best go." His words sounded petulant and childish, even to himself. Even though they were exactly what he needed to say. She responded to them as if he were eight years old.

"No, baby. That's why I should stay. You need me. C'mon. Listen to Lynda, okay? She'll take care of you. C'mon." She put the pipe back to her own lips, drawing steadily until the tiny coal shone bright and unwinking as a cat's eye. She held it in, making small throaty sounds of pleasure, then letting it stream slowly from her mouth. She fell against him, her body a warm weight, and pushed the pipe at his mouth insistently.

"No. I don't want it." He caught her wrist and held the pipe away. She smiled at him mischievously. Her other hand moved slowly, like smoke, to take the pipe from her captured hand. She took a short hit of it and then poked it at his lips, saying, "Come on, baby, it's nearly all gone. Loosen up a little. You take the last one. Better hurry now."

"I said no!" He caught the other wrist, gave it a shake that sent the pipe spinning away into the darkness. He heard the thump of its bounce, saw a tiny shower of sparks and a glowing coal hit the floor. Within seconds it winked out. He drew his eyes back to Lynda, making several efforts before they focused properly. *It never takes much to stone you, does it?* someone had laughed a long time ago. Laughed 'til it hurt him. *A long time ago,* he reminded himself.

He was confused to find that he still held both of Lynda's wrists. She was not struggling but was leaning into her captivity. She rested her face against his, her cheek pressing his cheek, her breath streaming past his ear. "You smell good," she muttered, rubbing her cheek against his. "You smell wild. I am so damn tired of tame men. I like a man who has spirit and passion. Not like that damn Booth. No balls. I swear, he only hit me because he was too dumb to think of anything else to do. He couldn't handle me and he knew it. I was too much for him. But I like you. You tell me 'no'. And you're quiet. But you do what you want to do. I like that in a man. I don't want to know every little thing about him; takes all the mystery away. And you feel just a little bit dangerous to me. I like a man with secrets and claws. I told that to my sister once. Damn bitch told me to go watch a vampire movie. She didn't understand. She's got a man like a fat poodle, curly black hair and all. But I've got a man here with secrets and silences. I like you, Mitch. I like you a lot."

Her mouth wet his face, her tongue trailing lazily across his cheek to his mouth. The warmth fled from her touch, leaving a cold trail of saliva across his skin. He thought of silver slug tracks on sidewalks in the morning. She put her wet mouth against his, her lips moving as if to devour him.

"Stop it!" His grip tightened on her wrists as he twisted his face away from hers. She laughed lightly and sagged against him. Something unhooked in his brain and his equilibrium went. He fell back on the mattress and she landed heavily atop him. She giggled at his game of reluctance. Her harnessed breasts nosed against his chest aggressively. She let her head loll forward on her neck so that the weight of her long hair fell across his face. He released her wrists and foundered beneath her, feeling trapped and entangled in her body. Lynda giggled again. The sound galvanized him.

"Get off me!" He struggled madly, pushing her from him as he rolled away heedless of her tangled hair. She didn't care. She was laughing helplessly as she rolled across his mattress. He tried to sit up, but the directions of the room changed around him. He closed his eyes and it spun even faster.

"Let me be on top," Lynda begged, very close, her breath warming his face. He pulled back from her, slapped away the hands at his throat. Her busy fingers dropped to his belt. "I'll do all the work," she offered, pulling his shirttail free. Ancient urges rolled down his spine to squirm in his belly and erupt unnervingly. Earlier today, his magic had been shut down, the switches thrown to plunge him into emptiness. Now Lynda was reactivating this other part of him, putting systems on-line whose flashes and thunderings he had stilled long ago. He groped within himself for control, but it was all set on override. His hands gripped her hips.

He squeezed his eyes tight shut, reaching for sanity and order. He found only her weight on his thighs, warm and solid.

"I don't do this," he said, but his voice sounded far off, even to himself. He wondered if Lynda could even hear him as he tried to explain. "There are certain things denied to me. Things I must not do if I am to retain my controls and my magic." Her hands were cold on his belly, sliding around under his shirt and up his chest. She pinched one of his nipples, hard. He divorced himself from the pain-pleasure. "I must not carry more than a dollar in change. I must not harm pigeons. I must listen to people and tell them the Truth when I Know it. I must not harm pigeons. . . ." He caught himself circling and tried to find his track again. He couldn't remember the other taboos. It didn't matter. She wasn't listening. Only their bodies were in the same room. He was just a warm prop for her in her fantasy game of seduction. He coughed and felt her fist grip him.

"Feels ready to me," she chuckled throatily. "Isn't it always the best, the first time with someone new? And stoned. It puts all the magic back into it."

"All my magic is lost to me," he corrected her. He was aware of his body's betrayal, but he scrambled frantically away from it, trying to keep the memories out, to block away the sensory input that stirred up such strong images from the past. All the forbidden and dangerous things came pressing out from the corners of his mind, to leer and snicker at him. There were so many things he could not bear, things severed from his life with the cold precision of a surgical scalpel. Now they came, one by one, to hook their claws back into his flesh, to press their sucking greedy mouths against his veins. He lost track of where and who he was. The thing he must not do became the thing he must do, a sightless appetite to appease before he could know peace again. The world was rocking with the rhythm of a railroad train picking up speed. He was along for the ride, on the night express back to the black pit.

"Mitchell," sighed Lynda.

"Yes," he confessed.

11

MORNING AVALANCHED INTO HIS EYES when he opened them. Gray light was pouring through the window, drenching the mattress and touseled blankets and the cardboard and blanket from the window on the floor beside them. He stared out through the cracked pane at the dark silhouette of the building across the alley and the overcast sky above it. None of it was coming together. He groped vaguely after the tails of memories, but they scuttled back into corners. He pressed his palms to his eyes until two things came clear. He should phone home today. And check with the damn VA office again, to see if they'd straightened out the mess they'd made of his records.

Temporal continuity ripped suddenly, spilling him from its sling into chaos. This was no cheap motel room. His pants were not slung across a chair under a cheap painting by a bureau with a Gideon bible on it. He sat up, staring around. His brain bounced sickeningly against the top of his skull. He must have gone drinking last night. He knew he had to quit soon. He eased back down onto the flat and stinking mattress. A gray pigeon took sudden alarm and swooped into the next room. From one corner of the room, a scrawny black cat regarded him with flat eyes. A damn zoo. A wave of stress rose in

Mitchell, pressing his headache to the top of his skull. He was
tired of mornings that started at the bottom. His whole body
ached; his mouth tasted foul. Something very bad was going
on here. He squeezed his eyes hard shut and tried to put his
mind in order. What had he done yesterday? How had he gotten
to today?

All that came to mind was phoning home. The number
loomed large in his mind, spurring him. He hadn't called in a
long time; he hated to call when all he could say was that he
was still working on it. He had promised to get it all straightened
out, once and for all. They were counting on him. He was
going to make it right with all of them.

There was a phone booth in the train station, with a decent
chair in it. He had used it so often he had memorized the
graffiti. He leaned into the privacy of the booth, telling the
operator to make it collect. The ringing sounded very far away.
He couldn't identify the voice that said so softly, "Hello?"

"Collect call from Mitch. Will you accept charges?"

He heard wind blowing in the receiver, that was all; as if
all the miles of wire between him and home were taking a long
and steady breath. The operator repeated, "There is a collect
call from Mitch. Will you accept charges?"

"I . . . wait a minute. Yes, I will. Go ahead, operator."

"Hello?" His own voice was so cautious he hardly recognized it himself.

"Mitch?"

"Yeah. I woulda called sooner, but this is such a fucked up
mess, every time I go in there—"

"Mitch. Wait a minute. Listen to me, Mitch. Just a sec."

She took a ragged breath and he suddenly knew she was
weeping. Weeping on the other end of the line. Why? "Look,
I gotta say these things. You don't want to hear them and I
don't want to say them, but I gotta say them now, on the phone,
while you're not looking at me. Listen." She cleared her throat,
but her voice still came out husky. "There's a lot of things.
There's Benjy, for one. He's back to sleeping all night again.
He's nearly back to how he was. He plays outside and his little
friends come over again. And he seems so sunny and fine, it
breaks my heart to think of how he was. He found one of his
old plastic army men in the sandbox yesterday. He wouldn't
touch it. He made me come out and get it and wrap it in a
paper towel and throw it inside the trash can for him. After we
did that, he asked when you were coming back. I told him I

didn't know. He seemed worried by that, so I told him pretty soon. Then he got scared and wanted to sleep in my bed with me last night. Mitch, it's too much for him. Too many blow-ups in front of him, too many weird-outs. Too many times of you going away and coming back fine for a month or two, and then a disaster. He's just a little boy, and it's too much for him. Do you know what I'm saying?"

"Yeah." The huskiness was in his voice now. "I do love him. You know I do. I love him and I love you and—"

"Mitch. Don't. Listen to me. We've had all our good times. I waited for you. And you came back a stranger, but I stuck with you. I really thought we could make it all better again. I waited through the dope, I waited through the booze, and when I thought we were finally safe and I could have our baby... Damn. You've been gone a while, and I can see things clearer. It isn't going to get any better for us. And I can't pretend anymore."

"No. Wait, please. I'll come home tonight. I can get this mess straightened out later. Baby, I'll come home tonight, we'll get my folks to babysit, and we'll go out and be alone together and talk. We can get it all talked out. And whatever you want me to do this time, I'll do it. I promise you. Whatever you think will make it work, whatever will be best for us all. I promise." He could hear her crying now, little gulping noises as she strangled for air. He needed so badly to touch her. His eyes stung.

"You promise."

"Yeah. I swear it. Please."

"Mitch... then don't come home. I won't be here. I can't be here anymore. You... you take care. I'm gonna drop your stuff off with your folks. They already know about it. I'm taking Benjy with me. Listen. I'm going to keep on loving you. I swear that. I always will. But I can't live with you, not anymore. I can't wait anymore for you to come back."

"I promise," he said softly to the empty line. The electronic winds blew his words back to him.

"I promise," said the man in the beige shirt at the huge desk, "that we are doing everything we can to straighten this out. But we need your cooperation. Did you bring your records this time?"

Mitchell set the document box on the desk beside the computer. The man looked at it with obvious relief. "Great. At last. Now we can get somewhere. Got your discharge papers?"

"In here." Mitchell tapped the cold box with his fingernail. He didn't like the sound it made, like clods of dirt falling on a coffin. He stopped.

"Let's have them, then."

"I lost the damn key. You got something we can jimmy it open with?"

The man at the desk looked disgusted again, and as tired as he had when Mitch had first come in. "No. That's not my department. Look, take the box to a locksmith and get it open. We aren't going to get anywhere without some papers to work from."

Mitch rubbed his head, hating the man, wishing he could take his head and shove his face into his fucking little computer screen. He put his fists in his lap, out of the man's sight. "Look. Please. Did you check on what I told you last week? Did you run down my name and serial number? I mean, listen, isn't that what these little gizmos are for?" He tried to sound reasonable, admiring of the computer technology that had caused this whole fuckup.

"Yes. And it came back the same. Mitchell Ignatius Reilly is listed as MIA. Missing in Action. He never came back from Viet Nam."

Mitchell's fist hit the top of the desk in short, hard jolts, punctuating each syllable. "I am sitting right here. Ask my wife. Ask my folks." The man's face went red and white. He began to rise. Mitchell hid his fists again. "Look. I'm sorry I did that. I know you're doing the best you can. Hey, did you check on that other thing I told you?"

The man settled back in his chair and looked at him in blank weariness. Mitchell wanted to punch his civil service mouth, to make him care. He controlled himself. He mastered it and held it down and strangled the impulse. He was in control of himself.

"You know. There was a guy in my company, shipped over with me, Michael Ignace O'Reilly. Weirdest damn thing. His serial number was within a couple digits of mine, they were always getting us mixed up, trying to give him my mail, that kind of shit. I shipped stateside before he did. Maybe he's the one MIA."

"Him." The man at the desk looked harassed. "I'd almost forgotten why I ran a check on him. It didn't help. He's not MIA, he came out in a plastic bag."

Cold panic squeezed Mitchell. "What? What are you trying

to tell me, that I got a choice between MIA and dead? Look at me. I'm here, man. Take my fingerprints if you want. The Army has mine on record, I know. That'll prove I'm me. Go ahead, take them."

"Look." For the first time, an edge of anger crept into the man's voice. "I know you want help. I'll even say that I can see you need help. But before we go to extremes like fingerprints, why don't we do what's simple? Go get that damn box opened! Get those papers to me and I'll have a fighting chance of getting this straightened out. Until then, I'm going to tell you to quit coming here. Every week I ask for your papers, and every week you have a different line. I can't do a damn thing without some papers. Give me a birth certificate, discharge papers, anything. Just go get those damn papers for me, or don't come back. Look, man, why don't you go to the state? There's a lot of agencies for people like you. They can help you. You need to get some help!"

The man stood up to call the words after him, but he didn't stop. He beat it out of there, leaving it all behind. MIA or dead. Great choice. Dammit, he was here, he was alive, he hadn't changed, but no one would accept him, not his wife, not the VA, he had no one. No one cared enough to help.

"Dad?"

"Mitch? That you, son? You still up in Seattle?"

"Yeah, Dad. Dad, I'm having a hell of a time. Nothing is going right."

"Well, you just stick with it. You'll get it all straightened out. I'd call Mother to the phone, but she's gone to get her hair done. Mary dropped some boxes here. You know about that?"

"Yeah. Yeah, she told me. Dad, what am I going to do? I'm losing it all."

"Son, you just stay right there until you get it all sorted out. I'm sure you'll be just fine. Say, did you catch the game last night? Did you believe that last play? Who would call a play like that? If I were the owner of that team, I'd take that coach and—"

"Dad! Dad, listen to me. I want to come home. I got to come home. Can you wire me some money?"

"Well, Mitch, I just don't think that's a good idea. Now, look, there's no sense in running away from this thing. You're up there, you may as well get it all sorted out before you come home. You know you brought this on yourself, acting so wild.

If you hadn't punched out those guys in the local office, maybe they could have cleared it up for you here. But as it is, you've got them all stirred up and they aren't going to do a thing for you. So you got to go through the Seattle office. You just tough it out and I'm sure you'll be all right."

"Yeah. Yeah, I guess you're right."

"I know I am. Now Mitch, I'm not going to tell Mother you called. This thing with Mary has her flying around the ceiling as it is, and she'd just get all upset all over again. So I want you to sit down and write her a nice note tonight and mail it off to her. She's been upset enough about Mary taking little Benjy away, and her stomach is acting up, so don't write anything that will get her worked up. Okay?"

"Is she going to be all right?"

"Yes, she's going to be fine, as long as she stays calm. Don't you give her any more reasons to be crying over you. Now, you do like I told you, and get better, and then you give me a call and let me know when you're coming home. I know things look pretty dark right now, but you've got to untangle them one knot at a time. Take care of the VA mess, get the help you need, and when you get finished with that, we can worry about what's next."

"Yeah. Dad? Dad, I've got to talk to you. When I called Mary—"

"Son, I'd love to talk with you about that, but I can't. Phone bill has been crazy with you always calling collect. I shouldn't have accepted this one. So I've got to hang up now. Remember what I said. Take the problems one at a time. Get straight with the VA and get some help. Then we can worry about Mary and the rest of it. I got to go now. You write your mom a nice note tonight, okay?"

"Yeah. Dad?"

"Good-bye, Son."

The bright sunlight through the window woke Wizard. Even in his sleep, it had been making his eyes water. He rolled silently from his bed, cursing the hangover and the weariness that had made him sleep in. He surveyed the damage. The den was a wreck. He dressed slowly, in silence, trying to move his head as little as possible. He wanted to lie down again, but forced himself to set his room to rights. He walked very carefully, setting his feet where the floorboards creaked the least. Black Thomas watched him as he shook and smoothed the blankets. They smelled like Lynda. She had left her mark everywhere. Thomas noticed it when he came over to lie on the mattress. He sniffed and growled softly before he settled, his raw stump hovering away from his body. When he had arranged himself, Wizard lowered himself carefully beside the cat and inspected the wound.

"Looks like it will heal, my friend." Wizard touched it with his eyes only, moving his pounding head to see it from all angles. "That was a foolish move you made, and I'm afraid you've paid dearly for it."

Black Thomas opened his red mouth wide in a meow of disdain. Wizard was forced to nod, humiliated. "I didn't say you were the only one who did stupid things. I'll have to pay for mine as well. I've got to find Cassie today. I've got to get this whole mess straightened out."

Moving with ponderous care, he tidied the rest of the room, taking no satisfaction in it. There was more shabbiness than he had ever noticed before. What Lynda's eyes had touched seemed to have changed overnight. The coziness of his retreat had turned to squalor, the privacy to isolation. He picked up the little pipe from the floor and dropped it into the footlocker on top of the bag of weed. He stared for a long time at the other things she had stacked on the floor. Daylight made them all real. Finally he brought himself to touch them, to stack them back inside the footlocker. But when he tried to drop the lid, he found the hinges racked. There was no shutting them away anymore.

He ate bread sticks and packages of crackers from his food supply. He thought of a cup of hot sweet coffee to wash them down. His hangover vetoed it. Why had he gone drinking with her? How could he have ever forgotten what the mornings after were inevitably like? He straightened the books on his shelves, moving always with a sleepy caution. He shook and refolded his clothes. He set the wizard bag carefully atop the folded garments, not daring to look inside the bag. He had betrayed them. He wouldn't look at them and wonder what he had lost.

When he had done and redone his small chores, he lay down on his mattress by the cat and stared around his tiny room. The pigeons had all left for the day. This time of year no young ones shrilled from the nests. No babies to handle, no setting parents to feed. The well worn paperbacks on the shelves were stale. He flipped through a Zane Grey, remembering every line of dialogue. It wouldn't do. He rolled over, staring out the sun-

stricken window. That was one thing he hadn't done yet. He
didn't think it prudent to take up his cardboard and blanket
again. Not yet. Wait until night when movement in a darkened
upper story would not be noticed. He wondered vaguely why
Lynda had taken them down. Or if she had. It must have
happened after he passed out.

His body stank. Sitting still, trying not to think, he became
aware of his own smell. Cleaning up was something to do, a
chore to keep his mind busy. There was fresh rainwater in the
coffee can on the fire escape. He scanned the alley before
reaching out the window for it. He made a ritual out of his
sponge bath, occupying himself with it for as long as he could.
He heated the water over his Sterno can and slowly sponged
his body as he shivered standing on a threadbare towel. He
was thinner than he remembered being. He rubbed at a spot
on his chest for some moments before recognizing the hickey
she had left. He re-dressed slowly.

The events of the night before came back to him slowly, as
elusive as last week's fragmentary dreams. He moved back
through them slowly, flinching at every stop. But when he
came to the image of Booth crumpling down the wall, it was
more than he could stand. He rose to pace his room with cat-
soft steps. Twice he went to the window. On the third trip, he
took his boots with him. He surveyed the alley, then slid up
the window and stepped out onto the fire escape. Black Thomas
raised a sleepy head from where he sunbathed on the mattress.
He gave a warning growl and lay back to sleep.

Wizard had given up all pretense at blending. Shaving in
the mirrors of the stainless steel restroom near the fire station
was something he did for his own comfort. He still didn't
recognize the man in the mirror. He wondered what to do with
himself today. He refused to try buying coffee again. He could
no longer feed the pigeons. If he went to Occidental Park,
Lynda would find him. At the market he would have to face
Euripides, at the Seattle Center he would have to deal with
Rasputin. For long moments it seemed as if his future was
made up solely of the things he could not do. Then he thought
of the Waterfall Gardens.

It was just across the street. It was a walled and private
place, an oasis of shade trees and flowing water in the middle
of the city. This time of year, it was usually empty. The gardens
were a tiny, walled-off area, no larger than a vacant building
site. In summer, people enjoyed its cool shade and the rising

mist off the splashing water. In Seattle's winter, shade and rising mist were in the public domain. No one went seeking them. Wizard sat at a little round table, watching the running water and trying to comfort himself with facts. The park was a memorial to the original headquarters of the United Parcel Service, which had been built on this site in 1907, convenient to Occidental Avenue and the whorehouses. That was how it had begun, with a handful of messengers whose chief customers were the brothels. He tried to picture it, and smiled vaguely at the running water.

"Does every little thing have to be spelled out for you?"

Wizard jumped at the woman's voice and spun, expecting to find Lynda rampant. Instead, it was a stout little black woman, her hair lacquered into an unnatural set of waves. Her dress was too long, but her very old shoes were well cared for. She had on a blue cloth coat, not long enough to cover her dress. She sniffed disgustedly as she stared at Wizard. As she sat down at his table, he immediately rose.

"Where are you going? Don't walk out on me, you dummy! We've got things to say. Hey! Don't try to run away from it, because it won't work. It's right on your heels now!"

He moved off rapidly, routed from the Waterfall Gardens. He had no magic to comfort them; why wouldn't they leave him alone? Away from the protective walls, the wind blew cold and stiff. It crept up his sleeve to chill his wrists, it stiffened his spine with achings. He coughed and it made his head pound. He had to find shelter, warm shelter, away from strange people talking to him. The bus.

The driver glared at him, but had to let him board. It was the Ride Free area. Wizard shivered his way to a seat in the rear, away from the doors that opened and closed to admit a gust of wind at every stop. He would ride it clear to Battery Street, then jump off and get back on a southbound one. He sat rubbing his hands and staring at his raw knuckles. For a moment he couldn't remember how he had skinned them. Booth. Oh, God! His mind teetered dizzily between Wizard and Mitchell.

The bus jerked and swayed from stop to stop. It had begun to rain, at first gently, then determinedly. The passengers on the bus increased, most of them damp, a few shaking drops from umbrellas as they boarded. Yet the bus was not full when a young man came down the aisle and took a seat beside him. Wizard slid over and leaned into the side of the bus, staring at the water drops on the window but heedless of the scenery beyond. He was so engrossed in his own misery that the soft voice of the man surprised him. He spoke in less than a whisper, his eyes fixed on the front window of the bus, his hands toying with a key chain.

"I think she's going to say we're through."

Wizard's body clenched. Mitchell receded. A tremble passed through him from head to foot. The magic was hovering, asking him to listen and balance with it, demanding that he give of himself what he could to those whose instincts sought him out. He began to sweat. It was here, and he had nothing to give, no Knowing, nothing to trade for these confidences. He had to force his shivering mind to focus on the words.

"She said we had to separate, just until she knew her own mind. She said she knew she still loved me, but that she needed space to figure out how our lives fit together. So I told her okay. What else could I say? I respect her. I didn't marry her to keep her at home in a box and take her out and look at now and then. Her independence was one of the things that made me love her. I didn't want our marriage to change that. So I said okay, and I moved in with a buddy for a while, and I tried to give her some space. I'd call her in the morning, and at night, and then she said that it made her feel like I was checking up on her all the time. I wasn't. I just wanted to hear her talk, hear her say she loved me and that I could come home soon. So I only called her twice a week after that. She talks to me, but I can tell she doesn't miss me. She likes being on her own again. She even comes out and says it, that she likes getting up alone and grabbing a quick breakfast and heading to work. And after work she can shop and eat out, or come home and watch TV, and she never has to worry if it fits in with anyone else's plans. She never has to hurry to be on time to meet me for lunch, or find a movie we both want to see, or wait to use the bathroom. She doesn't miss me. And she doesn't need me. So what I ask myself is, can you love someone if you don't need them? And is she happy and fine all on her own, or is there someone else? Can it be she doesn't need anyone, least of all me?"

The bus lurched into the next stop. Wizard waited nervously, but nothing came to him. Whatever comfort he was supposed to give this man was not appearing. The magic hovered just out of his reach. He steeled himself and leaped for it blindly.

"Love and need are two separate things," he murmured

softly. "A mother does not need her children, yet she loves them. Need may even destroy love. What have you been doing with your own life while she has been finding hers again? Are you still the man she loved, the man with his own interests and life, or are you standing in the wings, waiting for her to take responsibility for your happiness? Perhaps you should find your own life and resume it, so she can approach you without fear of being consumed by you. Your terrible need for her . . ."

The man was rising, getting off at this stop, without waiting to hear what Wizard was saying to him. Such a thing had never happened before, and Wizard gaped after him, feeling defiled and useless. The bus lunged and roared on through its route. He sat in silent misery. It began to get steamy inside from the cargo of warm, damp humans. The seat beside Wizard sagged with weight, and he turned to find that a slender Polynesian woman had settled in beside him. He turned away from her and stared out the window.

A manicured finger jabbed him in the ribs. "Pay attention!" she hissed. He knew that accent, but couldn't place it. It was from the bad times. "I've got you cornered now, and you are going to listen. So quit playing stupid with me. It's right in front of your nose, and you won't see it. There is no time left for me to be subtle and let you learn at your own pace. When you are irrational, you are vulnerable. And another thing: You substitute tears for action. You want to know what is wrong with you? You found out, a long time ago, that it is much easier not to care. You pretended a distance between yourself and others until it became real. You stopped hurting when people you loved got hurt. You threw your pain away. There is a part of you that fears pain and wants to go back to that numbness. But that is where your enemy is waiting for you. He will attack you with yourself."

She was rambling, he didn't know about what, but he did know he had nothing to give her. He didn't want to hear her secrets and her hurts. He had no balm for them. "Beg pardon?" In a flash of self-preservation, Wizard turned an icy stare upon the little woman. "Were you addressing me?"

She did not waver. "Yes!" she hissed. Another jab of the finger. "Pay attention. You are throwing away your weapons because you think defeat would be easier. You do not wish to take responsibility for yourself. You like to fumble and limp and be helped along. Winning would change all that. So you choose to forget that you are involved in a battle. You have turned your exposed back to your enemy. When you are defeated, you will say, 'There was never a war.'"

Politics were the last things on his mind today. He did not want to think back to that time. He spoke very softly. "You must understand. I have nothing useful to tell you. Beg pardon. This is my stop." Wizard dragged at the cord over the window, standing at the same moment. He clambered over her multitude of parcels to reach the aisle. He stood swaying by the doors until the driver could find a place to pull over.

There was no sanctuary for him today, he decided as he slogged down the pavement. The rain spattered him for two blocks, then he crossed the street and caught a southbound bus. The early dusk of winter was already claiming the sky. He felt relieved. He could go home. One advantage to sleeping in, he told himself, was that it made the whole day shorter. Less to deal with. The bus was crowded with early commuters. He stood for several blocks and then slipped into a seat beside a young student with her lap full of textbooks. She gave him a shy look and turned to her window. Wizard breathed a sigh of relief and sagged back in the seat.

The student fidgeted next to him. She flipped open one of her books on her lap and began to study. Her lips moved as she read softly to herself. Wizard closed his eyes and let his mind blank out. It was as close as he had come to peace today. The girl's sub-auditory murmurings were as pleasant a sound as water running over stones. He let it be a mantra for him, floating on the brushing sound. He began to make out words here and there. He listened carelessly.

"Only a fool is presumptuous enough to attempt to judge the relative merits of the different realities. Better to let them blend in a potpourri of life. Who can suavely deny that there are poets in our asylums and killers on our streets? We may never hear the sweetest songs because we were unwilling to accept a new scale. This reality that we treasure and call sanity may be the purest form of torment to those we try to impose it upon."

A philosophy course, Wizard decided. The thought irritated him. He shifted slightly to put his ears out of range of her soft mutter.

Her nails dug suddenly into his wrist. "All right!" she hissed angrily. "All right. I give up on you. Go throw yourself right back into it. But I'll give you one last gift, not a story or clue, but a question. If it was such a good deal, why did you leave it in the first place? What overbalanced your scales?"

It scared the hell out of him. He dragged free of her, leaving shreds of his skin under her fingernails. He stood up, staggering as the bus leaned into its stop. He pushed hurriedly past a fat man struggling to rise from his seat and was the first person down the steps. He fled.

The storm rallied as he emerged from the bus. From a monotonous gray pattering it became a downpour of leaden streamers. In less than a block, he was drenched. His coat dragged on his shoulders; his wet pant cuffs slapped his ankles. Hunger was asserting itself too, harmonizing with the residue of his hangover. His pace slowed to a trudge.

Streetlamps began to blossom in the dark. They dispelled the night, but not the rain that assailed him. His hair was plastered to his skull, and the scars on his scalp ached abominably. He passed brightly lit store windows where pilgrims and turkeys vied with Christmas trees for seasonal charm. The rest of the sidewalk traffic wore raincoats or carried umbrellas. They rushed past Wizard like lemmings, almost unaware of his passage. He watched their smooth plastic faces and tried to find some kinship with them. There was none. They were immune to misery such as his. They had homes, jobs, families, all arranged neatly in hourly slots of life. Not one of them, he told himself, was going home to a three-legged cat or a damp room haunted by a footlocker. No waitresses climbed through their windows. They would push open doors to warm apartments, to loving embraces and children playing cars on the carpet. He would climb through a dirty window into darkness and pigeons shitting down the walls. When had he made that choice?

Occidental Square was in bloom. Crews had worked all day stringing the lines of small white lightbulbs through the bare branches of the trees. Now they shone through the night, a spring of white blossoms in the November rain. Wizard turned up his face to look at them, the rain streaking down his cheeks. For a few moments he was eased by the beauty. Then something rolled over inside him, and he saw only bare bulbs on electrical wires, artificial and silly among the wet black branches.

He made a stop at the arcade to use the restroom. He drank cold water from his cupped hands and stared at himself in the mirror. His face had crossed the fine line between gaunt and cadaverous. His eyes were swollen and baggy above his hollow cheeks. A twentieth-century Grim Reaper stared out at him.

He did not wonder at the looks he drew as he left the arcade.

He took the pedestrian walkway that had once been a block of Occidental Avenue South. A tourist information booth sprouted up out of the bricks in front of him. But it offered no answers to any of his questions. He knew the booth had once been an elegant elevator car in some building. But the scrap of information fluttered away from his mind. He couldn't remember which old building it had come from. Suddenly it seemed less than trivial. He trudged on to the corner of Jackson and Occidental.

Across the intersection from him stood the building that housed his life. He stared at it. Wee Bit O'Ireland's windows were brightly lit and decorated for the season. It only made the rest of it drearier. The inevitable black fire escape twined up the front of the building. Great Winds Kites had one of its creations dangling from the lowest landing of it. The rain was battering the gay and fragile thing. He nearly yielded to the impulse to run and tap on their window and remind them of its plight. The energy for such a rescue drained from him. It seemed only natural that all things bright and airy should end up sodden and battered.

Faded white lettering gave a name to his home. The Washington Shoe Manufacturing Company. It hadn't been that for years, but back in 1890, it had held the business to go with the name. The sign would still be there long after he was gone. He was a passing bit of biological noise in the city, with no real place in its petrous existence. He could no longer see the faces in the brickwork, feel the underlying life in the crouching buildings. The facts and continuity he grasped at had no connection to him, any more than the scorching moth could claim the laurels of General Electric. He had tried to become part of Seattle, to blend with the streets and buildings. He'd failed. Such a ridiculous quest. Why should he persist now in so fruitless a task? When all was said and done, what did he signify, with his listening attitude and his ridiculous ministry to the pigeons?

He crossed against the lights and turned into his alley. Framed by the blackness of buildings, the King Dome glittered at the far end of the alley chute like a sagging faery toadstool. He tried to imagine himself down there, at whatever sports event was filling it tonight, cussing about parking his car, hurrying the family along to the game. Would he carry a little banner to wave and know all the team statistics? Would he tie himself into that as he had tied himself into the city? The brightness of the lights against the darkness made his eyes water until it shimmered like an underwater scene. Would it make any difference? There weren't many wizards left in the world, Cassie had said. Now he knew why.

His alley was as empty as his soul. He crouched beneath his fire escape and sprang. With weary expertise he hauled himself up and climbed to his fourth floor window. Crouching, he eased his window up.

A warm odor of food and hot candle wax flowed out to greet him. Wizard froze, not breathing, becoming part of the night. Then, soundless as any shadow, he eased into the room and slipped to his doorway. A yellow light spilled from his den, its source a candlestump burning on one of the pigeons' shelves. The birds had retreated from it and were eyeing it nervously. The cardboard had been propped in the window with his books. In the darkest corner where his mattress was, something sat up. Its single glowing eye bored into him.

12

"YOU KEPT ME WAITING," Lynda said petulantly. "Where have you been?" She dropped her cigarette on his floor and ground it out with her boot heel. Wizard came the rest of the way into the room, wondering if he were relieved that it was only Lynda. She caught him before he was halfway across the room, engulfing him in an embrace. She released him just as quickly, with a loud squeak.

"You are soaking wet and as cold as a fish! And listen to that cough! Now, you get out of those wet things right now. It's a good thing I decided to meet you here. I brought us some food, and a little something that will warm you right to your toes. I wanted to get you some clothes today, but I didn't know the sizes. Now I wish I had guessed. Look at you. I mean it now, get those wet clothes off!"

"Sshh!" he cautioned her frantically. "The stores downstairs are still open. They start staying open later this time of year. Don't talk loudly and don't thump around like that. Take your boots off."

"Oh, baloney! They're two floors below us. And if they're open for business, they'll be playing music and listening to customers. You worry too much. Now, are you going to take

156

off those wet things or do you want me to take them off for you?"

She must have taken the line from a movie. He stared at her. She stood hip-shot, her fists lightly resting on her thighs. He wondered what actress she was imitating. Her tone was maternal, her stance sexually threatening. He shivered in his wet clothing.

"I'll take them off myself," he said slowly. She would have taken any other reply as a challenge or invitation. With grave dignity he turned his back on her and slowly began to unbutton his shirt with chilled fingers.

"Aaw, rats!" Mock salacious disappointment was in her exclamation. "Well, if you won't let me help, I'll just get us something to eat over here. Let me know if you decide you want help."

He listened to her dragging things about. He glanced over his shoulder to see her turning his food box on its side for a table. Like a little girl playing house. He went back to staring at the walls. He pulled his soaked t-shirt off over his head. His wet hair draggled on the back of his neck, chilling him. She was still chattering at him, her voice not lowered at all. Her boots clumped with every step.

"Quiet," he warned softly.

She mis-heard him. "I said, did you hear about that murder down near the ferry dock?"

He stopped moving, his fingers clinging to the waistband of his pants. "Knife," he said dully.

"Yeah, that one. You heard, huh? But they don't put it all in the papers. A real mess. Only seventeen, they say. Some little girl playing hooker. Well, you can't say she didn't ask for it. Do you have any salt?"

"No!" He suddenly hated her, her callous, shallow attitude. A woman had died this day. Died of a knife because he hadn't been able to summon the magic to prevent it. Behind him, she went right on making domestic noises, rustling through his possessions with a calm assumption of domain. Why don't I get angry? he wondered. Why don't I turn and yell at her to leave, to get out of my life and leave me alone? Because I am tired and sick, he excused himself. From the back corner of his mind came the voice of the girl on the bus. "Because it's easier to let her do as she wishes, easier to let her take command and responsibility. You coward!"

"Because I am tired of being alone!" He defended himself

aloud. He had inadvertently injected the words into one of
Lynda's rare silences.

"Me, too, baby. Well, we aren't alone anymore, are we?
Here, put on your robe and come eat."

He hadn't realized how close she was. The warm dark cloth
cascaded over his head and down his shoulders. He found
himself shrugging into it, protesting as she tugged the collar
down over his head, "I don't have a robe."

"Then what's this?" she asked him indulgently.

Wizard looked down. The shimmering dark cloth fell to his
bare feet. Stars and crescent moons shone in the dim room,
sparkled in the light of the candle on the food crate. His wiz-
ardly robe draped his chilled body. He froze, waiting. It warmed
him. That was all. He smoothed his hands down the front of
it, waiting for some tingle of power. Nothing. He squeezed his
stinging eyes shut. Where had his mind been, and for how
long? What had he really expected of a discarded Hallowe'en
costume? He felt Lynda draping his shoulders with the cloak.
He raised his hands to tie the silver tassels at his throat. He
did not want her to step in front of him and see his face. His
mind fumbled back through his life. He had been in this den
for, well, he had seen the stores below him extend their hours
for Christmas shoppers twice. And before that? There had been
another den. The location was hazy in his mind now, but he
remembered the smell of boiling cabbage and rice wafting up
from a restaurant below. And before that? His sleeping roll
tucked up under an overpass or bridge; he recalled vividly the
rumble of the night traffic and the stretch-flash of passing
headlights. Years as lost and wasted as fresh rain falling on
oily city streets.

His life struggled to join hands with itself. He plucked up
two reference points. This was 1983, fast approaching 1984.
He had turned twenty in 1969, on his first tour in Nam. Thirty-
five years old, he guessed. He hadn't thought of his age in a
long time, hadn't related his personal span to the days and
weeks flowing past him. Half of the three-score and ten due
him were gone. Half.

Lynda giggled. He turned slowly to face her and she gave
a high scream of laughter. His face didn't change, so she slapped
him lightly on the cheek. "Old sourpuss. Well, you got to admit
you look funny. I should have guessed from the hat. Well,
never mind. At least it's warm and dry and comfy. Even if we
did miss Hallowe'en. Oh, baby!" She pushed into him sud-

denly, her face diving for his, her lips writhing against his mouth. Her sturdy arms enfolded him and trapped him against her body. She nuzzled his neck and then jerked back her face to look at him. "You look just like a sad little kid. Cold and wet and living in this hole. But we are going to change all that. Look, I got to thinking today. There's plenty of room at my place. It doesn't look like you have that much stuff. Tomorrow, after work, I bet I could come up here and have you packed in half an hour. Hell, from the look of it, we could leave most of it here and not take a loss. You could stay with me, get rid of that cough, get your head straight, and then you could look for work. Or sign up for unemployment or welfare or something. Honey, I look at you and I can see you weren't made for this kind of life. You're the steady, reliable type. I don't know why or how you came to this and I won't be nosy and ask. But I think it's time you got out of it. Back to reality. Now come and eat."

"You never give me a chance to talk." It was coming more easily. More and more often, the words came out of his mouth as soon as he thought of them.

Lynda was not impressed. "What's to say? Who in his right mind would choose to stay here when he could move in with me? Now come and eat, baby, before it gets cold."

He trailed after her to the makeshift table, the wizard robes wafting around his ankles. He stopped at his wardrobe box to pull a pair of socks on over his bare feet. He was warmer, but still shivering.

The food was in styrofoam trays on the table, still sealed. White styrofoam cups with lids squatted next to them. There were white paper napkins and thick plastic utensils. He could not remember when he had ever dined so formally within his own den.

"Hope you like oriental food," she announced and snapped open his dinner. He looked down at finely sliced vegetables swimming in a clear sauce, at slices of meat artfully arranged and cubes of tofu. Lynda was opening a little square paper bucket of rice. She scooped a double mound of it onto the lid of his container. There was a tiny cup of mustard and another of shoyu. The hot rice steamed. Lynda pried the lid off his cup for him. "Green tea," she informed him. "I always have it with this kind of food. Puts me in the right mood."

The tea was still scalding hot. Wizard sipped at his noisily and then attacked the food. The heat of it alone was comforting

to his abused body. The skillfully blended textures and flavors
nearly went unnoticed in his drive to fill his belly with something solid and nourishing. Lynda silently replenished his mound
of rice from the container. When his cup was empty and the
food nearly gone, she produced a short, stout bottle with a
flourish. "Plum wine!" Her eyebrows leaped at him. She poured,
and as the liquid filled his cup, the bouquet of it saluted his
nostrils. Memories of hot orchard summers drifted back to him.
When her cup was filled, they drank together.

He took his in a series of tiny sips, letting each moment of
taste flow and ebb over his tongue. When his shivering finally
ceased, he sighed and let the tensions go out of his shoulders
and back. "It's good, isn't it?" she asked, breaking into his
reverie. He nodded slowly and felt his own smile break free.
She returned it, and began to busily stack up the disposable
dishes and flatware. Wizard let her. She left the bottle of wine
on the table at his elbow. He refilled his cup. He slowly sipped
wine and stared into the candle flame. It was a long, still flame,
steady and unflickered by any wind. The dazzling of its light
reminded him of sunlight on the bright surface of a mirror
pond. If you looked at it one way, it could dazzle your eyes
and blind you. But if you tilted your head and half closed your
eyes, you could see your reflection in the black water. Like a
darker self looking up, mocking. And the more you looked,
the less it looked like you. Until, finally, if you stared at it
long enough, it didn't look like you at all, or anyone else.

"Well, he don't look like no wizard to me!"

Rasputin did a slow gyrating turn in his dance to his own
unheard music. Wizard stared at him in awe. Cassie had dragged
him up here, making him walk for blocks past the border of
the Ride Free area. They stood now on a sidewalk in the midst
of the Seattle Center. Grassy hillocks and imposing buildings
were everywhere, along with ducks and fountains and the Pa-
cific Science Center and the terminal of the monorail. He was
dazzled and confused by it all, and especially by the lofty spire
of the Space Needle. Cassie had told him all about the World's
Fair days here in 1962 as she had hurried him along. He had
been bored at first by her recital of facts and numbers but soon
had become engrossed in the bits of city history she spewed
out so casually. Yet she had not brought him here to view the
Space Needle or the Fun Forest Amusement Park or even the

ducks. She had brought him here to present him to Rasputin.

And Rasputin doubted him. Wizard did not doubt Rasputin. He was as impressive as the Space Needle. He was close to seven feet tall, and as black and shiny as anthracite coal. Not content with his natural stature, he had increased it by dusting his afro and painting his nails with glitter. Dangling earrings swung heavily from his earlobe. He wore a sleeveless shirt in the sweat of July, and his arms were wound with snakes of silver and eels of copper. His pants were raggedly cut-off Levis, and little chains of bells decked his ankles. His huge feet were bare and he danced. He danced always, every second. Even when he stood still to talk to Cassie, some tiny movement of wrist or ankle or neck or finger kept the dance intact, one continuous flow of motion. Wizard marveled.

"Nope. Don't look like no wizard, don't act like no wizard, don't even smell like no wizard." Rasputin made the litany a part of his dance.

"There's wizardry and wizardry," snapped Cassie. "A fountain doesn't look like a still pool, but they're both water."

"And I am the fountain!" laughed Rasputin in a voice as deep as the sea, but brown. "Leaping and splashing and flashing. You gonna tell me that you're the still pool, shining back a reflection, soft and green and slimy on the bottom. You gonna tell me that? Are you a wizard, man?"

Rasputin's eyes were not brown. They were black, blacker than his skin, and they crackled. Wizard flinched from their spark. "I'm not sure yet," he said softly. "Cassie says I am. I don't much feel like it. I'm not looking for power."

"Aho!" Rasputin leaped and whirled. "Not looking for power. Then you are starting at the right place, man. 'Cause the magic doesn't give power, it takes it. And it can't make you strong, but it can find your strength. Can find your weaknesses, too. Sounds doubtful, Cassie, but maybe you got one this time. Let me see his hands."

Wizard held out his hands, palms up, to Rasputin. Rasputin slipped his large pinky-black palms under Wizard's hands, moving them slowly and carefully as he studied them. Wizard's hands became a part of Rasputin's dance as he manipulated him. Slowly his own hands became strangers to him under Rasputin's scrutiny. They looked like pale fish. His fingers were long and thin, but the joints were large, like knots in skinny twigs. Odd little scars on the backs of his hands were like little landmarks in strange terrain. Suddenly Rasputin's hands flashed from under Wizard's to slap his palms with a loud clap.

"He's got the hands, man. The man's got the hands. Got the power in his hands. Power-handed man. He's got the power in his hands, and in his eyes he got the Nam." He had danced a shuffle-footed, hip-wriggling dance all around Wizard during his chant. But at the last line he stopped and stood still as his black eyes waltzed right into Wizard's soul. "And in his eyes he got the Nam, man," he whispered. Wizard stood steady. The afternoon was hot and still around them, the blue sky cupping them under its sweaty palm, holding in the secrets Rasputin whispered.

"Know why there ain't been so many wizards, lately? Know why? I got a theory, brother. Got myself an idea about that. Back in the Middle Ages, them Dark Ages, they got plagues and battles and poverty and tyrants as far as the eye can see. Know what else they got? Wizards. That's what makes us, man. Gotta take a man with nothing else left; then you can make a wizard out of the leftovers. That what you got to have to make a wizard. They got the Black Death, and we got the Nam. But one part of my theory I don't got done yet. Maybe we're all wizards, see, but you got to have a Nam to wake it up. Like a catalyst, see. And maybe we all came back wizards, but only a few of us crazy enough to know it. Or maybe only a few of us can be wizards, but it don't develop without a Nam. Like steel. We got hard in the fire, and wizardry is the cutting edge we put on ourselves. Other guys melt, other guys don't even feel the flames. Not us. We feel the flames and we hurt until we're hard. And we come back and we cool down, and then—wizards! What you think, Wizard?"

"I don't know," Wizard replied foolishly.

Rasputin danced away in disgust. "So you got a wizard, Cassie. You got an I-Don't-Know Wizard. What the hell good is that kind? What does he do?"

"He feeds the pigeons," Cassie retorted. "People know they can talk to him, and he listens to them. The Truth comes out of him. And sometimes he Knows. Isn't that enough?"

"What do you do?" Wizard, made bold by Cassie's defense of him, dared to ask.

"I dance!" Rasputin retorted loftily. "And that's enough, the way I dance. While I dance, I keep the bogey-man away. You got a bogey-man, I-Don't-Know Wizard?"

Wizard shivered. "There's something gray," he confessed, and the summer air turned cold.

"Sounds about right. Well, what you gotta do is this. You got to feed the pigeons. Pigeons sacred to you now, hear me? Never harm a pigeon. And you got to listen to people that come up and start talking to you. Can't turn away when what they say hurts. You got to tell them what they need to know. And you got to speak the Truth inside you. And when you Know, you got to admit you Know. Got to balance the magic, I-Don't-Know Wizard. Got to give away more than you get, all the time. If you don't, that gray thing going to get you. And if that happens, don't yell, well, Rasputin didn't warn you. Now get him out of here, Cassie. I got to dance."

They watched him leaping and whirling away, flashing black and silver in the sunlight. "Is dancing all he does?" Wizard had asked Cassie naively.

"Yeah," she said mockingly. "All he does is Dance. And look at derelicts and find out if they're wizards or not. And give wizards the rules of their magic. And keep the bogey-man away from the Seattle Center. Come on, Wizard."

He trailed at her heels as they moved on the paths between the hillocks of grass. She stopped at a bench that overlooked water and ducks. She dropped into it gratefully and he copied her.

"Well?" she demanded suddenly. "What did you think of him?"

Wizard shrugged. "What I think of Rasputin is that what I think of him makes no difference at all. It's like asking what I think of Mount St. Helens. It's there, and it's a hell of a lot bigger than me."

Cassie laughed softly. "I never thought of him quite that way before, but you're right. What I really meant was, what did you think about his theory on wizards?"

"Just what I said. I don't know."

"And you don't want to make any guesses, do you? Well, I do. I have my own ideas on it. Think about this for a minute. Think about the threads of color in a tapestry. When you need a bit of silver, for the shine on a river or the snow on a mountain top, you bring the silver threads up to the surface where they can be seen. Or if you need gold for the sheen on a princess's hair, or the spark in a unicorn's eyes, you bring that thread up. But it's not like the threads come and go. It's more like they're seen and unseen."

He gave another shrug. He could tell she was getting into one of her obtuse moods. It was all going to be stories and parables for the rest of the day. "Maybe. I don't know."

Cassie laughed wryly. "Rasputin named you well. Well, that's how I think of us. And another thing. Imagine these special threads, silver and gold, say. The tapestry weaver doesn't need them often. Maybe they're hardly ever used together, but there they are, running along together behind the tapestry, and sometimes coming out on the front together to light up a mountain or deck the princesses' robes. Think of what it would be like for those threads. Do you suppose they miss one another while they're apart? And when they come together in the tapestry, do you suppose they'd remember the times before when they'd been woven together?"

She had lost him again. "Do you suppose," he asked, "that we could scrounge some lunch? I'm starving."

"I suppose," she had laughed easily, but her eyes searched his with a hunger that was not for food.

Wizard opened his eyes and stared down at the pipe in his hand. He held his throat shut against the hot smoke and passed the pipe to Lynda. "You are feeling fine," she told him. "I can tell by your eyes. Isn't it funny, Mitch? When we get stoned, I talk even more and you get even quieter. I don't think you've said a word since you finished the wine. Are you still in there?"

"I don't know." He gave her a sad and foolish smile. The I-Don't-Know Wizard. That was him. He watched her drawing on the pipe and holding it down and then whistling smoke. She passed it back to him and rose languidly.

He was still holding his hit when she flapped the hat in front of him. "Put it on," she demanded with a giggle. "I've just got to see you in the complete outfit. When I first saw the hat in the bag, I didn't realize it went with the robe and cloak. Let's see it on."

He set the pipe down on the table. He took the midnight hat from her hands and gazed in melancholy at its bent tip. "I don't think I want to," he said softly. Just looking at it filled him with the sadness of opportunities lost. "Put it away," he requested, and handed it back to Lynda.

"Oh, come on!" she urged, and before he could protest any more, she set it atop his head. He cringed his eyes shut, expecting the flash of magic and the tingle of power against his skull. Still expecting it. Fool. He heard only Lynda's drawn-out giggling. He opened his eyes to her.

"It's perfect," she gasped. "Oh, geez, it's perfect. You really do look like a wizard. I never would have believed it. But with the robe and the cloak and the hat, I mean, your eyes have that mystic look, that kind of sad and weary look you see in old fairytale books about kindly wizards. It would be even better if you had a beard and mustache. But even without them, you really got the looks for it. Come on, sorcerer, work me some magic. Draw me one of them pentagon things and summon a demon. Do me a magic trick. Got any rabbits in that hat?"

"That's a magician, not a wizard," he told her, trying to smile with her. "And they're pentagrams, not pentagons." He tried to bring the words out lightly. But the skin of his face was stiff with dread, and a chill had invaded him when she spoke so lightly of summoning demons. His required no summoning. They lurked always, chill on the back of his neck. Would he ever feel warm again?

"Oh, come on, magic man," she pleaded in a voice gone husky. "Do a trick for me." She paused infinitesimally. "Or turn a trick with me." She giggled suggestively. "I shouldn't tell you this, I really shouldn't." She dropped down beside him and put her hand on his knee as she lowered her voice to a naughty whisper. "You'll think I'm kinky or something. But that outfit kind of turns me on. It makes you look so strange and wild somehow. And just now, when I looked at you, I remembered that you had nothing on underneath it. And I felt this kind of a tickly shiver that began you-know-where. You know, I always wondered why men were turned on when they found out a woman didn't have a bra or panties on. Now I know. It's the thought of you just being kind of loose and reachable under there." Her hand dropped to his ankle and began to creep up under the robe.

Wizard flowed to his feet. He removed the cap from his head and let it drop with a thump upon the table. His new-found verbal skills rescued him. "Don't you think you're asking a bit much of me? You feed me a big meal after I've been cold and wet all day, pour a bottle of wine down me and then get me stoned. About all I'm ready for is eight hours of sleep."

"Oh, you!" Lynda rebuked him, but she looked more tantalized than refused.

Wizard stood looking slowly around the room. He felt a

lucidity upon him, an awareness that had been missing for a long time. He could not remember what had so engrossed him that he had been blind to his own life passing. Things were going to be easier now. What had he been thinking of, to try and live like this? For what? He was letting it go now, with relief. He was moving in with Lynda, flowing back into the stream of reality. She'd help him. He'd get some clothes, sleep in a bed at night, find a job. . . .

"Lynda, what kind of a job should I look for?"

She shrugged lightly. "What did you use to do?"

"I was a sniper." The words came quickly, without any thought. They extinguished the flames of change that had burned so brightly just an instant before. But Lynda laughed.

"No, dummy. Before the army."

"I was a kid." Those words came heavily. Truth was on him, he thought to himself, and then tried to chase the phrase away. No magic about it. It was simply true and he had said it.

"Well, baby, hate to tell you this, but there's no money in being a kid these days. I haven't seen any Help Wanted: Sniper ads, either."

"Neither did I." A jacket of ice squeezed his soul. The scene leaped up in his mind, as bright as the flame. He was signing the papers, nodding as the recruiter reminded him that he couldn't guarantee he'd get the engineering training, but that there was a good chance of it. No more money to finish college, so what the hell. Such a deal. So he hadn't ever built a bridge or a road. He'd blown up a few. He'd learned things in the military he'd never have learned anywhere else. And he had been good at them. Damn good. Better than anyone else in his outfit. He'd gone places no one else would go. Eyes like an owl, nose like a wolf, walking softer than a spider in the night. He'd been so damn good. And proud of it; they'd all been proud of him. Until he came home.

The high was evaporating. He looked for the pipe, but it was out. He waggled it at Lynda, who took it and began to fill it for him. He watched impatiently as she lit it and drew on the weed to glow. But when she smiled and handed it to him, he just stared down into the bowl. "It's not here," he said softly.

"What isn't, baby?"

"Peace. Love. Freedom. Bullshit. There's nothing in here but burning leaves."

"Buds, baby. That makes all the difference." She took it back from him and sucked the smoke into her lungs. She swayed slightly as she exhaled and gave him a softly unfocused smile. "Hey, magic man," she said huskily. He looked at her. "Hey," she repeated low. "Come here."

She advanced on him and embraced him. He stood cold within her arms, suddenly wondering why he had been so passive as to allow her into his life this way. He hadn't been looking for this type of involvement, still didn't feel ready for it. Didn't want it, he admitted reluctantly. So why go along with it? Because the lady wasn't taking a polite no for an answer. She bumped against him and he staggered back a step. She was not a dainty woman. It was like being nudged by a cow. The edge of the mattress brushed his ankles. "Take me down, magic man," she whispered urgently, rubbing against him.

"Not right now." Games. She was playing a romance game, with him as a prop; he was playing a delaying game. She had fed him and stoned him and wanted her due. But he needed to think carefully right now, not be a toy for someone else's passion. Couldn't she see that? Was she so oblivious to his moods?

"Don't fight it, baby. Go with it. I'll make you feel good." Her wandering hand groped through the robe. His pulse quickened in spite of himself.

"No!" he growled, feeling the sudden high rush of anger. Strength coursed through him and his frustrations focused on her. He gripped her wrist tightly, putting a turn on it. The pain put a slight twist at the corner of her smile.

"Do it, baby," she whispered. "Hurt me a little and love me a lot. Show me your claws, magic man. Make me do what you want. Make it wild and new for me."

"Stop it!" he hissed through clenched teeth. "Stop it now!" She was the one summoning the demons that could destroy him. The instant he released her, she reached for him again, her mouth wide with laughter. He seized her shoulders and shook her violently, her head snapping on her neck, her long hair whipping with the motion. Self-disgust stopped him. He dropped her onto the mattress and turned aside from her. She shook the hair from her face and peered up at him. He felt his own nails rake his cheeks.

"I'm sorry," he whispered. "I'm so damn sorry, and always

sorry. But it's always there, right behind me, reaching for the controls. I don't know what brings it out. But you're not safe with me. I want you to go. Now."

Her face was flushed, her mouth wet. She took a gasping breath. "Rough doesn't have to be bad, baby." She licked her mouth. "If you're so sorry, prove it." Reaching up, she caught at his hand and dragged him down. His heart was beating thunderously in his chest and his legs felt rubbery. He couldn't get the air down to the bottom of his lungs. He sagged onto the mattress beside her.

"Don't tell me sorry," she murmured against his chest. "Show me sorry." He closed his eyes to her brushing touch, blacking out the memories.

"I don't like the man I was," he tried to explain. "It's him or me in the gray place. I won't go back to being him. I don't have to, and I won't."

"All right, baby, all right. It doesn't matter, it'll be fine now. Lynda's not angry." She wasn't listening to him, any more than he was tuned into her hands and mouth on him. He kept himself divorced from it, holding back the touching and feeling that could unleash the pain. It was a fair trade. If he let himself be reached, she would hurt him, would drive him with agony until he destroyed the source of the pain. No touch of pleasure, no touch of pain. Being numb was the key to it all. He found the balancing point again and felt a certain bitter satisfaction with it. He was safe from her now. She'd get nothing from him. He felt her squirm against him, heard the rustle of clothing as she arranged her body against his. He let her, unworried. There were other things he could think about, things that were safe to remember.

13

"IF YOU COULD DO ANYTHING, be anything, what would you do?"

It had been an expansive afternoon, roaming the city with Cassie. He was beginning to get the hang of this new life, starting to realize the possibilities. It was a heady sensation. She was in a tweed skirt; he wore a corduroy jacket with leather patches at the elbows. They had gone everywhere that eccentric scholars could go, with numerous side trips en route. They had merged unnoticed with a group touring underground Seattle, and had nearly managed to be left behind in the dank dark below the streets. She had shown him a bakery where a kind-hearted assistant set out the discarded baked goods on a tin foil tray atop the dumpster to save the street people the trouble of digging for them. They had explored what was left of the old plant at Gas Works Park and sampled five kinds of coffee at Starbucks. Cassie had taken him to the Klondike Gold Rush National Historical Museum on Main, and introduced him to the ranger there as her associate, Dr. Reynolds. The ranger had shown them films and opened the display cases for them, to let them handle the relics of that remote time. Wizard had promised to return soon, and spend more time talking about the

Gold Rush era and how it had affected Seattle.

"Especially on rainy days," Cassie had offered as soon as they were on the sidewalk again, and they had giggled together like wayward truants.

It had been a very mellow day. No schedules to keep and no assigned tasks. They had turned down every street that had appealed to them, in their conversations as well as in their wandering. He had learned that she loved roses and pansies, but thought orchids a cold flower. She knew that he liked green grapes more than wild blueberries, and commercial blueberries not at all. So now, as they strolled, he asked her the childish question, and waited for her answer. She disappointed him. "I'd be Cassie, and do what we did today," she replied blandly.

"Not me!" Wizard had been expansive, risking her displeasure. "I'd be a hero, a saint, or a mystic. When I was small, I always wanted to be a prophet. Sackcloth and thunder. I'd drive violence from Seattle and let peace reign."

Cassie snorted. "And under your protection, no seagull would peck another, no children would quarrel over marbles, no drunk would bloody another drunk's nose over a baseball pitcher's reputation."

"Not that kind of violence. You know what I mean."

"No. I don't. You keep acting like I'm some sort of mystic myself, some seer who knows all. Well, I'm not. I'm just Cassie, and while I know more than some, I don't know it all. I've only just met you, though I've been noticing your presence in Seattle for weeks. I suppose you could say our paths have crossed before. But that doesn't mean I know you from the soul out. So tell me. What kind of violence do you mean?"

"The sickest kind. I mean the kind where someone strong finds someone weaker and hurts him. And hurts him and hurts him and hurts him. Hurts past the point of damage, past retaliation, hurts him past the point of resistance, and beyond. Like parents who beat infants, like rapists who batter bodies and minds, like men who turn on other men too confused or different to defend themselves, and hurt them. . . ."

"Which end were you on?" Cassie had muttered the question, looking at him with eyes both sympathetic and wary. His voice had thickened as he spoke, some emotion choking him, but the words tumbled from him, refusing to stop until he clamped his teeth and closed his eyes. Cassie slipped her arm under his, drew him aside to a bench and sat him down. He sat far-eyed, kneading his hands together, rubbing at the tiny scars that marred them.

"I'm sorry," he said finally. "I don't know..."

"Me, neither," she cut in. "But listen. Number one. You are taking on too large an opponent. Do you think you're Saint Patrick driving the snakes out of Ireland? No. At most you're Saint Wizard, feeding the pigeons. Number two. You're too close to it to fight it. Not yet. I won't ask you how or why you're so close to it, but I'll remind you of this. When the enemy's on top of you, you can't win by bombing his position."

He wished she had asked him then. Back then, he might have been able to tell her about it, while she was still the stranger Cassie, before she became so important to him. In days to come he swallowed his secrets in large, choking lumps, lest she discover his flaws. He struggled to learn it all, to be the best at it as he had been the best at his tasks before. His failures he kept to himself. He coped, living hand to mouth at times, trying to believe her when she told him the city would open to him as soon as he opened himself to it. At first she fed him often, and he was sheltered many a night in her various domiciles. But he began to feel overexposed, fearful that he might be revealing more of himself than he wished her to know. And he began to have days when he ached with a dull hunger to be even closer to her. Never mind that it would destroy all she had made of him. Never mind that it would drive her completely from his life. The depth of the sudden need that would come upon him was terrifying. Lust he could have dealt with. But this was the forbidden hunger, the desire to be less alone. He found his strength before it was too late; he knew he had to separate his life from hers.

His wits and the skills she showed him helped him create his own niche. If she missed his daily presence, she never rebuked him for it. He suspected she was relieved by his independence, and he worked for her respect. For an instant he wondered where she was this night.

His eyes rolled open of their own accord. Lynda lay atop him, her hair straggling across his face. Sleeping. Stoned or drunk, she had finally given up her attempts to arouse him. It gave him a perverse satisfaction to have defied her. Her body was heavy and lumpy, her perfume oppressive. He reached up to wipe her hair away from his nose and mouth. He shifted to heave her chin off his collarbone. She stiffened suddenly and wriggled to get her wrist up to her nose.

"Oh my god!" She peeled her body off his, letting the cold rush in to fill the places she had made warm. "Look at the time!" She shook her dress back down over her hips, tugged the hem straight. "It's okay, baby. Don't lay and worry about tonight. You were just tired, that's all. I read about it in this book, says it's normal, can happen to any guy when he's tired, and being stoned might have made it worse. Promise me you aren't going to get all depressed about it. I really don't mind. Really. Are you okay?"

He nodded, feeling the total hypocrite. He watched her scoop her pantyhose from the floor and ball them up to stuff them in her purse. She didn't seem all that disappointed. Was her lust a game she played with herself as well; the wild and wanton woman who must always be eager?

"I've got to get up at six! If I don't go now, I'll be too beat to shower and wash my hair before bed. That's another thing I bet you'll like about my place: hot showers and clean bedding. Look, I got the early shift tomorrow." She ripped a brush through her hair, sleeking it back from her face. "But as soon as I'm off, I'll come to pick you up. Just take the stuff you really want. Leave the rest of this shit here. One trip should do it. You want I should borrow my sister's car?"

"No," he replied absently. She sat down on the makeshift table to drag on her boots. He couldn't even remember when she had taken them off.

"Right. Look, I'll bring a suitcase for your clothes, put the rest in grocery bags, and we'll take the bus. Oh, the cat. I can't have pets in my place."

"I don't have any pets." Black Thomas belonged to himself. He'd been a resident of the building before Wizard moved in, and would be after he was gone. For an instant he worried about Ninja and the pigeons. A foolish worry; they'd all have to take care of themselves from now on.

"Good." Lynda had rekindled the pipe and was taking a farewell hit from it. She waved it at him, but he shook his head. She shrugged, then regarded him more closely. Her boots thumped as she crossed the room to suddenly crouch down beside him. "Look. You look so worried about it. Don't be. So we didn't make it tonight. It doesn't change anything between us. You told me you were tired and cold and a little too stoned. I should have listened to you and not pushed it. I mean, hey, if a woman can say no when she's too tired, why can't a guy? So it's not a big deal, okay? Not like a failure or anything. Okay?"

He nodded wearily, wishing she were gone. All he wanted was sleep. She rose then to snatch up the window blanket from the floor and snap it out over him. "Okay, then. Now don't worry. Sleep tight, baby. See you tomorrow."

"Tomorrow," he echoed. Irrevocable commitment. She snuffed the candle as she went and disappeared into the next room, closing the connecting door as softly as a burglar leaving the scene of a crime. He listened. There was the sliding of the window, then the thunk of her boots hitting the pavement. The city silence flowed back in as soon as she was gone. The traffic noises and far muffled voices of a sleeping city filled his ears. The street lamp light seeped in around the cardboard and bathed his room in a dark gray wash. Gray light of the city burning up the night with cold, dirty fire. It was hard to see the stars over Seattle at night. Too much light pollution and more every year. He wondered if the air pollution and the light pollution would ever meet in the middle. He imagined a city never night nor day, only a uniform grayness in the sky overhead. He envisioned gray people slipping through its streets, their voices swathed in fog, their clothing damp with gray mist. Gray as the ceiling.

He stared up at it and suddenly felt horrible. Guilty. He had cheated and deceived Lynda by not performing tonight. But he hadn't wanted to. Still, what must she be feeling now? Did she guess he did not find her desirable? But he did; it was only when she got close that he was repelled by her. She was an attractive woman, generous and willing. Only a crazy man would turn away from her. So what was wrong with him? He didn't know. He just knew that he hadn't wanted to be that close to her. So. Would it have hurt him to have given in to her needs, let her keep intact the image she had of herself? But what about his own feelings, his desire to keep his body private from her? Weren't they just as valid as hers? And if he had served her, like a cow brought to a random bull; what then would he be feeling? Would he be lying here, gazing at the ceiling and wishing he had not so shamefully deceived her? His mind chased the questions and guilts in a hamster wheel of bad feelings. "No right answers," he tried to console himself, and coughed. This was life back in the real world. The walls of it were closing in on him already. But this time tomorrow, he would be running through his own maze, back on the track with the rat race.

The ceiling was coming down on him. He blinked, willing the illusion away. No more playing games with my mind, he warned himself sternly. No magic, no Truth, no Knowing. No scary things in the closets waiting to get me. Kid stuff. Like being small and being afraid to close the bedroom curtains at night because you might accidentally look out the darkened window and see something. Never look in the bathroom mirror when you're getting a drink of water in the middle of the night; you might see what is standing behind you. But he was an adult now, and back in the real world. He wasn't going to play that kind of mental hide-and-seek anymore. He stared up at the gray ceiling, daring it to come closer.

It did.

It did not, he insisted to himself. He was just sleepy. That was true, he was tired, but now he found he could not close his eyes. For if he looked away from the ceiling, perhaps it would dare to come closer. Even with his eyes opened, he could see the grayness of his ceiling descending on him. Impossible. Summoning every ounce of courage he possessed, he extended his arm and hand straight up and touched . . . nothing.

"See," he told himself aloud. "It's an illusion." He let his arm fall back to his side. He was warm and incredibly sleepy. He closed his eyes and started to let consciousness slide away. A pigeon fell to the floor with a soft thud. And another.

Wizard sat up. His face pushed up into dense gray smoke that choked him mercilessly. He fell back onto the mattress, into a cooler strata of air. His mind raced. The pipe! Where had Lynda left it?

He rolled onto his belly and gazed around wildly. There seemed to be no flames yet, but he was sure that when they came, it would be as a single flash, engulfing the room in an instant. He had only moments to get out.

His cracked window might offer fresh air, but no chance of escape. The fire escape was under the other window, in the next room. From his window it was a sheer four-story drop. He began a wriggling belly-crawl to the connecting door. His seeking hand fell on a small feathered body. Its legs twitched against his palm. The cooler air near the floor was reviving it. He became aware of other thuds as more pigeons fell, overcome by smoke and fumes. He wondered where Black Thomas and Ninja were. But they were smart animals, smart enough to leave a burning building. Weren't they? Not like the stupid goddamned pigeons that couldn't take care of themselves. Stupid, useless, shitty birds. He scooped up another body from the floor. His burden made crawling difficult.

He crept on. The floor was getting warmer. And when he finally reached the connecting door that should have led to escape, he found the wood of it nearly too hot to touch. It must have started in there, somehow. He thought of the stacked cardboard boxes. He heard helpless flutterings on the floor behind him, felt soft pinions brush his bare legs.

"Oh, shit, shit, shit!" he roared suddenly, wasting precious breath. He scuttled in a circle on his belly, the stupid wizard's robe winding up around his legs and hobbling him. He gathered up the little bodies as he crawled, putting them into the sling of his cloak. He took the tall wizard cap from the table and filled it with birds. They were heavy. How many did he have? He had no idea how many roosted in his room at night. The idiot things struggled against his rescue, hopping out of his reach as the gray ceiling pressed ever closer.

At last he had them all. His cloak was a heavy sling over his arm, his bird-stuffed hat tossed in as well. The cooing, rustling, struggling load dragged beside him, snagging on the old flooring. He could feel heat on his bare legs. The air in the room was warming up, the temperature rising every second. He would have to crawl for the hall door and down the corridor and try to find a way to escape.

Outside his room in the foreign corridor, he kicked the door shut behind him. He came cautiously to his knees. But the smoke was thick here as well, stinging his eyes and choking him. He dropped again and resumed his frantic crawl. He didn't know this part of the building. He had never explored it other than to determine that it and the stories above him were unoccupied. Now he regretted his lack of curiosity. The loose fabric of the robe dragged and tangled around his knees, snagging against the floor. The sling full of pigeons occupied one arm completely. But at last he reached a door and felt cautiously up the wood for the knob. The cold brass refused to turn. Locked. He banged his fist against the solid wood panels. Good, sturdy, old-fashioned door. No exit this way.

He coughed heavily and could draw in no clean air to calm his lungs. To breathe now was to choke. His belly scraped the floor as he wriggled along with his cooing, rustling load. His eyes were running tears, and even if there had been light he would have been blind. The smoke smelled acrid and poisonous; he wondered what was smoldering. The basic structure of the building was brick, but the interior, with its hardwood floors and fine old paneling, would burn merrily. His groping fingers encountered another doorframe. He was so horribly tired. If only he could lie still for a moment and catch his breath. One cool breath of air and he knew he could keep going. His leaden fingers walked up the door panels. His wandering hand finally encountered the knob. He rattled it, but it did not turn. Locked. But above it he felt the smoothness of a pane of glass. This room had been an office of some sort once.

He dropped back to the floor and sucked in a long breath of the marginally cooler air. His lungs tried to cough it out, but he held it down as he reared up, a fold of the cloak looped over his free arm. The glass was thick, frosted stuff, but two blows of his elbow shattered it. He thrust his arm into the opening to turn the knob from the other side. The hot air of the corridor was flowing past him into the cooler room like smoke seeking a chimney.

He staggered into the room and stumbled into heaped boxes piled nearly ceiling high. He pushed toward where the windows must be, wriggling between towers of boxes and over lower stacks. He began dragging boxes away from the wall of them that blocked his way. Behind him, he heard the boom as his room ignited and the laughing roar of the fire as it rushed down the corridor after him. He threw boxes awkwardly, one arm still encumbered by the sling of pigeons. If he dropped them, he could . . . He choked, and then the pane before him was reflecting the orange of flames in the hall behind him. He didn't bother with the window catch. His elbow took out the glass and then he was struggling out the snaggle-toothed opening into the blessed cold of the night air. The sirens began. The fire department was only a few blocks away. They'd be here almost instantly, with the police right behind them. The iron railings of the fire escape were icy against his hand as he rushed down two flights, his sling of pigeons thumping against him as he fled. The next set of stairs was only a half set. He halted, some nine feet in the air above the Great Winds Kite Shop.

The bright kite was still tethered to the platform of the fire escape. Its gay streamers tangled around him as he made his leap. His stockinged feet met the cement too solidly, jolting him to the very base of his skull, but he could not have rolled without crushing his pigeons. The sirens weren't more than half a block away, screaming and wailing. He took a tighter grip on his sling of pigeons, hiked up his robes and ran, his bare legs flashing in the night. His socks became soaked at once, so that he splotted with every step. The lighted expanse of Occidental Square offered him no hiding place, but at least it led away from the firemen and police.

He looked back over his shoulder at orange and yellow flames shooting out the upper-story windows of the Washington Shoe Manufacturing Company building. The whole thing would be gutted. All his fault. On his next stride, the cold iron lamp-post leaped out of the darkness before his fire-blinded eyes. Cold iron smacked his left temple and thumped his ribs. He fell into a windy darkness full of the whirring of wings.

14

"FOR GOD'S SAKE, will you please quit crying!"

Wizard yelped like a kicked dog as the book bounced off his shoulder and skidded across the Indian prayer rug on the floor. He raised astounded eyes to Cassie, silenced by the sheer shock of her outburst. As she retrieved her book, he rubbed at his stiff face and wet eyes and took a deeper breath. His head felt less foggy, but he was still more than half-stoned. He knew there was nothing more unpleasant to be around than a drunk on a crying jag, but he was too confused to be ashamed. Cassie sagged back into her overstuffed chair and regarded him as if he were a wet dog in a freshly made bed.

They were in the library, a pleasantly dark room with bookshelves growing up to an unseen ceiling and fat furniture crouching on thick rugs. Floor lamps cast their puddles of yellow light near the chairs. It was a cozy room, if you ignored the cobwebs and the rustling of mice in the corners. Cassie did. So did Rasputin, who sat flat in a corner, swaying softly in his eternal dance as he teased Ninja with a string. They were ignoring Wizard, too. Or had been.

Euripides had left hours ago, right after he helped Rasputin drag Wizard up the endless stairs. After they had dumped him in the middle of the floor, he had looked at Wizard sadly, shaking his head. "I don't think it was entirely his fault," Euripides had begun cautiously, but the looks Cassie and Rasputin gave him silenced the defense. Euripides had tossed a shrug at Cassie and left. Wizard wished he had stayed. No one had spoken a word to him since then, though he vividly recalled Rasputin shaking him violently just before they dragged him in. "Acting like you the last wizard in the world, and the only one going to get hurt by your crap. You dumb shit fuck-head!"

"I know, I know!" Wizard had wailed, and that was when he had begun to cry. He hadn't wanted to, had been ashamed of it, but he was too drunk, stoned, and disoriented to do anything else. That was when Rasputin had slammed him up against the wall, not hard enough to really hurt him, but force-fully enough to let him know that he could just as easily have put Wizard through the wall. Only Euripides's hand on the black wizard's arm had stopped the demonstration. Euripides was the only one who had shown any sympathy at all for Wizard's plight. Fresh tears stung his eyes at the thought, but Cassie's glare dried them.

She set her cup of tea down on the lamp stand by her chair and rose to cross the room to him. She towered over him, a sturdy woman in her thirties dressed in jeans and a faded cotton shirt. "Get up!" she ordered him sternly.

He sniffed and dragged himself to his feet. "You are a mess," she observed without rancor. He bowed his head. The robe was torn from the jagged window glass and bloody where he had cut his elbow on the second window glass. Pigeon droppings streaked the fold of cloak where he had carried them, and he stank of smoke. When he rubbed his face again and looked at his hands, he saw stains of damp soot. "What happened to you?" she demanded, and he knew she was not asking about the fire.

"I don't know," he replied hoarsely.

"Ah dooooon't knooooow!" Rasputin drawled out in a mock-ing croon. He rose to waltz lazily around them both. When he reached the door, he said, "Hate to say, 'I told you so,' Cassie. This one's on you, like stink on shit." His dark eyes snagged for a moment on Wizard's doleful face. "Hey, Wizard. No hard feelings, huh? If you live, come see me. You'll be welcome." He curtsied gravely and spun out the door.

"Thanks for bringing him to me!" Cassie called after him. Wizard wondered if she was sincere. She dragged a bandana handkerchief from her hip pocket and handed it to him. He wiped his eyes and nose dutifully. "What am I going to do with you?" she wondered aloud.

"I don't—" he began.

"That was rhetorical!" she snapped, stopping him cold. "I've had enough of your crying and saying 'I don't know.' Say or do anything you please, but not that." She meant it. He took a ragged breath.

"I thought crying was good, especially for us inhibited males." A little of his frustration and anger leaked into his voice.

For a second Cassie looked pleased. "Well, at least you still have your wits. I was beginning to think your mind was gone. Sure, crying is good. It's a great tension relieving response to impossible situations. But when you substitute it for action, it's no more appropriate than beating your head against a wall. As Rasputin tried to demonstrate. What are you crying about, anyway?"

"I don't—" Her look stopped him. "Everything. I feel like I just fell down the rabbit hole again, Cassie. It's not that I don't like you or the others. But, Cassie, I had it all straight in my head, finally. I was going to move in with Lynda and get a job or welfare or something, and forget all this stuff." A frown divided her brows, but she was nodding for him to continue. "All this stuff . . . all this pretending about magic and Truth and Knowing and pigeons. I was going to be like everyone else. And then my place catches fire and burns up everything I own. And when I come to, Rasputin is hauling me up those damned impossible stairs of yours, and I am back to this . . . place." Words failed to describe for him the gears of his two worlds grinding together.

Cassie looked pained. "A job or welfare. Shit, Wizard. Look at yourself. You can't change your residence and put on new clothes and be what you aren't. You'd still be a wizard, and you'd still have responsibilities to your magic."

"My magic's gone, anyway." Wizard crushed his eyes shut as he made this final admission. He dangled once again in the abyss of that loss.

"Hold it!" Cassie's voice snapped him back from it. She looked incredibly tired. "What a tangle," she murmured, mostly to herself. She managed a tired smile for him. "Let's take this one thing at a time. Go clean up. Maybe it will sober you up a little, too. Go on. You'll feel better.

She picked up her book again. He blundered about the place,

discovering a closet and an office with dusty files and a type-writer and then a short corridor with a door ajar at the end of it. The bathroom was small, little more than a sink, toilet, and shower stall. He untied the silver tassels of the cloak slowly. He draped it and the soiled robe over the sink and turned on the shower to the hottest water he thought he could stand. He shut the glass door behind him and stood in the stinging rain, letting it batter his face. His brain slowly cleared. He began to soap himself, finding numerous small abrasions he had been unaware of. They stung. The hot water loosened the newly clotted blood on his elbow and it bled again, slightly. With cautious fingers he explored the tender lump on one temple.

He stayed under the shower until the water turned suddenly cold. Then he shut it off and stood dripping in the stall. It seemed so safe in here. Getting out of the shower and drying off meant facing up to whatever came next. But after a few moments he began to shiver. Best face it. He blotted himself dry and then glanced about for something to put on. There was only the robe and cloak. He slipped the robe over his head, expecting the smell of smoke and pigeons. But there was only the soft blue robe spangled with stars and moons. But for the small rips from the glass, the events of the past few hours might have been dreams. That was not reassuring. He pulled on his socks, slung the cloak over his arm, and emerged in search of Cassie.

He stood silently until she looked up from her book and nodded approvingly at him. "That looks better. Feel any better?"

"Some," he admitted, and suddenly he didn't want to feel better. As long as the events were overwhelming, no one could expect him to assume responsibility for them. Cassie seemed to sense his reluctance.

"So what is still so awful?" she demanded.

"Everything. My den is gone, with everything in it. And—"

"Wait. One at a time. What did you lose in that fire that you can't replace? You're wearing the only unique thing you possessed. The rest of it could be replaced by a few strolls down dumpster row. Am I wrong?"

She wasn't, but it seemed cruel of her to state it so baldly. He racked his brains for a defense. "Black Thomas. I got the pigeons out, but I didn't find him."

Cassie gave him a disparaging look. "Black Thomas! Come

here, tomcat!" Wizard followed her gaze up to one of the bookshelves. Thomas sat up slowly. He yawned disdainfully, showing a red mouth, pink curling tongue, and white teeth. He surveyed them both with disgust, then rearranged himself with his front paws tucked neatly against his breast. His stump was tidily wrapped in a clean white bandage. He closed his eyes to slits and made Wizard and Cassie disappear.

"He's still angry," Cassie observed. "At you, for bringing a stranger into his home. And at me, for holding him down while I dressed that stump. But he didn't even stick around for the fire to start."

Wizard felt relieved. And guilty. "He wouldn't let me clean and wrap it for him."

"You didn't even try," Cassie stated factually.

"Well, I was afraid I'd hurt him," he said defensively. Had she no sympathy for him at all? His magic was gone.

"Sometimes you have to hurt someone to help him. When I cleaned that stump with peroxide, he screamed like a baby. But it's clean now, and he won't get gangrene."

"I'm glad he's all right."

"I know. Now. What upsets you most? That your magic is gone, or that you got caught before you could run out on us?"

Wizard's breath caught. The question was as cold and unexpected as a knife in the spine. Cassie's blue eyes continued to bore into his.

"Well, what would you call it?" she asked him at last, sounding a bit defensive. "Only days ago, you and I discussed this gray thing of yours, this Mir. That it had come to Seattle, and that you are the only one that will have its balancing point. That it will come to you, and you must stop it. And if you fail, it will take us all down. What happens next? Next we have Wizard forsaking the duties of his magic, claiming that he has no magic, and contemplating moving in with a waitress, to watch TV and drink beer and line up for payments from a window. So what should we think? What were you thinking? That you could roll over on your back and Mir would pass you by? Even if it did, which you well know it won't, where did you think it would satisfy its hungers?"

The enormity of it settled on him. He could only look at her. The grave sadness in her eyes was more than he could bear.

"You know," he said slowly, "that those things never crossed my mind. I never saw it that way, that I was abandoning a position. I only saw that my magic was gone, that I was Wizard no more. Somehow, I . . . forgot about it."

"I know," she conceded. She walked away from him to drop back into her chair, but then waved him into its mate on the other side of the lamp stand. His legs and back were stiff, and his ribs ached from the collision with the lamppost. The wound her words had dealt him was worst of all. He was glad to ease into the chair instead of standing. He smoothed his robes over his knees.

"You look like you're already comfortable wearing that," Cassie observed softly.

He looked down at the soft blue cloth. "It seems natural," he admitted. "Right."

"Are you sure your magic's gone?"

He nodded, tired of repeating it.

"Then the worst part is that you are sure. How did you lose it?"

He heard a test in her question. Did she think he would lie about it? "I broke the rules," he said simply. "And it went away."

Cassie was shaking her head slowly. From somewhere, a bit of needlework had come into her hands. Embroidery. He watched her bite off a thread and select a new color. "You're wrong, you know," she said conversationally. He leaned forward to catch her words. "The rules broke you."

He bowed his head to that rebuke. "I suppose I never really had the strength, the discipline, to be a wizard."

Cassie snorted. "Idiot. No. You knew what would break you. You knew what rules you couldn't keep, so you made those rules and then you broke them. To get away from the magic. It's scared you shitless since the first day I told you it was yours."

"What?"

"You heard me."

"No. No, you don't understand. Cassie, I broke the rules that had brought the magic to me, and so it went away. I kept more than a dollar in change, I've lain with a woman, I've turned my strength loose upon others." He was babbling, close to falling apart again. Cassie poked her needle through the heavy linen. He heard the rip-drag of the embroidery floss as it followed. She kept her eyes on her work, making no reply as he catalogued his sins, but only shaking her head. He told her all, all since the night she had done the Seeing for him, croaking out the tale when his mouth grew too dry to speak. When he finally ran down, she spoke.

"Where did you get the rules?"

"The magic gave them to me."

"No. Not those ones. You invented those ones yourself, knowing you couldn't keep them. You wanted to break yourself so the magic would go away, so you wouldn't be a wizard and have a duty to it. But even in your desire to be free of it, the magic went too deep in you for you to destroy it. Otherwise you would have taken the easy way out. Stomp one of those stupid pigeons. That would really have done it, really have blown the magic away. Or turn your back and walk away when one came seeking you. But you didn't. You made up your own rules to break. We all knew you were in trouble the minute you started putting extra rules on yourself. Rasputin thought he could rattle you out of it. Maybe I should have let him. But I said you would snap out of it on your own. So we watched you, hoping. Until it was damn near too late."

He was staring at her, refusing to believe her. She met his eyes calmly.

"Think back. What rules did Rasputin give you? Hold the pigeons sacred and never harm them. Listen to the ones who came to talk to you, and when you have comfort for them, speak out. Tell the Truth when it comes on you, and when you Know, admit you Know. That was all. Those were the rules of your magic, given you by the only one of us who can look at a wizard, see his magic, and tell him the rules of it. The rest of it was your own petty fences, put up to keep others at a distance. When you came to me for a Seeing, I hoped you would see how silly they were. Even Estrella tried to warn you."

"Didn't anyone ever think of just coming out and saying it?"

"You being such an easy person to talk to and all?" Cassie asked sarcastically.

"I'm not that hard!" he replied indignantly.

"Oh, aren't you, now?" There was something else in her voice now. A more personal hurt that baffled him. He didn't want to explore it. Cassie stabbed her needle into the cloth and dragged it swiftly through. She didn't look at him and he sat without speaking. At last he heard her give a long sigh. When she spoke again, it was in her ordinary, well-modulated voice.

"Are you still sure your magic is gone now? Remember, you haven't broken any rules."

He hated to disappoint her. "I'm sure. It's gone, Cassie. I can't feed the pigeons. When people talk to me, I'm not sure what to say to them. I was helpless against Lynda and what she did to me."

Cassie snorted. "Lynda. She's another matter entirely. Don't blame it on her. So you're sure it's gone. Then you're a fool and no one can help you." She finished a leaf and knotted off her thread. She suddenly crumpled her work into her lap and sat up straighter. "I have an idea about you. I may be completely wrong. Want to hear it?"

"Why not?" What could she say that would be worse than what had been said?

"This gray thing, this Mir. It scared the hell out of you. So, rather than face it, you tried to pretend it was only imaginary. Something inside your head, some neurotic disorder from your past. It isn't. It's as real as I am."

"How real is that?" he asked lightly, but she brought a pointing finger to bear on him.

"Never doubt me, not even in jest. I'm real, real enough to kick your ass if I hear another comment like that out of you tonight. That would have been the next step, wouldn't it? And you damn near took it. You would have convinced yourself that Rasputin and Euripides and I were all—I don't know what—imaginary, or fragments of your own disordered mind. I think you could have actually made yourself believe it, too. You're a very young wizard, as wizards go, and tonight you nearly lost your chance to get any older. But you had better believe this, now. This gray thing of yours, this Mir. It's real. Real enough to tear you into shreds. Real. And smart enough to start with your mind first, if you leave it an opening. Or it can stand back and watch you chase your own tail until you're exhausted, and then it can step in and take you without a fight. And use you for its own ugly ends."

"I think it's already begun," he admitted cautiously.

"Bullshit." Cassie smoothed out her needlework and picked up a skein of yellow thread. "You're scaring yourself. Searching your soul for bogey-men. So you have a temper. So your body has been trained as an effective weapon and steps in to save you when your mind is out to lunch. Maybe you even have a few kinks that the right person can trigger with the right sort of behavior. Well, don't we all? Don't blame the gray thing or the magic. Don't even blame Lynda, though she sounds like she could piss off a saint. Blame yourself. You set it all in motion."

"Meaning what?" He demanded. He didn't like the way this was going. Not matter what he said, Cassie seemed to circle back to where it was all his fault. But she couldn't know what it was really like. She hadn't been there.

"You deliberately unbalanced your magic. When Lynda came to you on the bench that day, she had a problem. You listened to her, but you didn't tell her what you Knew. Nor did you turn her away. You kept what you Knew to yourself, like it was some ponderous secret. Hell, even I could have told her the answer. I would have said, 'Lynda, it's fine to like men, any number of men, as long as you still like yourself.' But you didn't. So you owed her, and she became a danger to you. Mir has used her as a channel to get to you. Hell, didn't you wonder at a waitress that could jump up to a bar and chin herself up to a fire escape? Mir used her to move you away from the rest of us, to get you out on your own. But even though the magic was unbalanced when you didn't give more than you got, it didn't go away. Didn't you Know that Booth would follow and attack?"

"It wasn't the same. I couldn't feed the pigeons."

"Did you try?"

"She took the fucking bag!" he roared in sudden exasperation. "What was I supposed to do? Make popcorn appear out of nowhere?"

"Exactly. Did you try?"

"No!" he snapped. "I just knew I couldn't. And you can't shrug it off like it's nothing when I say that I've been hurting people. I had stopped doing that."

"I know. Because you didn't need to. Who did you hurt? A mugger? A murderer? A man who attacked you from behind?"

"And Lynda. And I hurt them all more than I needed to."

Cassie shook her head. "You hurt them as much as you had to, to make them stop what they were doing. In the case of the knife-man, not quite enough. And Lynda? Lynda is like a rat pushing a bar to earn a feed pellet. She sized you up right away without even being conscious of it. She can push your buttons and you give her a little scare that puts an edge on things. If you were really a danger to her, do you think she'd stick around? She was already smart enough to dump one man that got too rough. You're the key to the candy store for her. She sets the scenes and you say your lines. While the gray thing uses her to undermine you."

"You don't understand anything!" He rose so suddenly that he nearly upset the lamp. Fists clenched, he paced the room twice and stopped in front of her chair. "It's different for me. Maybe you can never understand. I don't just lose my temper and slug someone. I know what I am capable of, in a way most people never realize. I've killed, Cassie, with a rifle and with my hands. And I'm good at it. Very good. So good that when I am crossed, it's the first solution I think of, not the last. And Lynda. I don't like what she triggers in me, what she makes me want to do to her."

Cassie shrugged easily. "Then get away from her. Find someone else. But don't blame it on the magic."

He shook his head. It was so simple for her. And so hard for him. "I'm a violent man."

"You are also a man sickened by violence. A man triggered by violence to violence. Do you suppose I am so different? If I saw a mugging in progress, do you think I would turn away? If I were attacked, wouldn't I defend myself? Wizard, there is only one rule about violence. Do whatever you must do to make it stop."

He was so far beyond what she could imagine. It made her seem vulnerable and young as he told her, "I can't agree with that."

"I can't make you. I can't force you to believe that the magic hasn't deserted you, either. And because of that, you just may die."

His eyes snapped to her face. She suddenly looked very old. He crossed the room to her and sat at her feet, looking up at her. There was something in her eyes he knew. "Were you in Viet Nam?" he asked suddenly.

"My friend, I have been in them all since the wooden horse was dragged into Troy. They haven't improved them any."

"Viet Nam was the worst."

"It was different," she agreed. She leaned her cheek on her fist and looked at him sadly. "Do you know, since I met you, I haven't eaten a pigeon."

He was touched. "Don't look so sad. I feel like you're saying last words to me. I've listened to you, I really have. I'm going to go back and get it all straightened out. It's going to be all right."

"Fool," she said fondly. "The time I can shelter you here is ticking away. Then I must put you out, back into the streets. And Mir will have you. Tonight. This is the night it takes you away."

"I'm not ready." His mouth was dry.

"You threw away your weapons to pretend there was no war."

"Cassie, what am I going to do?"

"You're going to get yourself killed. And maybe take down the rest of us as well." She slid forward off her chair to sit on the floor beside him. "Why didn't I ever see what a child you are?"

"I'm not."

"You don't think so, perhaps." Her fingers traced the pattern on the rug. "But when did you really have the chance to grow up? You were just a kid when they took you. And when you came back, you were older than God, but without the wisdom. Only the knowing. Not adults, but wizards. You and Rasputin and Euripides. The difference is they found themselves sooner, and have put in enough time to do some growing. You're not going to have the chance."

Her words were chilling. He wrapped himself in bravado, leaning back against her chair as he spoke. "And just what makes you so different, then?"

"Me? I remember the befores." Soft as a challenge, those words.

A silence fell. Meaning hummed in the words sinking into the quiet, but Wizard could not quite extract it. He only knew it had immense importance to him. It dangled tantalizingly out of his reach. There were only Cassie's eyes begging him to pick up on it. He shook his head at her. "So what should I do?"

"Pick up your weapons. Call out the allies you've groomed for this battle. Stop pretending that you've been pretending."

She was talking in riddles. Despair washed over him. "I don't know how. I don't know what you mean. I don't know what you want me to do."

"The I-Don't-Know Wizard." There was no mockery in her voice. She leaned forward to put her hand against his cheek. The touch of her skin against his tingled, like an exchange of electricity. It was both heady and familiar. Yet he could not recall that she had ever touched him before. He found himself leaning into it, moving his face against her hand.

"Why can't you just tell me?" he begged in frustration, and was surprised at his own words.

"I've tried, in every way that I'm allowed. Don't you think my magic has its own rules?" A fierce edge to her voice.

That stopped him cold. "Oh. Then there's nothing left but for it to happen. I suppose I should leave now."

"I suppose." Her hand fell from his face. She picked up both of his hands in hers and looked at them, as if marveling at their emptiness. A tear fell into his hand and the wet touch galvanized him.

"Don't. Please, don't. I never wanted to make you sad."

"You never wanted to make me anything!" she accused suddenly in an anguished voice. She pushed suddenly into his arms and he found himself holding her. She smelled like spices, ginger and vanilla. Closing his eyes, he pulled her closer. She pressed her face into the side of his neck and her arms clung to him. Startled, he loosened his hold. She didn't. He patted her awkwardly. Her voice came from the hollow of his shoulder, sounding below his ear. "Do you remember the first story I ever told you?"

He cast his mind back. "No. There have been so many. Wait—about a little girl in a garden."

He felt her nod. It rubbed wetness against his neck. He sighed and pulled her in close again.

"That's all you remember of it. You don't remember the rules she was given." She probed hopelessly.

"Not really." So long ago, and it had seemed like a pointless little story at the time. Her breath caught raggedly as he admitted his lack of memory. Could it have been that important to her?

"They were all about giving and taking," he hedged. "She couldn't take what she wanted most because it wasn't offered to her."

"Until it was freely offered. Not that it makes any difference now."

"And she couldn't offer anything . . ."

"She could offer . . ." Cassie hissed angrily.

"Right," he amended. "She could offer, but she couldn't give, because . . ."

"Because no one wanted it." She pushed away from him abruptly, but he caught at her wrist and dragged her back down to his side.

"Because someone was too stupid to know what was being offered. And too scared to accept it. And too afraid of what might come of it if he did; afraid of himself."

Her eyes met his, stubbornly hurt. Refusing all comfort that he offered now, too late.

"Cassie," he said brokenly. "I never meant to refuse what you offered. I didn't realize it. Or maybe I did, I suppose, but it was forbidden to me. I don't do—"

"Yes, you do!" she replied fiercely. "You just refuse to enjoy it. Or to do it with me!"

"It's not safe to be with me."

"Nothing is safe anymore. And the time is gone." She began untangling herself from him. The finality of her words slapped him. The feel of Cassie moving away from him was more grievous than the departure of his magic. As she rose, he clutched at her hand.

"Cassie. Come back."

She turned to his words, her face strangely uncertain. Wistful. She looked down at him. "You don't remember the garden at all," she said sadly.

He was confused. "Not the whole story, but—"

"Never mind," she said abruptly. For a long moment she stood stiffly apart from him. Colder than frozen. Then she turned to look at him, and a sudden smile flooded her face. A decision had been reached in her mind and her face mirrored it. She came back to him and he rose to take her in his arms. She was trembling.

"Are you scared?" he asked her.

"Not as scared as you are. And it's not you I'm scared of."

She was right. He held her and as she put her arms around him, he felt her magic wrap them both like a mantle. Within that shelter, all was safe and right. Her breathing became slow and steady as the sea swells, calming them both. He closed his eyes. This was right.

And more than right, her magic promised. It was the pathway back to where a touching was not a hurting. It was the missing arc of the circle that took him back to an unspoiled beginning. To a garden on a summer day, with bees buzzing in honeysuckle on the garden wall.

"Cassie?" he asked, the last of his uncertainty in his voice.

"I'm right here," she whispered. "I've always been right here."

He journeyed to the heart of woman's magic, and found it was the journey home.

15

THE RAINY STREETS shone under the streetlamps. The squall
had passed, leaving only an icy wind wandering the streets and
alleys. He heard the final click of Cassie's door as it closed
behind him. He turned back to it, but it was already gone,
fading into darkness. She had left him alone to face it, turned
him out like a stray cat to take his chances with the street dogs.
He knew that she'd had to. But the night still seemed the colder
after Cassie's warmth.

At least there was nothing about. Whatever gray Mir was,
it wasn't bold enough to strike on Cassie's doorstep. He shivered and began to walk. He sensed the city around him, the
living entity of each building he passed, the vacant windows
that nonetheless watched him. He had not felt it so alive since
the night Cassie had come for him through the snowstorm. Nor
so ominous. It was as if he walked through a maze of spectators
come to witness his execution. "Bring on the hatchetman," he
muttered to himself. He had screwed his courage to the pitch
of being able to go forth and meet Mir. But he didn't know
how long it would stand up to the tension of having to seek
Mir out. That wasn't something he had prepared for.

His socks soaked up the rain water like wicks. The hem of

his wizard robe and cloak dragged slightly. Soon they had absorbed a weight of mud and water that slapped unpleasantly against his ankles. He squelched along, feeling uncomfortable and slightly foolish. It was either very late or very early. Traffic was less than sparse, and the vehicles that did pass did not slow at the sight of him. He settled his wizard's hat more firmly onto his head.

Cassie's words replayed endlessly in his mind, and he fancied for an instant that he could still feel the warmth of her touch on his skin. She had left her scent upon him, like the colors of a high-born lady on her knight-errant. There had been a few precious moments when he had fancied himself in the garden she had mentioned. He had felt the grass and fragrant leaf mold under his palms, and a summer sun warmed his naked back. Her mouth had smiled beneath his. Never had he felt so full of a woman.

Or so clear in his mind of what he must face now. He was going to his death, Cassie's certainty of his magic notwithstanding. He wished he had been able to make her understand before he left her. He could tell her what he had done and felt, but he couldn't make her feel what he had. Did she think he hadn't tried to reclaim his magic? Could she imagine that he didn't ache for it? Gone and beyond him now. Despite her calm certainty, he was sure he knew more of Mir than she did. Mir had touched him; had already bent him to its will. He shuddered with the knowledge. It had touched him as intimately as she had. It would again.

"But when?" he asked aloud of the watching city, flinging the challenge to the night. Nothing answered it. He passed gray parking meters with empty faces, reviewing the cold and passionless troops of the streets. Faces in the brick alleys and the black storefront windows changed and stretched as he passed them, peered after him until he was out of their sight. He felt no heaviness of evil in the air. Where was Mir hiding? The wind kept the night clear of the gray fog he had come to associate with its wickedness. A reckless boldness settled on him. So he was going to defeat, was he? Gray Mir wasn't making it easy for him to meet his fate. He shrugged his shoulders and drew his cloak more closely around himself. It was warmer than he expected it to be, and for an instant he imagined he felt a rippling of power through it. But it was only the wind tugging at the blue cloth. He paced on.

He could always run away. He tempted himself with possibilities. He could hide from it, could leave the city on foot and take to the woods. It would have to come and hunt him down. He shook his head. He had been hunted before and remembered it only too well. He would meet it face to face in the night, not be dragged out from behind some dumpster in an alley.

He had been walking without thinking, but his feet had led him well. He stood at the mouth of his old alley. It was littered with charred rubbish from the fire. Well, why not here? He had felt it here more often than any other place. He ventured into the alley and turned his eyes up to his fire escape. There was a terrible smell here, of wet charred wood and melted plastics. It was the burned odor of ruin and decay. No heat remained of the fire that had gutted the upper stories of the building. All was silent and dark. More than hours had passed since the fire. A day and most of a night, he guessed. That would fit in with the lightheaded weariness he felt. He was running on nerves and adrenalin, his reserve energy long spent. He wouldn't last much longer. It seemed to him that his strength had been slowly leeching away from him since the day Estrella had warned him. When Mir chose to attack, it would find him no adversary at all, crushable as a dried-out eggshell.

"Where are you?" he called out bravely into the darkness, but the alley swallowed his challenge without an echo.

He crouched beneath his fire escape, tensing himself for the spring. Then he straightened slowly and shook his head. Not up there, on charred floorboards, if any remained at all. Not before the burned specter of a footlocker, if it had survived. No. He would not be hunted, but he would not be lured into ambush either. He turned soundlessly and let his body do what it had been clamoring to do. He opened it to the night. His senses expanded and he walked as one with the darkness. No magic this; a skill learned in a night that had shrilled with insect noises and screamed with sudden silences. An easy awareness spread out around him, searching as any light of flare. It had guided him alive through trees and vines and grasses. Could brick and steel and glass be any worse? He moved with slow grace, in no hurry at all. Let it come to him.

He could not have told what made him turn and look up. There might have been a rustle of cloth, some scuff of skin against metal. He was in time to see the figure leave the fire escape, see it silhouetted, however briefly, against the far lights of the King Dome. It landed lightly, its legs bending nearly double to take up the shock. He pivoted slowly and silently to meet it. He had not expected a human form, but he sensed it, an electric prickling along the edges of his perimeter. A chill of readiness ran over him. He smiled in the dark, and when he felt it looking at him, he gave a slow nod of acknowledgment. Mir.

"Oh, there you are!" she cried and rushed at him, her arms held wide. In the next instant she had engulfed him and was covering his face with wet, panting kisses. "My god, I am so glad you're safe! I saw it in the papers this morning, and it said signs of recent habitation, but no remains discovered yet, and when I read the address I just about collapsed. The first thing that hit me, was, oh, god, he did it on purpose because we didn't make it last night! and I felt like I had killed you myself. I had to sit down and the boss asked if I was taking my break now, and I couldn't even talk, all I could do was point at the paper and shake. I guess I really looked bad, because he told me to take a day off, sick time. So I did and I looked for you everywhere. I musta fed those stupid pigeons ten pounds of popcorn, hoping you'd show up, and everyone kept walking by and staring at me; I guess I looked pretty stupid, sitting on a park bench feeding the pigeons and bawling. I am so glad you're safe."

As she talked, she kissed, hugged, and shook him at intervals. He could conjure no emotional reaction to her greeting. It reminded him of the noisy greetings of a sheepdog he had known in his childhood, complete with wet tongue and cold nose. He knew he had to feel something for her, but all he could find was a quiet acceptance of her. This was what she was. No more than that, but certainly no less.

"Lynda!" he told her firmly. He put his hands on her shoulders and moved her out to arm's length. She waggled happily in his arms and tried to move into his embrace, but he held her back. After an instant of struggle, she calmed and looked at him. He tried to catch her eyes, to peer past the dumb devotion and electric lust to see what else might be lurking there. But she focused on his clothing instead and gave a squawk of dismay.

"Have you been running around dressed like that all day? It's a wonder they didn't lock you up! Look at your feet! Poor baby! Come on, you're going home with me."

There was an energy to her that verged on a natural magic. She had taken his arm and turned him and was walking him away before he realized that she was taking command. Her tongue was rattling like a pocketful of loose brass, and she plowed down the center of the sidewalk as if nothing in the world could wish her harm. Wariness was impossible with her around. When he tuned in to her words, she was still going on about hot showers and clean sheets. He dug his heels into the sidewalk and brought her around to face him. The look on his face stopped her chatter.

"What is it?" she demanded. "There's nothing back there to go back for, if that's what you're thinking."

He took a deep breath. "Lynda. There is nothing wrong with liking men, any number of men, as long as you still like yourself."

Annoyance creased her brow. "What's that crack supposed to mean? Hey, I've been walking around down here all day, crying my eyes out over you, and when I finally find you, you say something like that. What do you think I am? Do you think I'd take in just anyone?"

"That's not what I meant!" he protested.

"Then just what the hell did you mean?" Color was staining her cheeks, and with amazement he realized he had hurt her. He was surprised at the strength of the remorse he felt. He touched her face quickly, stroking the hair back from her cheek as he might smooth a pigeon's rumpled feathers. She quieted under his touch. He took a deep breath.

"There's no way I can explain that you will understand. But I'll tell you anyway. I've got to put the magic back in balance. That means I have to give more than I get, always. There were questions you asked me when we first met. You asked me why you should keep on going, you asked me if you had to live like a nun because your sister thought you should."

"I don't remember any of that," Lynda began, but he put a soft finger over her lips.

"Maybe not in those exact words, but you asked me. And I had things to tell you, but I didn't answer because I didn't want to talk to anyone who might endanger me later. I unbalanced things, and I owed you. The more you gave me, the further unbalanced it became. After tonight, there may never be another chance for me to put things back in balance. So I have to do it now."

"You are really sweet, you know that?" She leaned forward to kiss him again, with no more regard for his words than if they had been empty sweet-talk. She didn't know the difference, he realized. Had other men tried to reach her mind, only to have her shelve their words as verbal foreplay? He felt pity for her and wondered who had taught her that men and women never really spoke to one another. She was rattling on. "You don't have to say thank you to me. It's okay. Let's get you to my place now and run you through a hot shower and head for beddy-bye. I've got to work tomorrow, baby. Hey, it's already tomorrow, isn't it? I was going to say we could talk about all this tomorrow, but I guess it'll have to wait for the next tomorrow. Hey, that sounds funny, doesn't it?"

"This is the last tomorrow I have," he told her desperately. He was selfishly relieved to find that he felt only pity for her. Loving a woman like her would have been hell. She believed all the old myths: Men have no feelings such as women harbor; they can share your home, your bed, and your money, but not your life. She knew all about 'how men are,' but she had never really spoken to one. She wasn't going to let him get through. He made a final effort. "Lynda. I have things I have to say to you. For my sake, if not for yours, let me. You are a giver, and it brings you joy. Don't let your sister shame you out of it, for the world would be a barren place without those who give as you do. But it can also be a form of giving when you take. Let them give to you, the men that come into your life. The giving must flow both ways for the bond to be real. All your life, you've believed in only one kind of relationship; that in each pair, there is one who is loved, and one who does the loving. It doesn't have to be that way. Give yourself by taking. Then you'll find—"

"Can't we at least walk while we're talking? I'm freezing, baby, and I've got to get home and get some sleep before work. I'm going to be dead on my feet as it is."

He fell silent, allowing her to take his arm and tow him along. Perhaps the time for him to speak to her had passed, irretrievably. Perhaps the magic granted only that one moment of exchange, when the strange man with the pigeons could have spoken to her and she would have felt his words. Now he was too close. He was just another man to her, to feed and support and screw and, on occasion, when bored, to pester and irritate to the very edge of a violent confrontation. She would never hear him again, and he would never know any more of her than he did at this moment. Why was he going with her?

He stopped abruptly. She rounded on him. "Now what? Baby, I have to—"

"I'm not going home with you, Lynda. We have nothing for one another. There is a thing I have to do tonight, and I have to do it alone. Go along, hurry home to where you'll be safe. And if you can remember what I said to you, think about my words. I meant them."

"I don't believe this! What's the matter with you, are you crazy or what? You can't just walk off like that, running off in a Hallowe'en suit with no shoes on! You can't just walk out on me. You can't treat me this way! You've got no right to treat me like this."

"I've got no right to treat you any other way, either." She wouldn't hear him. How can you say good-bye to someone who never even heard you say hello?

For a moment she stared at him, her face an ivory mask in the darkness. Then she burst into tears, stamping her feet on the sidewalk. When he impulsively reached to comfort her, she hammered him with quick, forceless blows of her fists. "Go away, then. Go away! Leave me alone! I knew you would anyway, sooner or later. Everyone always leaves me, or makes me throw them out! All men use me! And you're no different."

She continued to hammer at him wordlessly. He caught one of her flying wrists and restrained it. With her free hand, she dealt him a slap on the side of the head that clapped his ear painfully and stung his cheek. "Lynda!" he protested, but she swung again, a backhanded slap that smashed his lips against his teeth. Damn, she was strong. He tasted blood. Anger coursed through him and he squeezed the captured wrist and began to turn it. The night pressed close all around them. Electrically gray.

He let go and sprang back from her so suddenly that she fell. "No!" he told her frenziedly. "No!" He turned and ran from her. She shrieked obscenities after him and the sodden hem of his robe flapped against his ankles as he ran. He fled through the night, a hunted thing. Mir had stalked him well, from a perfect blind. Its raking claws had touched his soul and marked him. It would have him this night.

The city marked his cowardice and turned on him. He collided with dumpsters in alleys. At an intersection a yellow light winked suddenly green, and a car roaring from nowhere blasted its horn at him. He raced up streets that were all uphill. A passing squad car suddenly lit up like a Christmas tree and squealed a u-turn to pursue him. He darted up a crowded alley, knocking over garbage cans as he fled, then turned left and ran half a block before dropping to roll into hiding beneath a parked truck. He lay flat and still, the front of his robe absorbing an oily puddle of rainwater. He held his breath until he could force himself to breathe silently. He thought of Lynda's eyes gone huge and gray and hungry in the night. He shuddered. Cassie had been wrong. It was hiding, not only in the city, but within him. Like was calling to like, and when they united, it would have him. Lynda had come perilously close to letting it out. It had been stalking him all this time.

The cold water met his skin and chilled it painfully. He endured it, lying still until he was sure that the patrol car was far away. Then he rolled from under the truck and stood again in the bitter November wind. There was a heaviness inside him, a sense of carrying as if he bore the seed of a deadly disease. It hid in his chest and in the muscles of his back, questing tentatively into his biceps, probing into his wrists and hands. Waiting. It could materialize in his fingers, or use his feet as its tool. His body was rotten with it. The knowledge disgusted him. It was worse than the idea of internal parasites. He would have preferred intestines full of tapeworms or the cellular anarchy of cancer, leprosy, or plague. But he had not been given a choice.

"'And if thy right hand offend thee, cut it off,'" he muttered. He laughed bitterly. It was past the stage of a hand or an eye. He would have to cast his whole body aside to be free of it. Now, how did one go about that? The word was like a snake sliding through dry summer grasses. Suicide. The cold certainty of it settled on him even as he denied it. Cassie would never have sent him out to face it if that were the only way he could win. But, then, Cassie had not known as much as she thought she did. She would not believe that it lurked inside him: not as a figment of his imagination, but as a fragment of himself. Maybe Estrella had known more than she had been able to tell. The Hanged Man. A helpful suggestion from your friendly neighborhood fortune-teller. But it wouldn't be his foot in the loop. The plan did not please him, but there was a bitter satisfaction in knowing that by losing, he would win.

One detail disturbed him, and it took him a moment to find it. There it was. He did not want anyone weeping over his body. Not Lynda, dramatic in black, not Cassie, shaking her head. A vision came to him, clear and cold as ice. He saw himself standing on one of Seattle's bridges, the rope looped several times around his throat, simply looped, not a noose at all. He would jump, and the weight of his body at the end of the rope would be enough to break his neck. Then the slow turning of the body at the end of the rope from the natural torque of the woven strands; the rope unwinds itself from the throat, and the body drops neatly down, to be carried away by the moving water. In the morning, an empty rope dangling from a bridge. He was almost positive it would work. If it didn't, he'd never know. Tidy, he congratulated himself, and tried to ignore the gray chuckling in the back of his mind. As for the rope—had not the dumpsters of the city always provided him with all his needs before? So would they this night. His stride was purposeful.

The scream ripped his decision. It was a strange cry, thin and short, terror with no breath to vent it. He could not decide if it came from deep inside himself or only echoed there. It was a sharp sound, pained and despairing and gray. He crossed his arms on his chest, holding it in and muffling it. He heard three quick scuffs, soles against pavement, and the gong of a heavy body colliding with a dumpster. Then silence. Fear roiled through Wizard. He wanted to stopper his ears and keep walking. He had reached a decision for his gray Mir, and he wanted it to be a final one. He doubted he had the strength to face anything else this night. But his traitorous ears brought him the harsh breathing of a predator on a blood trail. It came from an alley mouth, less than a half a block away.

Wizard kept walking, his steps reflexively silent. He would reach the alley mouth and pass it, search for his rope elsewhere. His own burden was all he could carry, and his mission was clear in his mind. If other evil walked in Seattle, that was no affair of his. Someone else would have to handle it. He was already doing as much as he could.

The alley loomed on his right, blacker than the night itself. It was a deadend alley, walled up so that it offered no light or escape at the far end. Entering it was a one-way journey to the pit. Coldness emanated from it. He kept his eyes down and straight, watching the sidewalk in front of him. He walked soundlessly past the mouth of the alley and continued walking. The grayness wriggled inside him, chuckling. He clenched his arms tighter around it.

"Oh, please!"

The cry, whimpered with no hope of clemency, halted him. The stalker had found his prey and was upon her. The grayness giggled inside him, rejoicing in wickedness and the turmoil in

Wizard's soul. If it was no affair of his, why did he Know that the plea was directed to him?

"Ah!" A soft little sound, beyond terror or pain. He knew it well. Once, in a small hot black place, he had made that sound, not once, but many times. Death was better than the uttering of such a sound. He had to turn to it.

The alley was black, the grayness inside him a cold, heavy thing he must guard. He stepped with care, straining all his senses. Soft, ugly sounds were coming from a far black end. With no warning, he felt the knife. It was hot and keen, and its razor edge was being scraped slowly up and down his throat, paring away layers of skin that left exposed new cells stinging. It had not drawn blood yet. It made a paralyzing whispering against his skin that left him powerless to think of anything else, not even the fingers that prodded and probed in a parody of tenderness.

It was too real. It froze Wizard for a long instant, until he realized it was a Knowing. This was happening, but not to him. To someone who lay amid the trash at the end of the alley, knowing that to scream was to die, and that to keep silent was to die more slowly. The magic had come back to him, but he could not rejoice in it. What it was showing him was too great an atrocity. "If this be Knowing, I would rather walk in ignorance," he muttered soundlessly. And Knew it was not the first time he had made that decision. But this time the magic ignored his wishes and pressed the Knowing into his brain. If he touched the man, the knife would kill her. He must draw the attack to himself.

"Stand up!" he barked. "Drop the knife and put your hands above your head."

He didn't expect obedience and he wasn't disappointed. But the man was quicker than Wizard expected a man interrupted in such a game to be. He turned, rose, and attacked in one motion. Wizard made the perfect counter, a kick that would take his attacker in the chest and keep his knife at a distance. It would have stopped the man dead, if Wizard had been wearing pants.

The robe was cut full and loose, but not loose enough to allow for the full swing of the kick. It snapped tight, jerking the balance from Wizard's other leg. He staggered sideways and the hungry knife went slipping past his ear. He caught himself and spun to face it, but the knife was already before him, weaving a song of blood as it hovered before his face.

Like a steel hummingbird, it moved faster than his eyes could follow. Feet planted, hands loose and ready, Wizard shifted and wove before it. The magic limned it for him, setting it glowing with a toadstool light in the blackness of the alley. He saw nothing of the one who held it and commanded the dance. The mind behind the blade trusted its cutting edge implicitly. There would be no kicks, no sudden jabs of fist to spoil the perfection of the knife's killing skill. Wizard's eyes followed the blade as hands hung loose and ready, slightly away from his body. He tried to remember there was a man behind the blade, but the magic forced his attention back to the steel edge. He struggled with it and then, with relief, let go. The knife, then. Counter to all his embedded training, he would fight the knife and not the man behind it. He relaxed and felt the tingling of power run over his limbs and up his spine.

From hand to hand the knife leapt nimbly in its wriggling, gliding dance. Wizard himself moved with it, in a swaying counterpoint that kept all parts of his body just beyond the knife's leap. The knife, the knife! Why was the magic focused on the knife? Was he supposed to grab the damned thing? He imagined a sudden successful clutch, and the fingers slipping silently from his hand. No. That couldn't be it. Silence but for two men panting, the soft scuff of wet socks against the pavement, and the far whimpering of the one who huddled at the end of the alley. The knife flickered and flashed, burning before his eyes. He reached and felt for it with the magic.

This knife was a Ruana, a fine old blade shamed by this new owner. Its tempered steel haft was enclosed on both sides by bone grips. It was balanced, it was honed, it was a joyous tool perverted to butchery. It fit the killer's hand like an extension of his body. He sensed the man's twisted soul pulsing in the blade.

So he froze it.

Swifter than any kick of leg, than any twitch of muscle could ever be, as swift as the flicker of a thought, the Knowing came to Wizard and he used it. As simple as snuffing a candle flame with a pinch. He reached and froze it, the metal cooling past imaginable temperatures and then exploding into icy shards in the killer's grip. The man screamed aloud, clutching at his wrist with his other hand and squeezing it, trying to hold out the pain invading his body. He doubled over with the agony of it, holding the mangled hand out away from his body as if he were bowing and offering it to Wizard.

Wizard stepped back from his glimpse of that familiar face. The killer bolted past him, grunting with the pain of every jolting step. Wizard smiled and followed him. The man heard his shadowing steps and moaned in terror. He staggered on, pain dazing him, the terrible warmth of his own blood soaking him as he tottered. When he fell, there was the awful shape of the man from his nightmares, the man cloaked and robed with the night sky itself. The stars and crescent moons glittered balefully, but the man's face was shadowed into blackness by the broad brim of his hat. He did not find the bent tip of that hat amusing. It pointed at him like an accusing finger. And when Wizard spoke, his eyes glittered like two chunks of blue glacier ice. He whispered.

"If ever thou takest up a knife in thy hands again, be it even for so innocent a thing as the buttering of bread, the metal of the knife shall find revulsion in thy touch, and break again into a thousand splinters. But those splinters will pierce thy eyes and thy heart. Go now. Remember I have granted thee mercy this time, but justice will be thine the next time."

He nodded, he wept, and in agonized fear he thanked the man who had maimed him, groveling away from his feet. Wizard stood, watching him go. Power swelled in him, pulsing through his veins. This was a better way, so much a better way. In the instant he had frozen the knife, he had seen the killer's maggoty little soul. He would take up a knife again; not tonight, or even this month. But when the hunger became too much for him, he would take up the knife and perish by it, even as Wizard had foretold. He had wielded his power fearlessly and permanently. No knife would tolerate his touch.

He felt more than satisfaction as he watched the staggering figure retreat. Exultation. The wheel of his existence had rotated a half turn, carrying Wizard from the bottom to the top. The magic was back, in such strength as he had never known. He who had been the prey was the hunter; from being at the mercy of circumstances he had risen to be the controller. He had found his strength and his dreams would fall into his hands. So heady was this feeling he could not keep the smile from his lips. Suddenly he had it all: the magic, Cassie, and the strength to conquer his enemy.

He turned his strength inward, found the lurking gray inside himself, and squeezed it to a thing of infinite smallness. So simple once one knew how and was not afraid. Was this what Cassie had been trying to tell him? Pick up your weapons, indeed! Had even she guessed at the new strength of his magic? Like a butterfly pumping fluid into his wet wings, he stretched to feel the limits of his power and laughed aloud.

The gasp of a quickly drawn breath recalled him to himself. A small shame nibbled at the edge of his conscience. So enraptured had he been by his vanquishing of the killer that he had forgotten the victim.

"Come out now," he called softly to her, peering into the darkness of the alley. "You're safe now."

There was no answer. Concern that she had been hurt more than he suspected creased his brow. He stepped quickly back to the place where the killer had crouched over her. "Where are you?" he called again, and spun as she broke cover behind him. He caught a fleeting glimpse of her under the streetlamp as she ran, her torn clothing clutched around her bruised body.

"Wait! I won't hurt you!" he called after her and started to follow, only to stumble over leather straps. He nearly fell. Reaching down, he untangled her shoulder bag from about his stockinged feet. Her purse, torn from her grip by her attacker and forgotten in her panic. He heard the jingle of keys, felt the lump of wallet inside it. She'd need it. He tucked it under his arm and ran after her.

By the time he reached the mouth of the alley and looked around, she had already turned a corner and was out of sight. He stood still, perplexed, flinching at the thought of her fleeing through the dark streets with no way to get home, not even a quarter for the phone. Who else might target her as a victim? Then he chuckled at his own foolishness. Could he forget so soon? He reached after her. There. The scent of her fear was as distinctive as perfume in the cold air. He ran lightly after her, his robe and cloak rippling soundlessly behind him.

Terror had spurred her, and she had fled like a rabbit, turning as corners presented themselves to throw off her pursuer. Wizard felt a touch of pity for her. She couldn't know as yet that he meant her no harm. Yet her pathetic efforts to elude him had a touch of humor he could not deny. It was like a toddler trying to hide from the night things by putting a pillow over his head. In his night, in his city, no one could evade him. For two blocks she eluded him with the winged feet of fear. He caught full sight of her at last and called to her. "Wait!"

With a smothered shriek, she was off again. He paused and took a breath in exasperation. The damp front of his robe clung to him annoyingly. With an impatient shake of his head, he dried it and chased the chill from his body. He stooped to pull up his socks, then wished them dried and water repellent. All was as he ordered it. Why hadn't he thought of it before? He supposed he had grown long accustomed to discomfort and inconvenience. Now, where had the girl gone? He closed his eyes and groped after her. He was getting better at this with every passing instant. He located her easily this time, running through an alley some block and a half distant and weeping as she ran. No need to pursue her. He could now predict, even guide her course. It would be child's play to cut her off. He lifted his long robe and ran lightly down the sidewalk to his planned interception point, chuckling soundlessly as he ran.

He appeared in the mouth of the alley before her, leaping out silently with outstretched arms to catch her. She screeched in horror, pursued beyond sanity. She stopped so swiftly she fell to her knees. Without trying to rise, she jerked herself around and scrambled away from him on all fours. The alley was cluttered with garbage cans and dumpsters. An inordinate amount of plain junk was scattered about, as if the contents of a room had been thrown down from above. She scuttled and hid from his eyes but he could see her. He didn't mean to laugh; she was so scared, when all he meant her was good. But it was too ridiculous a situation; no doubt when she realized she had been fleeing her benefactor she, too, would see the humor. And he was tired of the pursuit. Poor little fool; best for her if she were captured and it was over.

He waved his hand, and the other end of the alley closed before her. The wall he had called up glowed with a fungus light, and dark shapes coalesced beyond its translucence. She snatched herself back from it, breathing in little moaning pants. She fell and cowered upon the paving stones, huddled in on herself.

"Come here, now," he ordered her in a kindly voice.

She only whimpered.

"No harm will come to you if you do as I say. Come to me."

She rolled herself into a tighter ball. He frowned at her stubbornness. He began to pick his way through the junk and clutter, then halted. It would be better for her to come out and face her fears, he decided abruptly. For her own good.

Having been driven himself, he well knew how to drive. With a gesture he freed a sinuous gray shadow from the wall of light. It oozed toward her like a monstrous slug, elongating

itself to surround her and force her to its master. She screamed
at its touch and staggered up and forward a step before she
collapsed again. Wizard shook his head. She had so little stam-
ina. Was this the woman he had risked his life for? Idly he
held his creature in check to see if she would rally. She didn't.
Very well, then. He would have to go to her. He banished the
creature back to the wall and began clambering over junk to
the woman. But as he stooped over the cringing woman, he
realized his creature had not returned to the wall as he had
commanded it. Instead, the wall had come to it. It pushed even
closer.

He gasped in recognition.

Mir laughed in acknowledgment and surged forward to join
him over their prize.

He wavered then, in a moment as long as his life. Kinship
and camaraderie and the electrical excitement of being the
conqueror seethed within the wall. Come forward to join Mir
and be no longer alone. Nagging doubts would vanish, and he
would know, not peace, but headlong decisiveness and life
burned to the socket. At last they had found one another. His
long exile was over.

Revulsion, sudden as an explosion, rushed over him. He
threw his strength against it, every strand of power he had
discovered and tested this night. He flung it up before gray
Mir in a restraining web and rushed forward to lift the woman
with his human hands. She staggered up and leaned against
him, unable to stand. He could not bring himself to look into
that tortured face. A rush of shame burned him as he pushed
her purse into her nerveless hands. She took it, seeming scarcely
aware of what she did. Tottering free of him, she pulled in-
effectually at her torn clothes, trying with feeble hands to hide
her nakedness from the November wind.

Grayness lunged for her. Wizard pressed it back, feeling
the far snapping of restraints as small bits of his magic gave
way before it. It laughed like the wind booming through tattered
sails, and the world swayed beneath Wizard's feet. Impossibly,
the magic he had woven to hold it back was falling in on him,
like a net dropping onto a tiger. The chase had stirred its
appetite; it would have both of them this night. Wizard squeezed
his eyes to slits and threw the last of his power up before it.
The great mass of power he had so shortly wielded had been
thrown back against him. What was his own small magic against

that omnipotence? He could not win. It knew it. It leaned into him, enjoying the slow crumbling of his defenses.

"Run!" he gasped to the woman, but she only stared at him, blank-eyed. When his strength failed, she would be helpless before the grayness. His demon would rend her.

He reached to the silver tassels at his throat. His fingers were stiff claws that ripped them free of their knot. One-handed, he swirled the cloak free of his shoulders and over her. He felt a part of his strength go with it, a peeling away like a layer of skin. The woman stood up within the cloak, finding the presence of mind to clutch it around her chilled body.

"Run!" he commanded her again, and this time she seemed to hear him. Enough sanity returned to her face that her fear was rational. She saw Wizard with his hand upraised before the gray shape in the gathering mist. Her wide eyes smote him, echoing of Cassie's. She turned and ran away. He was glad.

Cheated of its second victim, Mir fell on him with the weight of the earth itself. Real, Cassie had said. She was right. A talon or tooth or blade penetrated Wizard's guard, slashing at him. Blood welled along his ribs. The cloak would have protected him, he realized vainly, and let the thought run away unconsidered. He tried to focus his own powers to a jabbing point, but it was like trying to roll a quilt into a spear. It could buffer the attacks of the grayness, but it could not prevent them, and it was no weapon. Mir surrounded him, its pressure building. His eardrums pressed in against his brain. He felt the leap of blood from his nose, felt his lungs squashing up high in his chest. He went as small and hard as a nut in its grasp. For a second he felt relief. Then the trick failed him. The pressure mounted again; he had nowhere left to flee. He could not close his eyes, had no breath left to scream.

A softness that smelled like ginger and vanilla settled over him, forcing Mir back and offering respite. He took a breath, opened bloodshot eyes.

Mir loomed over them both. Cassie was wrapped in his cloak, her black hair spilling down her back and gleaming like polished ebony. One of Wizard's hands clutched at the crumpled front of his stained robe; his hat with its crooked point was sliding down over one of his ears. Her hand was on his shoulder, joining them. He drew a breath, and with it Knew that Cassie's power was strained to its limits, was screaming with the load of the grayness against it. Even together, they were not enough.

She had come on a fool's errand, to go down with him. It was just as hopeless, but slower. He wished he had the breath to tell her so.

"Hold on!" she shouted, and her voice reached him from across a vast dark plain. "They're coming. Night makes it hard for them."

He gave his head a minuscule shake, taking no meaning from her words. But he took the last reserve of his power, the small bit he had not known he was saving, the piece that meant he expected to live, and flung it into the face of the grayness. Mir laughed with triumph.

And screamed with sudden pain.

Pigeons are not nocturnal. At night they are plump puffs of feathers perched in high sheltered places, sleeping more soundly than fat cats on sunny window ledges. They do not see well at night. They seem weaponless, lacking the taloned feet and hooked beaks of the raptors. But a mother pigeon can accurately crack the knuckles of an intruding hand venturing into her nest with a sharp stroke of her wing. The pointed pink or black beak that pricks out bits of popcorn from cracks in cobblestones occasionally jabs even the soft palm of one who offers largesse. And the battering wings and jabbing beaks of a thousand hungry pigeons in competition for food are not to be ignored. By anything.

They had heard, had received the call of Wizard summoning them to be fed. So they came, hungry always, blundering through the darkness. They dove to his feast, squabbling and crowding one another as they fought for the writhing threads and juicy gobs of grayness. Plucking and gulping, they dismantled it. Mir roared its agony through Wizard's bones. Its pain exploded inside him in the place where it had sheltered, burning like phosphorous in his guts. The night turned black and red before his eyes. To his ears came only the cooing and fluttering of pigeons, pecking one another in their eagerness as they snatched up wet, gray chunks. The agonized roar inside him became a shriek that rose up in pitch, passing through the scales of his hearing until it reached a shrillness that his ears could no longer perceive. Wizard sat rocking in the darkness, his hands over his tortured eardrums, wondering if it had stopped, or if it would scream on endlessly inside him, too high to be consciously perceived.

The wondering was his own. When he recognized that, he opened his clenched eyes to the grayness of city night. A simple grayness, unthreatening. Just the gray light of streetlamps, blessedly empty of any cognizance. He wished he could sit and bask in it and rest. Not yet. It was not quite finished. He heaved himself up, wiping blood from his face onto the sleeve of his robe. Cassie he saw leaning against the wall of the alley, beside the Great Winds dumpster. She looked drained, but he sensed that she strained still to hold Mir at bay.

He reached her side and touched her arm gently. "No need," he whispered hoarsely. "That part is done."

Her legs gave way beneath her and she sank to the cold pavement. He crouched beside her on nerveless legs that trembled with weariness. Together they watched the pigeons clean it up. It seemed to take forever, but Wizard did not mind. Cassie was leaning against him, warming him, and her soft hair beneath his chin smelled of the garden. They sat silently, watching the busy beaks of the pigeons. He knew they both thought of that summer day when he had left the cavalcade to find her. Threads of gold and silver, woven together so seldom, and always so briefly. He pulled her closer, thinking of the befores they shared.

When at last the pigeons were sated, no bones or teeth remained at the core of the thing. The plump birds sat about on the paving stones, blinking sleepy round eyes, full to capacity at last. In the center of the alley, untouched by beaks, rested a small gray document box.

"This part's for me," Wizard sighed. He dragged himself to his feet, reluctantly pushing Cassie back when she would have joined him. He stepped softly up to the box and stood over it. When he nudged it with his toe, he heard a ghastly scuttling inside it. "Still," he marveled. He lifted his foot and brought it down sharply, concentrating on smashing the paving stones that lay beneath the box. The shock of the blow jolted up through his spine. He felt the lock and lid give way, to crush down upon whatever was in there. The heel of his sock grew warm and heavy with his own blood.

But when he nudged the box again, all was silent within.

"What was in there?" Cassie wondered.

"You don't want to know," he assured her.

He picked it up with dirty newspapers from the dumpster and dropped it into a smoke-blackened footlocker lying underneath the fire escape. He touched the lid and it fell, to shut with a thud over the thing. He knelt before it to fasten the catches shut.

"Give me a hand?" he asked Cassie.

There were handles on either end of the fire-blackened foot-locker. The load within was heavier than it had any right to be. The shape of the footlocker was awkward and their disparate heights made it no easier. They walked side by side down the night sidewalks, each gripping a handle and dodging parking meters. Cassie did not need to be told they were heading for the public dock.

They spoke very little at all. Once Cassie said, "They were all sleeping in high places, or I could have reached them sooner. They would have come right away, if you had thought of calling them yourself. I used your voice, but they were still wary of believing me."

And once he observed, "This has been the longest night of my life," to which she replied, "The dawn is wise enough to wait some struggles out."

The sea splashed and heaved beneath the public docks. Wizard stared down at the lacy tops of the waves. "Is it deep enough here?" Cassie worried.

"I don't think it will stop at the bottom," he assured her. Together they swung it, once, twice, three times and away. There was no splash, no rising of bubbles. It was gone. The sea wind made streamers of their clothing.

Beside him, Cassie fussed with the silver tassels of the cloak. They came undone in her fingers and she slipped from its shelter. Bruises were shadows on her white skin, revealed by her own torn clothes. Wizard winced. She draped the cloak over his arm, but when he tried to put it again about her shoulders, she stepped away from him. "I've borrowed your strength long enough. Take it again, and give back to me what is mine."

Puzzled, he slung the cloak around his shoulders. The warmth of her body clung to it still, and he had to smile sadly as he met her eyes. Then he felt the slow peeling away of something, like a tight garment being drawn off his body. For an instant he felt naked and chilled, and then his own power rose to protect him again.

"I've been using your magic tonight," he said, finally grasping it. She nodded, looking down at the rough wood of the dock.

"I put it upon you when I held you, knowing it was for-bidden, but too fond of you to let you go unsheltered. If I had known the strength of the grayness, I would not have had the courage to do so. But I did not. I thought I was wise. I set my own trap for it, never guessing how easily it could overpower me once I had lent my strength to you. I did not guess the hold it had on you." She paused suddenly, shaking her head violently. "You had hidden your torment too well. You were right, you know. It was within you as well as without, just as real in both places. And when I saw it upon you, saw you transformed in it. . . .I thought I would go mad with horror. I fled. Even now, when I think of how easily it hunted me down using you . . . But it is done. You are free now."

She was giving him the pieces faster than he could fit them together. "It was your power I used, then, when I faced it down?"

She shook her head, not looking at him. "You used mine upon the knife; did not you guess that ferocity was woman's magic? The soaring rush you felt afterward; that was seduction of the grayness. I saw you swept away from me. But when you cloaked me in your protection and sent me away, I took my magic with me as well. I needed it, to find and rouse your pigeons, and call them to you. Then, when I returned . . . I know you felt me join you."

The spice scent. He nodded slowly, beginning to understand as Cassie fitted the pieces together for him. But Cassie never explained anything. Something was terribly wrong. He reached and turned her face up to his. Moonlight and streetlights touched her tears.

"Why are you crying?" Her tears hurt him as nothing else had.

"Because I am hurt!" She cried out. She pulled gently free of him, wrapping herself tightly in her arms. She stood so alone. "Why do you think the rules are given us, if not to keep us from hurting ourselves? But the decision was mine. I took it upon myself, to give you what you would not ask for. My magic. To call for you the allies you had prepared so well for this battle. I unbalanced my magic. But I could have done nothing else. Could I have watched you destroyed? Knowing that for all the times and tomorrows that might ever come, never again would our paths cross? Shall I be sorry for what I did? But it hurts. Yes. All the old scars have come unhealed. I had forgotten it could hurt this bad. All the old pains are new again."

He nodded stiffly, knowing what she meant. The pains that came out of the past and haunted, hurting past toleration. A pain that made you explode at a touch. He could not reach after her as she walked to the edge of the dock. The full moon was over the sea, sending a wrinkling silver path across the waves to them. Cassie gave him one anguished look and then stepped down onto that path. He hurried to the edge of the dock and stood looking after her. She walked steadily away, her small feet leaving no impression on the ocean's salty face. Her silhouette grew small against the moon.

"I'll see you later!" he cried after her.

She never answered.

16

"SEEN CASSIE?" asked Rasputin.

Wizard shook his head slowly. It had become a ritual greeting among them. Always one asked, and one denied silently. Nothing more than this was ever said about her. Wizard had all the memories now, and he clung to them. He had given up trying not to hope.

"So what you want me for, I-Don't-Know Wizard?"

It was June again, and Rasputin shone in the pleasant weather. Enameled red hoops glittered in his earlobes, and his bare chest was decked in successions of bright red seed necklaces. They rattled when he danced, and even when he was still, · they clicked softly against one another, maintaining the secret rhythm of his endless dance. A light wind rustled the leaves of the trees in Occidental Square.

"See her?" Wizard nodded at a bench acróss the way from them. He flung another handful of popcorn from the withered bag on the seat beside him. Pigeons fluttered and scrabbled around their feet. Rasputin nudged them away from his bare toes and scowled.

"See who?"

"On the left end of the bench. Move your eyes just a little, to catch her at an angle. See her now?"

"I don't see nothing but an empty bench. You getting snaky on us, Wizard?"

Wizard made an impatient motion of his head and caught up one of his pigeons. He whispered to it for an instant and then flung it aloft. It fluttered frantically, made altitude, then wheeled and came sliding down to light on the empty bench.

"A chameleon!" Rasputin gasped.

Her startlement had betrayed her. When she moved, she was visible. But as soon as she was still again, she began to blend back into her surroundings. Subtle ripplings of color crossed her. In a moment, she was invisible again.

"I'll be damned!" Rasputin whistled low. "Looks like maybe you found one. You talked to her yet?"

Wizard shook his head. "I've been watching her for about a week. She's completely unaware of what she is doing. I thought I'd get your opinion before I approached her."

Rasputin shrugged. "Ain't my department. You go talk to her, take her around a little. Run her past Euripides and see if she Knows him. The usual stuff. If she pans out, bring her by me. I'll give her the rules."

Two wizards leaned back on their park bench. The blue robes of one fluttered against his bare feet. The other's fingers twitched in his endless dance. No one gave them a second glance. It was a fine June day in the Emerald City.

URSULA K. LE GUIN

Award-winning author
Ursula K. Le Guin is acclaimed as
today's leading voice in fantasy.
Berkley is proud to offer Le Guin's
THE WORD FOR WORLD IS FOREST,
winner of both the Hugo and Nebula
Awards, LANGUAGE OF THE NIGHT,
a full-length collection of essays and
criticism, and MALAFRENA, her first
mainstream fiction novel. Don't
miss this chance to sample some of
the finest fantasy and fiction
written today!

07484-6	**THE WORD FOR WORLD IS FOREST**	$2.75
07668-7	**THE LANGUAGE OF THE NIGHT**	$5.95
08477-9	**MALAFRENA**	$3.50

Prices may be slightly higher in Canada.

Provocative and visionary tales from a Hugo and Nebula award-winning author

KATE WILHELM

"Kate Wilhelm's stories are smooth, provocative, moving and intensely alive. Her depth and range as a storyteller continue to astonish."

—Marta Randall, author of <u>Dangerous Games</u>

In LISTEN, LISTEN Wilhelm probes the dangers which lurk in a near tomorrow. The four novellas which make up the collection include "With Thimbles, With Forks and Hope" and "The Winter Beach," her terrifying look at the dangers of immortality. WELCOME CHAOS is an expansion of "The Winter Beach," and in it she unveils the horrors that everlasting life could bring to the human race.

____ **LISTEN, LISTEN**
0-425-07327-0/$2.95

____ **WELCOME, CHAOS**
0-425-07585-0/$2.95

Prices may be slightly higher in Canada.